Praise for Degr

'Fake engagements, nos
dilemma of falling for that g
of Engagement is sexy and heartfelt, about pursuing your passions,
and the people who are passionate about you. Be prepared to
fall in love with Hennessy's bookish heroine and her brooding
modern-day *Indiana Jones*'
ASHLEY POSTON

'Full of sweet heat, banter, and a beautiful, long-anticipated
connection, DEGREES OF ENGAGEMENT is an ode to
the many paths life can take-and what happens when you let
the right person go on the journey with you'
GRACE REILLY

'A swoony, horny heartache that Ali Hazelwood fans
will be clamouring for. I loved it!'
LIZZIE HUXLEY-JONES

'Academic rivals-to-lovers is great, but what about two academics
who deeply respect each other's intelligence but are completely
clueless when it comes to admitting their long-standing feelings?
Hell yeah I wanted Bianca and Xavier to get fake engaged and teach
everyone a lesson, but more than that I wanted them to finally see
how perfect they really were for each other. Jennifer Hennessy's
debut adult romance is a real treat!'
ALICIA THOMPSON

'Fast-paced and delightful, *Degrees of Engagement* is packed
full of fake-dating fun. A charming romance of finding
happiness and defining it for yourself'
EMILY WIBBERLEY and AUSTIN SIEGEMUND-BROKA

Jennifer Hennessy is the romance genre pen name of young adult author, Jennifer Iacopelli. By day she's a librarian and by night she writes books about ambitious women who know what they want and the men who love them for it. She lives in New York with no plans to ever leave.

Follow her everywhere **@jennifercarolyn**.

Also by Jennifer Hennessy

Degree of Engagement

FOR THE RING

Jennifer Hennessy

HEADLINE
ETERNAL

First published in 2025 by Headline Eternal
An imprint of Headline Publishing Group Limited

1

Cataloguing in Publication Data is available from the British Library

ISBN 978 1 0354 1324 9

Typeset in 11/14pt Minion Pro by Jouve (UK), Milton Keynes

Printed and bound in Great Britain by Clays Ltd, Elcograf S.p.A.

HEADLINE PUBLISHING GROUP
An Hachette UK Company
Carmelite House
50 Victoria Embankment
London EC4Y 0DZ

The authorised representative in the EEA is Hachette Ireland, 8 Castlecourt Centre,
Dublin 15, D15 XTP3, Ireland (email: info@hbgi.ie)

www.headlineeternal.com
www.headline.co.uk
www.hachette.co.uk

For Poppy and Grandpa, who loved New York
baseball as much as I do.
Sorry I became a Yankees fan.

FRANCESCA

Two Years Ago . . .

After seven hard-fought games, the New York Yankees cele-
brated their World Series championship win on the field at
Dodger Stadium, and the LA faithful were stunned silent.

I'd never heard fifty thousand people be that quiet before.

Helpless from my seat in the front-office suite, all I could do
was watch. Our players drifted from the dugout back through
the tunnel to the clubhouse, where there would be no champagne and beer waiting for them to douse each other sticky,
and no trophy to lift above their heads, no World Series ring
that would forever name them champion.

My front-office colleagues melted away too, one by one,
until I was left alone. With a long breath in and then out again,
I wiped the tears from eyes with the heel of my hand, grateful
I'd thought to put on waterproof mascara that morning.

It wasn't supposed to end like this.

Not again.

But no matter how hard I worked, it still wasn't enough.

I worked late a lot back then.

It was expected that all baseball operations staff stay until the end of every game, but I didn't do it because it was expected of me. I did it because I loved being there long after the final out, when all the fans are gone, the players and coaches too, when it would be just me in my office and maybe a few other diehards left.

Sometimes I'd even go into the empty stands and work with the field laid out in front of me. I'd compile my report on the next day's opposing pitcher and how our line-up matched up, determining outfield positioning for the other hitters, going over pitch selection for our starter and the guys available out of the bullpen.

Should I have been delegating that kind of stuff? Probably, but if Frankie Sullivan, the head of major league analytics, stayed late, it sent the clear signal to the rest of my staff that I was willing to put in the hours, and that, if I'm going to do it, they should too.

Is it healthy to feel that way about your job?

Most people would say no. They at least try for a semblance of work-life balance.

That's crap.

At least it was for me.

Hence my divorce. Though, I think that was probably more about him being a cheating scumbag rather than how much I loved my job. And it was actually one of the things my ex said he loved about me: how dedicated I was, that I was focused and driven and ambitious, and wouldn't let anything stand in my way.

As it turned out, not even him.

Because even after he left, I still had my dream.

And that was everything.

Five years with the Dodgers and I knew I was the best in the game.

You don't get to the top of the baseball world as a woman without not just being the best, but being *obviously* the best.

I put in the work and left everyone else in my dust.

But, in the end, the only thing that mattered was the result. A World Series championship. And there isn't an algorithm in the world that can predict what happens once you get there. Two teams, the best of seven games. It's too small a sample size with too many variables to predict.

Believe me, I've tried.

And so had he, the last player left in our dugout, watching the Yankees celebrate.

Charlie Avery, all six foot four, two hundred odd pounds of him, with eye black streaked across his face and dirt creased over his uniform, his wrists wrapped tightly, shaggy brown hair probably still damp with sweat plastered against his forehead and his sharp blue eyes staring blankly out onto the field.

He sat like a statue until the Yankees danced back to their clubhouse and long after the fans, even the stragglers milling around for one last gasp of the dying baseball season, were shooed away by security. He sat there and so did I, two levels up and across the field, like we were the last two people left on earth.

Charlie had played nearly twenty years in the majors. There'd been ups and downs over the years, but for two decades he'd been penciled in nearly every day behind the plate for the Dodgers, and now, though he hadn't made an official announcement, nearly everyone was sure this was it for him.

His knees were breaking down. And once a catcher's knees go, that's the ballgame.

Still, he'd put together an All-Star season and went on a hot streak in October, only for it to end with another team celebrating on his field.

He and I have had our differences over the years.

Guys with the kind of instincts, ability and work ethic that Charlie has have a hard time believing that their efforts can be boiled down to some numbers spat out by a computer. His words not mine, obviously, but, despite our battles, and they were many, I always respected the hell out of him.

And now it was over.

Twenty years gone, a Hall of Fame career for sure.

But no championship to show for it.

I didn't blame him for not wanting to leave the field.

He did eventually, though.

And so did I.

I caught his post-game interview as I was gathering my things from my office, half an eye on the TV. He stood at his locker, stone-faced and exhausted, taking question after question, patiently answering each one, his voice solemn, but his responses thorough, almost meandering, as if he didn't want the moment to end.

Interviews were always obviously his least favorite thing, but he was latching on to this one, the last bit of normalcy for a man who'd spent his whole adult life playing a little boy's game.

I couldn't stand it, so I switched off the set. Then the stadium lights went out – the cleaning crews were finished and gone. And I finished packing up my things.

Just for the night, though.

I'd be back the next day and so would dozens of other front-office types, but, for everyone else, the season was over. No baseball for six months, and then a new season would start and hope would spring eternal, just like it did when the team was back in Brooklyn, back when the unofficial organizational motto was: "wait till next year".

For Charlie Avery, "next year" never came.

His career was ending while mine was only just beginning, even though he's only a few years older than me, not even forty.

Baseball is cruel like that.

Young men in the prime of their life, ancient before their time.

The dream has a ticking clock. For some time expires early.

Mine expired when I started softball instead of baseball the year I turned twelve.

Charlie's dream at least had the decency to wait until he neared middle age to die.

All that said, I couldn't say I was sorry to see him go. We'd had more than one knock-down drag-out fight over his sheer inability to follow a game plan. The younger guys coming up through the minor leagues were always way more amenable to our analysis.

The click of my heels echoed in the cavernous concrete hall as I made my way out of the stadium that night. It was odd the way such a small sound made so much noise, especially in a place that had been raucous with tens of thousands of voices just a few hours ago.

"You're still here, Ms Sullivan?" Raúl, one of the security guards that's usually stationed by the employee exit, asked.

"So are you," I answered, with a grin, despite my bittersweet feelings from the loss.

"We're not the only ones," he said, and nodded his head back toward the field. "*He's* still here."

Raúl didn't need to clarify who "he" was.

I should have just left, should have gone home and let him sit there alone until he was ready to go.

Instead, I left my bag with Raúl and made sure those heel clicks echoed even louder as I headed into the stands so he'd know I was coming.

Down in the front row, just behind home plate, Charlie Avery sat unmoving with Dodger Stadium laid out in front of him. The field was pitch black except for the soft glow of the city behind us. Just enough light for him to see me when he turned at my approach.

"Sullivan," he said. He'd only ever used my last name in the five years we'd worked together. I was never sure if it was passive aggressive or begrudgingly respectful. And I'd never asked.

"Avery," I responded in kind, and lowered myself into the seat beside him.

It's a hell of a view. Even in the dark, a major league stadium is one of the most beautiful things I've ever seen.

"It's late. You should go home. You have things to do tomorrow."

"And you don't?"

"You and I and the entire world know I don't."

I hummed a non-committal agreement.

"You could always come back, if you wanted," I suggested.

"So my knees can collapse out from under me on the field? So that kid in Triple A can take my job from me? So they," he gestured to the empty stands around him, "can boo me when I can't keep up anymore?"

"So they can say goodbye?" I offered. "They cheered for you for twenty years. Grew up with you. Don't you think they'd want the chance?"

"The team'll do a thing next year, bring me out and I'll throw a ceremonial first pitch and that'll be that."

"Well, what about me, then? Who's gonna give me crap about my analysis before every game?"

"What, are you gonna miss me, Sullivan? I always enjoyed our little discussions."

He turned in his seat and, for the first time, met my eyes with his. The crystal blue is swimming with unshed tears.

Fuck.

I shouldn't have been there. It shouldn't have been me to find him like this. But it was, and I had to do something.

"Discussions? Is that what you're going to call them? You getting soft in your old age, Avery?"

And, thank God, it was the right thing to say. He barked out a laugh, but the suddenness of it had the tears drifting to his eyelashes, one and then another falling to his cheeks. He brushed them away with impatience and then waved off the apology that was about to spill out of my mouth.

"Fuck, I needed that," he said, a broad grin spreading across his face.

I had no idea what else to say, so I just smiled too before sitting back in the seat and letting out a long sigh. He followed suit, his knee knocking gently into mine, his large frame nearly too big for a stadium seat. His knee was warm against my bare one, which was only just peeking out from beneath my pencil skirt – Dodger blue, of course.

And for a moment we might as well have been the only two people in the world, breathing in the slightly chillier than normal autumn air.

"That last at bat," he murmured, his head turning toward me, drawing my eyes to his again.

"Your last at bat? The home run?"

"Yeah. What did that computer of yours say I was gonna do?"

"Not that you'd hit it out. I can't predict things like that, but odds were over fifty percent that you'd barrel it, though, which is basically as good as those odds get."

"Fifty/fifty shot, huh?"

"Not a bad way to end a career, with a World Series home run."

"Not as good as a championship, though."

"No. No, it's not."

"You're supposed to say it's okay, though, Sullivan."

"Am I? Sorry, I don't know the protocol."

"It's okay. Neither do I. Guess we'll just have to figure it out together."

"I lost one of these too, you know."

"A World Series?"

"A championship," I corrected him. "My senior year at Cal. We were an out away when that bitch from Oklahoma launched a homer and walked us off."

"Brutal. I didn't know you played."

"You never asked."

He had the good sense to seem abashed. "What position?" he asked, but realization dawned quickly. Like understands like. "Catcher."

"Yeah. Anyway, it's happened to me a lot. Runner-up at the Little League World Series and the California High School State Championships. Runner-up at ASA Gold Nationals. Runner-up at NCAA Championships and now . . ."

"Runner-up at the World Series," he finished for me.

"Second-Place Sullivan," I sing-song.

"No one calls you that."

"I do, in my head."

"Fuck," he breathed out, "my therapist would have a field day with that."

"Oh, mine does, believe me."

His laugh is a deep, rumbling sound and I join him just as a breeze kicks up and I shiver against it. I left the jacket to my skirt suit up with Raúl and just the camisole from beneath it isn't enough as the night grows ever darker.

"I should go." I stood up with a soft sigh.

"I'll walk you to your car." He stands too, his eyes trained away from the field in what I assume is a deliberate attempt to stop looking at it.

"You don't have to. Raúl usually—"

"If it's okay, I'd . . . I don't think I can walk out of here on my own."

"Oh, right. Of course."

The last time he'll leave Dodger Stadium as a player after the last game of his career. That would mess me up too.

"C'mon then."

He followed me back up through the suite exit, through the tunnels of the stadium, until we reached Raúl's desk. Then, from somewhere inside the dark brown leather of his jacket, Charlie pulled out an envelope with the security guard's name on it and handed it to him.

"Mr Avery, that's unnecess—"

"No arguments," Charlie cut him off, and grinned. "There's a little extra in there, you know, for all the years."

"You're done?" Raúl asked, and for a moment the tough security guard, fifty if he's a day, sounded like one of the little kids who line the edges of the stands before every game waiting for their favorite player to jog over during warm-ups to sign a baseball or a hat.

A lot of grown men felt like little boys once the news dropped.

But, in that moment, only the three of us knew for sure that Charlie Avery's career was over.

"Thank you for everything," Raúl said, extending his hand.

"Nah, thank *you*, man," Charlie said, taking it and shaking it firmly.

The reserved parking lot that the players and front-office staff use is empty except for our cars. His Grand Wagoneer in the reserved spot in the first row, my Audi set way further back. Our job broke our hearts tonight, but it does pay well at the top.

He bypassed his car and followed me to mine, waiting patiently as I hung the jacket to my skirt suit up in the back seat and then put my things into the passenger side.

"Are you gonna be okay tonight?" I asked him.

"Yeah," he trailed off, before he leaned up against the side of my car and looked up into the sky, the stars obscured by the city lights beyond Chavez Ravine. "I was just thinking."

"Don't you let your gut do your thinking for you?"

It's something he'd thrown at me more than once during our pre-game discussions. That his gut instinct was way more reliable than my algorithm.

"Who says I'm not now?"

"Fair enough, what is your gut thinking?"

"We don't work together anymore."

"No, technically your contract expired after the last out tonight."

"I was just thinking about what I always wanted to do after one of our discussions."

"I still wouldn't call them that. Nuclear implosions I think is probably the closest I can . . ."

But I didn't get a chance to finish the thought, because he kissed me.

Almost.

I'd always assumed Charlie Avery was the kind of guy who didn't ask permission, who took what he wanted because he could, just like he did out on the field.

I was wrong.

Because in an empty stadium parking lot after the worst loss of his career, with one hand at my hip, the other gently cupping the back of my head, his mouth hovering just over mine, he whispered, "Can I?"

"Yes," I whispered back, and he smothered the sound with the press of his lips to mine, firm and insistent, his hand tangling into my hair to tilt my head to the side as he deepened the contact. His tongue nudged at my bottom lip and then flicked against mine as I opened up to him, my body following the same signals. I pressed into him, his broad chest and strong thighs easily holding me up.

He spun us around, my car a solid surface at my back while I held on to his shoulders to keep my balance and surrendered myself to it, his hot mouth and his firm hands sending my heart into a frenzy, juxtaposed with how entirely safe I felt enveloped by him. His lips never drifted from mine; his hands never explored places they weren't welcome.

And then he was gone, pulling away, steadying me on my feet before striding away to his car, hands shoved into his pockets, shoulders hunched against the weight of whatever complicated cocktail of emotions were running through him, all while I tried to catch my breath.

It was just a kiss, but I'd never been so thoroughly ravished in my entire life.

Chapter 1

FRANCESCA

Two years later . . .

I speak four languages with varying degrees of fluency. English was my first, spoken at home with my parents, and I was surrounded by it in my suburban Los Angeles neighborhood growing up. Spanish was my next, a slow slog during middle and high school, with a few classmates who could speak it better than our teachers, and then way more vigorous study in college, which got me to conversational level. My third, after a few classes in college, is Japanese. I am in a constant battle with it in my Duolingo app.

The app is mostly winning.

Which is why I don't really understand the people around me in the Tokyo Dome. At least I don't understand their words.

But I do understand another language, my fourth, and one I share with everyone in this stadium tonight.

Baseball.

The crack of the bat and the smell of the dirt or the leather of a glove, the rhythm of the game – building, always building to something – is so deeply ingrained in my soul that I most definitely speak the same language as the other fifty-five thousand people packed into the stands for the final game of the Japan Series as Kai Nakamura, the ace of the Yomiuri Giants, stands alone in the center of the diamond.

Ninth inning.

Two outs.

Nobody on.

Two strikes on the batter.

I've been here before, on the other side of it.

The Giants are up one to nothing, but it might as well be five or ten or a hundred runs.

The other team hasn't reached base, not once. Not hits, no walks, not even a fielding error or a hit by pitch.

A swing and a miss.

Strike three.

Sutoraikusurī, in Japanese.

And that collective inhale explodes into a roar that I understand perfectly.

Baseball isn't my first language, but it is the one I'm most fluent in.

I can't help it – my gaze drifts across the field, past the delirium of the victors, to look in the visitor's dugout, where I see a team that has just been dominated by the best pitcher in their league. Their season is over, with nothing to show for it but their memories, tarnished by this final one of watching another team celebrate the championship they've coveted all year long.

That feeling? That's one I know better than most.

And it's enough to remind me of someone who knows it as well as I do, back in Los Angeles, where we parted on a night a lot like tonight – an unexpected bonding moment, the bittersweet ending of a career and an unexpected kiss that I sometimes still relive with startling clarity.

"Sullivan-*sama*," a stadium worker says, interrupting me before the memories take over. And I'm back in the Tokyo Dome, rather than more than five thousand miles away and two years ago at Dodger Stadium. "Sullivan-*sama*, your car is here for the airport."

My flight isn't back to Los Angeles, but to New York, to my new team: the Brooklyn Eagles, the team that had replaced the Dodgers when they left for the West Coast in 1957.

As their assistant general manager, I'm going to help make sure next year *finally* comes.

And Kai Nakamura is the arm we'll ride all the way to the World Series.

I don't stay for the celebration.

He knows I was there. I was right behind home plate for the whole game. The cheeky kid even had the audacity to tip his cap in my direction before the first pitch. He'll want to celebrate with his teammates, enjoy his championship, but, in a few weeks, when he's ready, that will be my moment.

Until then, I've got work to do.

Conventional wisdom would be to sleep through most of my nearly thirteen-hour flight. There isn't a lot of business getting done quite yet, just a week after the World Series. Most people who work in the league are taking a day or two to regroup before they evaluate their season and start executing their plans for the next one.

But I'm not going to wait. So, instead of sleeping, I'm bolt upright with a coffee cup that the flight attendant in first class never allows to get below half empty, working on my pitch for Stew.

Stew, whose real name isn't Stew or Stewart, but who picked

up the nickname during his playing days, where he went on a hot streak and only ate stew for four weeks, until his bat went cold, is the general manager and vice president of the Brooklyn Eagles and, more to the point, my direct boss.

My only boss, really.

When he brought me on last year, the Eagles were dead last, not just last in their division, but held the actual worst record in baseball. A disgrace by any measure, but, in New York, it was wildly unacceptable.

Last season the goal wasn't to win it all.

It couldn't be.

Worst to first stories might work great in fiction, but they almost never happen in real life.

In real life, you have to scrape and claw your way from of the bottom, and last season we made moves.

But, to get the team to the next level, we'll have to really take a good hard look at who and what we want to be in the coming years.

Which means my pitch to Stew has to be perfect if I'm going to talk him into the massive amounts of money he'll have to pry out of the tightly clenched bank account of our ownership group to get the deal done.

Millions of dollars.

Tens of millions, just for the right to sign him.

Hundreds to lock him up for the next decade.

The kid is worth it. Now I just have to convince everyone else.

And I won't be alone.

Every team is going to be gunning for Nakamura, but my real competition is clear. It'll be the Yankees and the Dodgers. New York and LA. Other teams will express interest, to make their fanbases happy, but ultimately the deal will be too rich for them.

The Eagles are usually one of those teams.

But they won't be on my watch.

So, it's more coffee and dozens of spreadsheets analyzing data from Nakamura and his opponents, his injury history – hell, even his social media activity – and comparing all of it to what his production might be in the major leagues, and then feeding all of it into the algorithm I designed myself in order to have it predict the most likely outcome for his tenure.

Every single time, no matter what I enter in for variables, my results are the same.

He's just that good.

After my analysis is complete, I'm back into my files, making notes about Japanese customs. I've worked on signing free agents from there before, but I need to make sure I'm as well versed as possible. Particularly regarding how to walk the fine line of courting someone's business: what's too passive, what's too aggressive, things that will convey respect and others that will risk giving offense.

Kai Nakamura is going to dominate Major League Baseball.

And I'm going to make sure he dominates for the Brooklyn Eagles.

When the plane touches down at JFK, I've consumed enough coffee to make my skin feel like my soul is vibrating inside of it, but the analysis is complete, and my pitch is written, edited and fine-tuned, and I'm absolutely ready to do what I need to do when I see Stew later today.

I'll just head straight to the ballpark and grab a shower in my office (I negotiated that into my contract when they were desperate to lure me away from the Dodgers and they had absolutely no idea I wanted out maybe even more than they wanted me here). And once I don't smell like an increasingly dire combination of ballpark, airplane and terrible coffee, I'll be ready just as Stew swings into his office. I can pitch him right here and now and get the gears into motion before anyone else.

Accepting my coat from the flight attendant, who is still clearly horrified about the amount of caffeine I've consumed in the last half a day, I deplane briskly and head straight out to the car that will be waiting for me.

I catch a glimpse of myself, ever so briefly, in the glass of the automatic doors just before they open to the sharp chill of November air and, cringing just slightly, I pull my hair, a bit matted and slightly greasy, onto the top of my head in a messy blonde bun.

My neck protests as I lower my arms – creaky joints were inevitable, no matter how comfortable the seats are in first class.

One of the many joys of simply existing after the age of thirty.

Another is the ache in my feet. I was able to take my shoes off on the plane for a while, but now the pinch in my toes is making itself known as I balance on the heels I wear despite my height, or maybe in spite of it.

Who says tall girls can't wear heels?

Not Francesca Sullivan.

And if it gives me the advantage of bringing me up to eye level or above with the men I constantly come up against in an industry they dominate, they'll just have to deal with it.

Stretching my neck, I peer over the heads of the people hovering near the curb waiting for their rides to pull up. The team will have sent a car, probably Vladimir, one of our regular drivers.

Holding tight to the handle of my suitcase, I spot him a few yards away, my last name written on a white card with a tiny Eagles logo at the top in the passenger window.

But before I reach it, a man and a woman with several large suitcases and a baby in a carrier approach the car, waving it down.

Vladimir makes eye contact with me, but stops the car to avoid running over the family.

They must be confused.

Maybe they're tourists, thinking the car is a cab to flag down, or maybe they have the same last name as I do. Sullivan isn't exactly rare . . . My mind tries to calculate the odds of that while I stride toward the car, when something else clicks in her head.

The man . . . I know him.

And, yes, we do share a name.

. . . Sullivan.

My ex-husband.

And his wife.

And their baby.

The odds of that are even worse, hundreds of thousands of times worse.

Unfortunately, my brain is too busy reeling to focus on stopping my feet. I just catch the last of Vladimir's protests that they aren't the Sullivans he's supposed to be picking up as he motions toward me.

Shane turns around and, well, at least he looks as stunned as I feel.

"Frankie," he says.

And it's the first time I've heard him speak in years.

Two years.

Two years, two months, six days and, if I really, really think about it hard, probably five or so hours.

The last time I saw him was during the brief time just after the divorce was finalized but before I blocked his number and every social media account I could find. Okay, maybe my best friend had done that for me. But in person? The last time I saw him in person was the day he came to clean out the last of his stuff from our house back in LA.

I hadn't said anything and neither had he.

Though there was plenty I would have liked to say. I'm not really the kind of person that censors myself, but that day I kept silent, because I knew once I started I'd probably never stop, and what good would that do? Probably just give him the satisfaction of knowing how much he'd hurt me.

And after the lying and cheating he put me through, he didn't deserve to know about my pain.

"Is this your car? Babe, I think this is her car."

His wife.

The woman he'd cheated with.

The woman he'd married almost as soon as our divorce was final.

The woman he'd had a baby with less than a year later.

A baby that, he insisted to me years before, wasn't something he wanted.

Oh God.

I'm spiraling and they're just staring at me, waiting for me to say something.

Fortunately, Vladimir is a saint among men. He's out of the car and by her side.

"Ms Sullivan, I can take your bag," he says. "I'm sorry, folks. This is a private car."

"Right," his wife, Jessie, says, biting her lip and glancing down at the baby in its carrier. I'm not even sure if it's a boy or girl. "Sorry, we were waiting for our car to take us, but it's a half hour late and we thought . . ."

"Take the car," I hear myself saying, though I can't quite believe the words as they fall off my tongue.

"What?" Vladimir says.

"What?" Shane says at the same time.

"Oh, we . . . we couldn't. We'll just wait," she says.

"No, no, you have a baby out in the cold and it's probably going to rain. Vladimir can take you wherever you need to go. I'll just get an Uber to the field."

Shane blinks at me, his vision seeming to clear for the first time. "The field?"

"Russell Field."

"You work for the Eagles now?"

"For about a year," I say, but shake my head. "You should go . . ."

"Wait, you live in New York?"

Seems like maybe he cut me out of his life just like I did him.

Not that it bothers me. It really doesn't. It just reaffirms that leaving him, leaving that life behind, was the right decision. No matter how much it hurt.

"For a little over a year now."

Shane and Jessie look at each other, eyes wide like they don't quite know what to say to that, and I can't imagine why it should matter.

Then something in my head pings, like a timer going off.

One of the reasons I'm so good at my job, why I can predict down to the smallest percentage point exactly how a baseball player is going to perform in a season, is because my brain tends to analyze the data it's given and arrive at the most probable outcome.

And the only reason I can imagine either one of them would care about me living in New York is because they also live here, or maybe . . . are about to.

They really do have *a lot* of luggage.

Too much for just a vacation.

And who vacations in New York in early November?

No one.

"I didn't think anything could get you out of LA," I manage to say.

"We don't want Kaydance growing up there."

"I grew up there," I protest, though I have no idea why I'm even responding. Who cares why they moved to New York? I just need to get out of here. They can take the car, like I said. I'll just get an Uber and maybe I won't go in straight to work. Maybe I'll just go home for a little while and take a long hot bath and then sleep for a few hours.

Yeah, that's it. I'll be refreshed and ready to pitch Stew and can pretend this never happened.

And then spend the rest of however long pretending that they don't live here.

Shane doesn't respond and we're all still standing there. Him, his wife, the baby . . . Kaydence, a girl probably, Vladimir and me.

"Go, I insist. Vlad take you wherever they need to go. You should get the baby out of this chill."

"You're sure?" he asks, his face wrinkling into a deeper frown than usual.

"I'm sure."

I'm already taking a step and then another back to the sidewalk and glancing around to find the sign for the cab line.

"Frankie," he says, and I look back over my shoulder. "Thanks."

Shrugging, I send him a tight smile, the kind you use when there's way too much to say, but you're absolutely not going to say any of it.

Turning away, so I don't have to watch Vlad help them into the car and secure the baby seat and put their luggage in the trunk, I pull out my phone to start ordering myself an Uber.

"Ms Sullivan," Vlad calls out from behind me, and I stop, not keen on making the older man run to catch up.

"It's really okay, Vlad, I promise."

"No, no, I understand. I will take *that man* to where he wants to go." Ah, so Vlad put the puzzle pieces together. "But there is another car."

"Another car?"

"Yes. The team sent another car this morning to pick up a guest from Los Angeles."

"A guest."

"Yes, from Los Angeles. Just behind you, ten minutes."

He motions back toward his car where another has pulled up behind, black and sleek, just like all the cars the team employs.

I can't see a name in the window from here.

"Who is it for?"

Vlad shrugs his large shoulders. "I don't know, but if you wait, you can share."

Okay, so keep to the plan. Get in the car and wait for whoever it is ownership is flying in from LA, get to the office, shower, a change of clothes and then pitch Stew.

That's my priority: get Stew on board with signing Nakamura and then go from there.

Dragging my luggage back toward the cars, I avoid looking into the tinted windows of Vlad's car and allow the other driver, a man I vaguely recognize and who introduces himself as Sam, to take my bags and load them into the trunk before he holds the door open for me.

Just as I'm about to climb into the backseat, a voice calls out from the sidewalk.

"You jackin' my ride, Sullivan?"

That voice.

I know that voice too.

Closing my eyes, as if I don't see his face he won't actually be there. No stupid ever-present five o'clock shadow, no ridiculous broad shoulders and thighs to match, and definitely not eyes crinkled with a shit-eating grin, and the slightly premature lines from spending most of his life on a baseball field.

Charlie Avery.

What is he doing here?

Chapter 2

CHARLIE

I've always liked New York.

Always liked playing here.

There's something about the city, about the energy, that makes me feel like I can do anything.

And boy, did I.

My bat always got hot when we were in town. Mets and Eagles fans loved to hate me, still do probably. It's only been a couple of years. Not long enough for that hate to have run its course.

The city is different from LA, sure, but not as different as people from either place want to believe.

They're both a hell of a lot different from Canton Creek, Iowa, the place listed on the back of my baseball card. Now the mathematics of life have me out of there longer than I was ever in. I can't even remember the last time I went back. More than a decade ago, for sure, when they named the high-school field after me.

Mom and Pop were still around, proud as all hell, maybe

prouder than at any other moment in my career. And Gemma was there too.

That was a good day. One of the last really good days before things went to shit. Before my folks got sick. Before Gemma wanted out.

Reaching up to rub at the back of my head, the cool air hits me as I step out into the sharp bite of the late fall, with a mist that feels like it's appearing in the air instead of falling from the sky.

Yeah, definitely different from LA. I let that train of thought fly off into the early morning hours, the only time this city is even semi-quiet.

I'm not used to a quiet New York. It wasn't back when we played the Yankees in the Series.

Not even my hot bat could push the team over the finish line, however, and that elusive world championship I chased my whole career slipped through my fingers.

Yankee fans don't hate me the way Mets and Eagles fans do.

It's easier to have respect for someone you beat, I guess.

"Hey, are you . . ." a slightly quaky voices asks from my left. I know that voice. Well, not the voice specifically, more the tone. I've heard it hundreds, maybe thousands of times in the last twenty years.

A kid, maybe nineteen or twenty at the most, is squinting at me through the soft mist that's started to fall.

". . . are you Charlie Avery?"

"Used to be."

"Ha! You were my favorite player when I was a kid!"

I let out a soft snort, but allow the kid to think he's grown.

"You mind taking a selfie with me? My dad won't believe it. He used to let me stay up to watch when the Eagles were on the west coast swing."

"Sure." I lean in while the kid raises his phone, giving a half smile.

"Thanks, man, I really appreciate it. What are you doing in the city? They gonna hire you to do one of those desk gigs on TV?"

At that I really do snort. There's nothing I'm worse at than TV commentary, following some kind of script to gin up conflict where there isn't any, except what's about to happen on the field, like baseball isn't a game mostly about whose pitcher has a bad day, and if the guy in the lineup you never expected to do a damn thing happens to run into one.

The silence gives it away and the kid changes tracks. "Wait, no way! Ae you here for the job?"

"What job?" I ask, but the kid has me and we both know it. I've always been a terrible liar.

The Eagles have been looking for a manager since their last game of the season. Their old skipper, Stew Reynolds, is headed to the front office to take over as general manager. He's been getting on in years and his wife has been on him to retire. So he compromised. An office job.

"No way. That's insane."

"Kid, I'd appreciate it if you . . ."

"No worries. I'll keep it locked down. No one would believe me anyway. Why would you want to manage the Eagles?"

That's the real question, isn't it?

I've got my reasons – more than one, really – but they aren't anyone's business. Definitely not a stranger's I just met on the street, even if he is a fan.

"You have a good night, okay?" I say, and shake the kid's hand before turning and looking at the cars as they pull up. Stew said the team would send a car, but there's a sea of sleek black SUVs and luxury sedans jockeying for position, even this early in the morning.

There's one, and, yeah, it's got an Eagle logo on it, subtle to avoid attracting attention, but definitely there. Except there's a woman getting into the car, a foot encased in a stiletto heel that leads up to a long, shapely calf and then a black skirt that just skims her knee, but it does nothing to disguise the curve of her thighs and the absolutely incredible rise of her ass.

I'm not ashamed to admit that it's a familiar ass.

Frankie Sullivan, former VP of major league analytics for the Dodgers, before she left last year to take the Assistant GM job with the Eagles.

Our battles were legendary. She was always so *sure* that her equations and whatever answers her computer spat out should be taken as gospel, even when my gut, the thing that got me to the majors, the thing that kept me there, was telling me otherwise.

Then there was that last night in LA, the last night of my career, after everyone had gone home – one hell of a kiss.

I haven't seen her since then, not even the next season, when they retired my number. I wondered then if she was avoiding me, but that day was such a whirlwind I never got the chance to track her down.

"You jackin' my ride, Sullivan?" I call out.

She freezes at the sound of my voice and then turns, eyes wide, her hair falling out of a loose bun at the top of her head, strands of her long blonde hair sticking to her cheeks, her generous mouth open in a small o, as the rain starts to fall harder around us.

Yeah, she definitely had no idea I was coming.

Interesting.

I assumed her boss would have warned her, that maybe she

even gave the okay to bring me in for an interview. I'd be lying if I said that thought hadn't intrigued me. That maybe, in her time away from LA, her philosophy had shifted toward an approach that prioritized on-the-field decisions made by actual human beings.

"What are you doing here?" she asks, and I assume she's censoring herself more than a little bit. I can practically hear *the fuck* that she left out.

Oh, I'm going to enjoy this, probably more than I should.

"Stew didn't tell you?"

"Tell me what?" she asks, but the question is barely out of her mouth before it clicks for her, just like it did for the kid I just met.

"No."

"No?" I ask, unable to stop a corner of my mouth from lifting, and she glares at the mere hint of a smirk.

"No," she repeats. "Absolutely not."

"I don't think that's your call, is it?"

"Why would you . . . you never said that you'd be . . . how is this . . ."

My grin grows wider and wider every time her thoughts cut off and change track.

"Uh, folks?" a new voice, lower and a little gruff, cuts in. "We should get going. The cop's gonna kick my ass if we keep blocking this spot."

The driver gestures toward the open door and then goes to take my suitcase from me.

I let him and then give the still stunned woman in front of me a nod as I move toward the car and wait for her to climb in.

"Are you gonna get in," I ask, "or are we just gonna stand here in the rain holding up traffic?"

She gives herself a little shake and a droplet runs off the

tip of her nose and lands on her bottom lip, where her tongue darts out to catch it.

A jolt runs through me, the same kind of feeling I used to get when a runner would arrive just behind the throw home and blast into me to try and knock the ball loose.

That's what that kiss felt like two years ago. At least some things haven't changed.

Thank God she's already turning and stepping into the car, balancing on those heels as she climbs into the SUV and then slides across the backseat to make room for me.

"You never answered my question, Sullivan."

"What?" she asks, like my voice pulled her out of some deep thought. Her mind always seemed to be whirring at a hundred miles an hour and I never could get a read on her, even after working together for five years. At first it was an irritation, but, as time went on, it morphed into a real problem. We were never on the same page and I couldn't predict what kind of shit she'd pull, always somehow talking the front office around to her way of thinking. And making my life harder in the process.

If I take this job, I'm gonna need assurances from Stew that she won't be able to overrule my calls on the field. I'll have it put in my contract if necessary.

I'm not getting back into the game just to be undercut over and over again by someone who never played at day at the major league level.

And if that makes me the asshole, so be it.

"I wasn't jacking your ride," she insists. "Or, I am, but . . ."

Frankie hesitates and I look over at her, her hair still damp, easily the least put together I've ever seen her.

"We're going to the same place, so I thought . . ."

"It's fine. You can admit it: you just missed my face."

Her jaw drops open again, the second time I've made her

do that in as many minutes. I might start a tally. I wonder how many times I can make it happen before the season starts.

If I take the job, that is.

Because I still don't know if I'm going to do that.

I retired for a reason and it wasn't just because my knees broke down.

I was tired. Tired of the long plane rides and the bland hotel rooms, of my body breaking down and of trying to fend off kids half my age from stealing my job, of never being able to figure out if a woman wanted me for me or because I was Charlie Avery, Los Angeles Dodger.

Twenty years, a lifetime really, and I was done.

But you can't do something your whole life and not miss it. And I do; I miss it a lot. The game itself. Baseball has always been more of a calling than a job. Some guys just happen to be good at it. Some guys love it more than anything. I was both.

I missed it almost as soon as I hung 'em up.

Everyone told me it would pass, though, that I was just used to it and that I needed to move on, find something else outside of baseball to spend the rest of my life doing.

But there wasn't anything. No wife, not anymore, and Gemma and I didn't have any kids. My friends were scattered across the country and some around the world. I never planned for life after baseball. And so, after baseball, I didn't have a life.

I tried, though. I tried golf and I tried travel. I even tried, for one fucking shitshow of a summer, to do some broadcasting.

Nothing stuck because it wasn't the same.

And then, a couple of weeks ago, Stew called.

Stew managed me in the minors, back when I was just a struggling kid, signed right out of high school and absolutely terrified that I'd made the wrong choice and should have gone to college. That was the first time I considered being a manager.

But then everything clicked, both at the plate and behind it, and I never looked back.

Until now.

The Eagles need a manager. They need someone to pull the sorry excuse for a Major League Baseball organization out of their decades-long rut as third-class citizens in their own town.

And Stew thinks that guy might be me.

He's built a first-class front office, poaching the best of the best in baseball operations, analytics, minor league development and scouting from all over the league. But now the real changes need to happen on the field.

Not that I'll actually be *on* it. In the dugout is as close as I can get.

I frown down at my knee and then stretch my leg out as far as I can without kicking the driver's seat in front of me. The cold, damp weather mixed with a six-hour flight didn't do it any favors and, even after years of physical therapy, yoga and not squatting for a few hours a day, six months out of the year, it still aches and probably always will.

When I look back up, Sullivan is following the motion, her lips pursed, probably holding back a scathing comment or ten.

That's a pretty good look for her too.

"Where are you coming from?" I ask, and it throws her off enough to elicit a non-sarcastic answer.

"Tokyo."

Tokyo, where the Japan Series has just wrapped up. I watched it while staying up late for my red eye to New York. Are the Eagles in on Nakamura? That would be a step up from their usual free agent budget for the off season.

"Nakamura was otherworldly," I say, and I mean it. That kid has all the makings of a major league star.

"And I was right behind home plate in his line of sight the entire time."

So, he *is* a target.

Interesting.

Because Nakamura is a Japanese player, there's a complicated posting process he has to go through in order for him to sign with a major league team, so it'll be a while until the Eagles, or any team, will be able to pitch him as a free agent, but with everyone else still taking a few days off after the World Series, Sullivan might have put us into an early lead to sign the phenom.

Us? I need to chill. I haven't agreed to anything yet. Haven't even talked to Stew.

"A nice touch," I say, and I mean that too.

"Thank you," she says primly, crossing her legs and I try my hardest not to follow the motion with my eyes.

I nearly succeed. "You think he'll sign with you?"

"I think it's none of your business."

"Might be in a few hours."

"We'll see."

It sounds like a threat, like she thinks she'll be able to talk Stew out of hiring me.

She'll be disappointed if that's the case.

If I want the job, it's mine, and we both know it.

And with every minute that passes, as the car slides through the relatively still Brooklyn streets before the sun rises, I'm closer and closer to having to make that choice.

Russell Field appears from almost nowhere at the end of a residential street, the neighborhood now pretty different from the working-class one that built up around it during the latter half of the twentieth century.

During the season it's a bustling hub, but right now, at just past seven in the morning on a Monday in November, it's eerily quiet, as if the baseball gods have gone to sleep for the next six months, waiting for spring.

Getting out of the car, I take a long leap over a puddle starting to gather at the edge of the sidewalk. I reach back to hold my hand out for Sullivan. I can feel her in there, hesitating, not taking it. I can just picture her eyeing the puddle, doing the math on whether her heels are high enough to keep her feet dry.

With a resigned sigh, her hand slides into mine. She lets me take her weight for a split second as she follows my leap with one of her own, landing with improbable lightness beside me, feet dry. She draws away instantly before I can really register how soft her skin feels under the callouses on my fingertips.

"It's a hell of a ballpark." I gaze up at the landmark, seeing it in a way I never have before, like a potential home.

Russell Field was built on the same spot where Ebbetts Field used to stand, named for the old railroad family that founded the team in the 1950s after the Dodgers fled for the west coast. The team is owned by a group now, a few corporations and bored billionaires looking for a tax write-off and to be able to say they own part of a major league team, but its original owners did their best to make it a great place to play.

"It is," she agrees with me, a rare enough occurrence that I don't know how to respond. But it's hard not to remember the last time she and I stood outside an empty ballpark together.

Glancing down just enough to take in her profile, I see a strand of silky blonde hair has escaped, and I resist the urge to reach over and tuck it behind her ear.

"Was a great place to play," I add, and cringe at how bland

and generic I sound. Really? I couldn't come up with anything better than that?

"Practicing your answer for the reporters when they ask you about it?" she retorts, rightly mocking me.

I'm off my game. It's been too long since I sparred with her like this and she never holds back.

It's one of the things I respect about her.

"And how does Russell Field compare with Dodger Stadium?" I ask, recovering, in my best imitation of a nasally sports reporter.

Sullivan lets out a short huff of laughter before cutting it off with a cough I'm pretty sure is fake.

"C'mon," she says, "Stew's around here somewhere. If you're here for an interview this early, it's because neither one of you want anyone to know, and standing out here admiring the ballpark is bound to get you seen."

Dutifully, I follow her toward the entrance reserved for players and the front-office employees, where an assistant she calls Gregory is waiting to take our luggage and escort us to the executive elevator.

"Ms Sullivan, welcome back," Gregory says, and then, as he turns toward me, "Mr Reynolds requested you join him and Mr Avery in their meeting once you've been able to freshen up."

I glance back at her and, yeah, she looks a bit worn around the edges. Half a day on a plane from Tokyo would do that to anyone, but, despite that, I have to admit it doesn't make her any less gorgeous. Just a little disheveled. It's a good look on her.

I manage to mostly control the direction of my gaze while she stands in front of me in the elevator, before getting off on the floor below where I'm headed.

"Don't get too comfortable," she calls back, as she walks

away, and I allow himself to appreciate the silky slide of her skirt over her curves.

"Wouldn't dream of it," I shoot back, but she's already rounding the corner and out of sight.

Gregory clears his throat roughly, the younger man sending me a narrow-eyed glare as I lean back and allow the elevator doors to close.

I shrug one shoulder in mock defeat. "Not my biggest fan."

The glare doesn't soften.

Right. Okay. She's got allies here. Strong ones, if Stew's personal assistant is in her corner.

There's no reason why she shouldn't.

In all our showdowns, I never accused her of being incompetent. It would make sense that what she's helped build in the last year would have made people loyal to her. The Eagles were a joke at the end of last season, and since she came on board they're a team on the rise. But they need more than just people crunching numbers to make them into a championship-caliber team.

And that's why I'm here.

Ding!

The elevator arrives and, when the doors open, Stew is on the other side, a broad grin spread over a tanned face with more lines than I remember and a swathe of hair, grayer and a bit thinner than the last time I saw him too.

He looks good, though. Really good. And happy to see me. I'm only a step out of the elevator when he pulls me into a bear hug, quite the feat since he was always at least half a foot shorter than me and has lost an inch or two more in the last twenty years.

"Hey kid," he grumbles, in that gritty voice of his, forever made rough by years of yelling at umps and corralling baby hot-shot ballplayers who thought their shit didn't stink.

"Hey, Skip." He'll never not be my old skipper, the man who taught me so much about what it meant to be a professional baseball player instead of an overgrown kid playing a child's game.

"Been a minute since anyone called me that. C'mon back. Let's get started and maybe, by the time I'm done, I'll be calling *you* Skip."

Oh, yeah. I'm in.

Chapter 3

FRANCESCA

Sleep helps.

I knew it would, but that doesn't make it any less annoying.

For our players and the fans our season is over.

For me, it's just getting started.

And sleeping in?

That's a waste of time.

It's been so long since I've woken up with the golden glow of dim afternoon autumn sunlight pouring through the sheer curtains. I clearly forgot to pull the thicker blackout drapes closed when I collapsed into my bed.

But it isn't the sun that woke me up. It's my phone, buzzing on the nightstand, and just before it vibrates off the edge, my hand shoots out to catch it.

"Hey B," I mumble, as I accept the call, letting my eyes fall shut again as I hold the phone to one ear and burrow the other side of my face deeper into my pillow.

Bianca's been my best friend since childhood and lives in

LA with her husband, so her calls get answered, but she gets the version of me that's still kind of asleep.

"I'm ignoring the fact that you flew right over me without stopping and staying with us for a day or two. Nothing is going on right now at work and you could definitely take a couple of days off, but I'm preemptively forgiving you because I just saw the alert on my phone."

And just like that I'm fully awake, immediately rolling over and propping myself up against the headboard, putting Bianca on speaker and scrolling through my phone, trying to find it.

But I've been asleep too long. There are way too many texts and alerts.

"Which one?"

"The Eagles hired Charlie Avery?" Bianca isn't a sports fan, at all, but she does keep her alerts set for my team, even back during my first job in baseball with the Rancho Cucamonga Quakes, one of the Dodger's minor league affiliates.

"Ugh, did that drop already? I was hoping we'd be able to keep it under wraps for at least another couple of days."

"Nothing official. He's been seen around Brooklyn and apparently there's a team source too."

That'll be Gregory. Stew must have asked him to leak it to the press. They've probably already even hammered out the broader details of his contract. Stew works fast when he wants something and, only God knows why, but he wants Charlie Avery in the Eagles' dugout.

"Yeah, there'll be a press conference soon, I guess," I say, finishing my thoughts aloud.

"You knew?" Bianca asks, and I can picture my friend, all the way on the other side of the country, her dark eyebrows lifting toward her wild riot of brown curls.

"Yeah, I knew. I—" I could talk about how I saw him, about how he was the exact same arrogant son of a bitch I worked with back in LA, but despite the sleep doing its job, I don't quite have the energy. I just let the sentence trail off, but Bianca picks it up for me.

"I know you hated working with him when you were both here, and then there was . . ." she trails off.

"It was a kiss, B. It's not a dirty word."

"The kiss, then. Are you okay with it? Did you talk to Stew about it?"

"I absolutely did not tell Stew about that. Besides, he loves Charlie, managed him in the minors. It's . . . it is what it is, and I have some time before I really need to work with him on the day to day, not until Spring Training, so a few months until I'm ready to strangle him."

"Got you. Okay, changing the subject. How was Japan? How was . . . what's his name?"

I always love when Bianca asks about baseball, because she has absolutely no idea what I'm talking about, but she's my best friend, so she still asks.

"Kai Nakamura. Twenty-five, left-handed pitcher and he's *so* good, B. I'm going to lose my mind if we don't get to sign him. He can spot every pitch and I swear his curve ball just drops off the table. He pitched a perfect game in game seven to win a championship. I've never seen anything like that before in my life."

"I don't really know what any of that means," she admits, just like she always does, "but I'm glad he lived up to the hype."

"Now I just need ownership to pony up the cash."

"How much?"

"Probably in the three hundred million range, maybe more."

"Just to throw a baseball?"

"To throw a baseball better than anyone else when your teams' yearly revenue is nearly two hundred million dollars and signing a player from Japan of this stature means an estimated revenue increase upwards of thirty million dollars a year."

A lot of people have issues with how much professional athletes get paid. Bianca's an academic librarian, so I'm sure she can imagine a million uses for that kind of money. But I've always argued that the money being in the hands of the players instead of just sitting in the billionaire owners' respective bank accounts is a net win.

"And Stew's on board?"

"Yeah, I think so, but listen, I've gotta go. I need to head back into the office."

"Back in? Did you go there straight from the airport and then work all day yesterday?"

"Maybe."

"Frankie!" she scolds. "What did we talk about?"

I scoff lightly. "I can do the work-life balance thing when I have a ring."

"I assume you mean a World Series ring?"

"What other kind of ring could I mean? Wait, is Bianca 'I waited literal years after I found the love of my life to get married because we had things we wanted to accomplish first' Dimitriou asking about my love life?"

"I just worry about you. You were never like me. I was always happy being single before Xavier and I finally figured everything out, but there hasn't really been anyone since Shane for you, right? Not anyone serious anyway."

I ignore the question because she knows the answer. "B, I appreciate the concern, but I promise you, I'm fine. I'm more than fine, and I'll be better than fine if I get ownership to sign off on a competitive offer for Nakamura."

"Okay, but promise me you won't go in for at least another couple of hours. Give your body time to adjust to the time change or you're going to be a mess for the rest of the week, and I know you have a couple more work trips coming up soon. Promise me."

"Fine, I promise. I'll go for a run, clear my head a bit."

"I guess it would be too much for me to ask you to rest a little more?"

"Definitely."

"Okay, fine, have a good run."

"Tell Xavier I said hi."

"I will and, listen, if you need to talk about the Charlie Avery thing, you call me, okay?"

"Yeah, okay. Love you, bye."

"Love you, bye!"

Sliding out from under the covers, I press my feet into the carpet beneath my bed, the one that came with the place. Beige and nondescript, but plush enough to make fists in with my toes, grounding me after a long-ass few days.

The taupe nail polish I got at my last pedicure is looking pretty rough as I stretch my legs out and then rotate my ankles, both of them cracking in a satisfying way as I turn them one way and then the other.

Then, with a groan, as my spine echoes those cracks, I stand up, stretching my arms over my head.

And that's it. I'm up and moving with purpose to the closet to find running tights and a long-sleeved t-shirt to wear for a quick mile around the park.

Running was always my least favorite part of being an athlete. It was something to be avoided at all costs, a punishment for lack of performance on the field, for messing around at practice or, occasionally, for being a little too mouthy with a coach.

Now, running is a sanctuary, physical activity to make the constant whirring of my brain quiet to a gentle hum and, with my apartment just off Prospect Park, I have a place to escape to that nearly silences the city that never sleeps.

I jog down the stairs and groan at the Open House sign in the main entry of the two-family brownstone that I own the top two floors of, making a mental note to barricade myself in my upstairs unit when I get back to avoid the influx of people desperate to move into this neighborhood. They need to be willing to hear me pacing the floor of my apartment all hours of the day, though, because even when I'm home, I'm working.

The air is brisk when I make it outside and I switch my Apple Watch to a workout and choose a run. After a quick tap, I set a brisk pace down the block before crossing over Ocean Avenue. I head straight into the winding paths shaded by trees bedecked with orange, red and yellow leaves; their fallen brethren crunching steadily and satisfyingly beneath my feet.

And there it is, the silence I needed to focus my mind and keep it from spinning out of control.

Okay, so the plan for next week.

I wanted to pitch Stew my Nakamura strategy, but that got foiled by Charlie Avery's audacity to make today the day he decided retirement wasn't for him. I'm still not sure what his deal is. He's a multimillionaire and not an idiot, so he was probably smart with his money. He definitely doesn't need a job in the sense that most people, including me, need their jobs. So why is he doing this?

Everyone always thought he'd be a great manager after he retired. His people skills are generally good, our relationship notwithstanding, but getting back into the grind of a major league season is a lot for someone who did it for two decades and called it quits.

He's old in baseball years, but young for, you know, life. Not even forty. He could have an entire existence doing something else, anything else, if he chose.

Then again, what's better than a life in baseball?

I can't think of anything else I'd rather do.

Maybe we have that in common?

Maybe it's the only thing we have in common?

Except . . . that kiss.

I drove home that night my lips tingling. Well, every part of me tingling. No one had ever kissed me like that, not even my ex. Or, at least, I'd never *felt* a kiss that way, like he was trying to see into my soul. Desperation and passion and skill.

It was the skill that stunned me more than anything. There was never not a gaggle of female fans hanging out in every ballpark and hotel bar, ready to shoot their shot, in the time I'd known him, and that was toward the end. It was probably even worse at the beginning of his career.

So, the fact that, despite not having to work for the attention, he took the time to be really, really good at kissing . . . it said something about him, something unquantifiable and, therefore, incredibly confusing.

I don't like things that don't add up.

I'm circling past the dog beach, the little alcove where dogs roam on the rocks near the smaller of the park's two lakes. Turning around, I grin, knowing that on my right will be the Long Meadow Ballfields, seven baseball and softball diamonds nestled into the park, empty aside for a few retired men's slow-pitch softball games, the only thing that can be scheduled for the middle of a weekday afternoon in the fall.

The men on the field closest to me look to be in their late sixties, or even older, strapped up with braces on their knees and ankles, some looking more likely to fall over than stay upright. But there they are, in their sixth or seventh decade of life still out there, still playing the game they've loved their entire lives.

The same game I've loved since I was a little girl, nestled in my dad's lap to watch Mike Piazza and the Dodgers power their way to a division title, hooking me for life.

Okay, that's enough sentimentality.

I'm barely two or three strides into the jog home when my eyes catch two men waving from the field.

I don't get recognized often, but I live just a few blocks from the ballpark and there are some fans dialed in enough to know who I am and what I do. New Yorkers, even the ones who can pick me out of a lineup, mostly leave me alone, though there are moments when they want to chat.

Normally, I don't mind, but right now I really need to get back.

The two men aren't wearing uniforms, aren't geared up for a game, but my eyes aren't strong enough to make out anything other than their business casual clothes and their general frames. Large, athletic, one fair skinned, one darker and, as I squint in their direction, I'm able to focus just enough to make out Charlie Avery's grimace and the broad grin plastered across Javy Vasquez's face.

I should have known.

Those two were inseparable during their playing days. Why would it be any different now?

Javy lives around here somewhere. His wife's business is in New York – fashion design, if I'm remembering correctly. I've run into them on occasion. He does some spots on MLB Network and he was at the ballpark for a few games last season with his kids.

As they draw closer and I take a few steps in their direction, a realization passes over me and I know without even having to ask exactly why they're wandering the baseball fields of Prospect Park.

If Avery's agreed to be our manager, there's no one else he'd want to be his pitching coach.

"Vasquez," I say, acknowledging him with a nod and a grin.

We always got along back in LA, though I'm pretty sure any objections he had to my analysis were just filtered through Charlie. Regardless, he almost always stuck to the gameplan I devised. Not that it ever really changed. Some players are an analyst's dream because they're so consistently good that what they perceive as their own strengths and what the numbers bear out are virtually identical.

"Frankie, it's good to see you," he says, and that's when I finally notice the glove on his left hand. Charlie has one too, with a ball nestled into the webbing. Despite myself, it makes me smile. Still just two little boys playing catch.

"You too. Welcome to the Eagles," I say, holding a hand out to him.

Vasquez grins broadly and shakes it firmly. "You always were one step ahead of the rest of us."

"I assume you're going to need a suite for Maria and the kids this season?"

"Nah, this one won't be using his, so we'll just mooch off of his ass."

"Who says I won't be using it?" Charlie cuts in, mock offended.

"Dude, you didn't use the one in LA and you won't be using the one here."

"So, what did he say to talk you into getting back into the game? Last I checked you were a hard no to every single feeler every team has put out."

Javy shrugs. "When your best friend calls and asks you to coach with him, you say yes."

"And you decided to play a celebratory game of catch?"

"Obviously," Charlie says, and slides his mouth into that megawatt grin that had paparazzi constantly clamoring for him outside of every nightclub and hot spot in LA.

"How's your arm feel?"

Javy laughs. "Right now, great, but ask me tomorrow. I haven't actually thrown a baseball in more than a year. Shoulder might fall off in my sleep."

"You're sure? We could use another arm," I say, only half joking. Nakamura's the goal, but not a guarantee, and you can never have too much pitching.

He winks at me and shakes his head. His career is over, was over when the final doctor shook his head and agreed with what all the other doctors before him had said.

Just like what the doctors said about Charlie's knee.

I glance over their shoulders to the old men still roaming the fields, moving with aching slowness to run the bases and chase down a weakly hit foul ball.

Guys like Charlie and Javy won't do that, they can't, their pride won't allow it, not after playing at the highest levels, competing against the best in the world, day in and day out, but the gleam in their eyes is the same: the brightness, the joy, it radiates off of them, even after a simple game of catch.

So, they'll do whatever they have to do to keep baseball in their lives, even if it means seven months of the year crisscrossing the country in cramped airplane seats and watching other, younger men do what they once did, if not quite as well.

"How much do you know about Kai Nakamura and what do you think it'll take to teach him your sinker?"

The guys laugh and I join them, but then my phone buzzes

in the pocket of my leggings and a voice in my earbuds tells me it's a call from Stew.

"Hey, boss, what's up?" I ask and mouth *Stew* to Charlie's mouthed *who?*

"I just got a call from Daniel Wilson," Stew says, without even saying hello.

"Ugh," I groan. Wilson is the most powerful sports agent in the game and the most notorious, particularly for demanding way more money than his clients are worth. "And what did that sleazeball want?"

"To give us the heads up. Tomorrow morning Ethan Quicke will be opting out of his contract."

"What? But the last time we talked with him, he said he had no intention of leaving."

"Seems that Quicke was watching the Japan Series last night and caught sight of a familiar face in the stands. Since he thinks we'll be offering a substantial contract to Nakamura, he wants to ensure his compensation as our current number-one starter is . . . how did Wilson put it? Commensurate with his past and future contributions to the organization."

It's going to cost the team extra millions to sign Quicke if they have competition from other organizations.

Extra millions that were supposed to go to Nakamura.

Damn it.

This is my fault and I need to figure out a way to fix it.

Chapter 4

CHARLIE

"We're going to open up to questions now," Juan, the Eagles' head of communications says to the sea of media sitting out in front of me. We're about the same age and I remember him running press conferences whenever we were in Brooklyn. I didn't know his name back then, but I plan on making friends. There's no one more important to have on your side as a manager, especially in a major media market.

Sitting at the dais in the Eagle's press room, I have on a creamy white jersey with a blue BROOKLYN across my chest in all caps over my crisp dress shirt and a cap with the NY in block letters on my head. I signed my contract about an hour ago in Stew's office. Now I'm being introduced to the local reporters and a handful of national media types. There are more than a few familiar faces. I haven't been out of the game long enough for there to be a total changing of the guard.

Back when I first got to the big leagues there was pretty extensive media training. A bunch of guys from the press office taught us how to deal with the gaggle of reporters that would ask us questions after every game. LA's obviously a big city and with that came a pretty hot spotlight on us, on and off the field.

One of the things they teach you is that the things that trip you up won't always be obvious, that a good reporter will come at you sideways and, before you know it, you're saying things you never meant to say.

When the question comes, it follows the ones I expected. It's like I was being lulled into a false sense of security.

There was the meatball starter question, "How does it feel to wear a different jersey for the first time in your career?"

"There's some poetry to it, I think. After starting with the Dodgers, the original Brooklyn franchise, having this new part of my career beginning with the team that brought baseball back to Brooklyn feels fitting."

And then the obvious follow up of, "What does it feel like to be here as part of the team instead of the opposition?"

"I'll let you know once we actually play a game."

"How will your tenure be different given the organization's historical lack of success?"

"The Cubs and the Sox managed to get off the schneid after what? More than a hundred years each? I think I can say the Eagles'll do it before we get that far."

There are a few amused guffaws at that.

Maybe that's what had me letting my guard down.

The next reporter is sitting dead center a couple of rows back. Pete Bruckner, the Eagles beat reporter for as long as I can remember, one of the most famous writers in the game. His hair is entirely gray now, almost the same color as the jersey I'm donning, no sign of the thick black curls he sported when I first came up to the big leagues.

"After a modicum of promise shown toward the end of last season, are you looking forward to building upon it with the addition of some new blood – Kai Nakamura for example?" Pete asks, pen at the ready to jot down whatever I say despite his phone recording the session as well.

I can't help but dart a glance to my right, where Sullivan and a few other geeks from the analytics department are seated up against the wall.

"Nakamura's a fantastic pitcher, but we already have a good mix of guys here who, like you said, showed a lot of promise toward the end of last season. And I'm excited to see what they can do."

I'm ready to move on, but Pete gestures that he has another question. "Just a follow up. What about Ethan Quicke? I have his agent Dan Wilson quoted as saying, 'If the Eagles have enough money to lure Charlie Avery out of retirement and pursue the top prospect out of Japan in recent memory, then they have enough money to pay my client what he's worth.' What do you say to that?"

"I say that I know Dan Wilson well enough to know that what he says and reality very often don't coincide."

Pete's bushy gray eyebrows shoot up toward his receding hairline and he leans forward. "So you're saying that the Eagles *don't* have enough money to sign you, Nakamura and Quicke?"

"No, that's not what I . . ."

But I'm cut off by Juan. Thank fuck. "Only one follow up each or we'll never get out of here."

The interruption is too late, though. Even as they move on to another reporter, I can't take my eyes off Pete as he sits down, ignoring whatever the next question is, scribbling furiously into his notebook.

Fuck.

The rest of the press conference blends together and then we're breaking up for pictures, but I just hear that question over and over again on a loop in my head. What I should have said is simple: *Our front office is dedicated to putting a championship-caliber team out on the field. Obviously, pitching is an area of need and I have full confidence it'll be addressed before we break camp in March.*

It's saying something while saying absolutely nothing at all.

Exactly what I was taught all those years ago.

After there were pictures taken of every possible combination of me with a dozen or so guys representing the ownership group – their names have already flittered out of my head – plus Stew and a few other executive types from the organization.

I look around for Pete, but he's already gone, probably to file his story about how frustrated the Eagles' new manager already is at their budget constraints.

I move out of the press room, the fluorescent overhead lights set up for the cameras at the back of the room now replaced by the high ceilings of the large halls. They make up the outer edges of the Stadium, bracing the stands on the other side of the cinderblock. Light shines in from the upper levels, casting angular lines of shadow over the concrete floors.

"This way," Stew says, leading us away from the people still milling around after the press conference.

Frankie's a couple of steps ahead of us and, as we get farther and farther away from everyone else, I get the sense that she's actually leading us.

A little pit of dread swirls in my gut when we make it to a large dark-wood-paneled entrance that looks like it's from an era gone by, compared to every other steel door in the wide walkway.

The clubhouse: the locker room in every other major sport but, in baseball, we still call it a clubhouse, a word, like the door, from another time.

Carpeted floors, lockers trimmed with the same stained wood as the doors we just walked through, large comfortable executive chairs in front of every locker. They're all empty now, but come April they'll be fully stocked with everything a ball player needs: gloves, bats, warmups, uniforms, cleats, hoodies and jackets, all in the distinct cream and blue the Eagles have been wearing since the middle of the twentieth century.

And in the center of it all, Frankie is down near the floor in a squat. She's in one of those skirt suits again, her personal uniform, I guess, the deep blue skirt hugging her hips, knees pressed together as she balances on those high heels. Head down, staring at the pristine carpet, her blonde hair is pulled into a knot at the back of her neck.

I know that position, I was in it often enough. She was a catcher before she was an analyst. It's exactly what we do when we're thinking, when we've got the batter on the ropes and our pitcher needs the right call to get that strikeout.

It's the sexiest fucking thing I've ever seen.

I don't have long to admire it, though, because she looks up and absolute thunderbolts are firing out of her blue eyes.

Standing slowly, her voice is low and measured. "What were you thinking? You know better than that."

"I misspoke," I say, attempting to downplay it. "It happens."

Tilting her head to the side at my blithe dismissal, her volume rises as she goes on. "That's crap. You were the blandest, most boring interview in the whole league for twenty years and you decide on your first day on the job as a manager to completely undermine me?"

"What?" I ask, baffled. "I'm not undermining anything. I misspoke. It happens."

"It can't happen. Not here. What don't you get? We have *one chance* to make this work before we become a shiny tax write-off again. Why would you comment at all?"

"Okay, easy Frankie, he gets it," Stew says, and I whirl around. He's sitting in one of the chairs, tie loosened and collar unbuttoned. Does he agree with her? He's pale and there's a bead of sweat dripping down from his hairline above his temple.

"Does he?" Sullivan asks, and I turn back to her. "*Do you get it?* Because we have to be a united front on this. It's the only way we're going to convince the guys we need to sign here. You don't think Nakamura and his agents are going over every single thing that comes out of every club before he posts for the free agent market? You don't think they'll hear that and think, *Wow, the Eagles aren't committed to winning, better go to the Yankees or the Dodgers?*"

She's right. I know she is, and I'm halfway to opening my mouth to admit it when Stew cuts in again.

"Enough," Stew says, through a gasp, and when I turn again, he's slumped back into the chair. "You two can fight it out later. Call an ambulance. I think I'm having a heart attack."

"Is he going to be okay?" Javy asks, as he plates up the steak he's been grilling on his back patio.

I don't have a place in the city yet, so Javy and Maria offered me their guest room. Guest floor, actually. Their house has an entire floor they put together for Maria's mom when she comes from Puerto Rico to stay. It's so nice I might just move in for good, which would save me the trouble of dealing with Brooklyn real estate.

"I don't know," I say, taking a long swig of my beer. "Last update I had was that he was going in for surgery."

That was hours ago, when Rita, Stew's wife, sent us home.

The steak smells amazing, but, shit, I can't stomach any-thing right now.

I lost my dad when I was in the minors, and Stew stepped in back then, taking a scared kid under his wing. I'm scared again right now, and it's been a long-ass time since I felt that way.

"We have a guest," Maria says, coming back out onto the patio. Sullivan is trailing behind her. I pop up out of my chair.

"I'm sorry to intrude. I was going to call, but I didn't have your number," she says, actually looking sheepish. It's not an expression I'm used to from her. Immediately the fear becomes sheer panic.

"Stew . . . is he . . ."

"He's okay," she reassures me.

"Thank fuck," I say, and let out a shaky breath before lifting my beer and chugging the last of it.

"He's out of surgery and kind of spacey, but he's insisting on seeing us and won't calm down about it. So the doctors called Rita and she told them to let us in before he has another heart attack."

"Yeah? Let's go."

She has a car waiting for us and I open the door and hold it for her. She slides past, her shoulder ghosts my chest. There's a scent she wears, light and soft, like baby powder and . . . laven-der, maybe? It contrasts so entirely with the hard edges of her personality that I actually let out a soft snort.

"What?" she asks, smoothing that pencil skirt under her knees as I climb in after her.

"Nothing. Just glad we didn't kill our boss on my first day." She opens her mouth and I can *feel* her sharp retort coming, but I shake my head. "You were right. I fucked up."

"Yes, you did," is all she says, and it's what I deserve for giving in, even an inch apparently. Silence reigns for a couple of blocks, the neighborhood relatively quiet until we turn past the stadium and the sidewalks are lined with people walking to dinner and their local bars. "I killed the story."

"What?"

"I had Juan call Pete and had him kill the story about your Daniel Wilson quote."

I can't really believe what I just heard. Is she calling a truce?

"What's the catch?" I ask.

"Nothing big. You'll do an exclusive sit-down with him in the next couple of weeks in return, but you don't have to worry about it."

"Except on TV and sports radio."

"Yeah, well, don't listen to it. They'll move on by tomorrow. It's football season."

"It's that easy?"

"No, but it'll drive you insane. New York isn't LA. They lose their minds over *everything*. You gotta learn how to tune it all out or it'll become a self-fulfilling prophecy."

"Thanks."

"Don't do it again," she says. No "you're welcome" or "no problem", just . . . "don't do it again".

So, not a truce then. Just damage control.

The hospital is operating like it's the middle of the day. Bright lights, people everywhere in the waiting rooms, walking the halls, doctors and nurses hurrying to their next patients, EMTs heading back out in the night in their ambulances.

I've always hated hospitals. I lost both my parents in one and if that isn't enough to make me loathe them, the only time I was really in one myself was when I tore my lat midway through my career and had to sit out nearly an entire season because of it.

Apparently, Sullivan knows where she's going, confidently

heading straight for the elevator instead of stopping at the desk to ask.

When the elevator doors close behind us, there's a short gasp, followed by a "Yoooooooo," drawn out under the breath of whoever is standing behind us. And then the voice follows up with: "Are you Charlie Avery?"

I turn and nod with a smile at the young man behind me, standing there with his wife or girlfriend, who doesn't look like she has any idea who I am. "Yeah, man. It's nice to meet you."

"Bro, do they, like, make you get a physical to be the manager?"

Sullivan snorts next to me and murmurs, "We probably should."

"Nah, I'm just here to visit a friend," I say, ignoring her.

"Shit. Everything okay?"

News of Stew's heart attack must not have gotten out yet.

"Yeah, turns out he's gonna be fine."

"Glad to hear that, man. My sister just had her baby, so we're gonna go see her, but can I get a pic real quick?"

"Of course," I say.

"I'll take it," Sullivan volunteers, just as the elevator dings.

We pull in tight, the guy holding his hand up in a peace sign while I point at him like he's the man.

They get off the elevator and the doors close before Sullivan lets out a chuckle.

"Is that your whole life? Just everywhere you go people want to take a picture with you?"

"Pretty much," I say, sending her my best million-dollar smile and a wink before dropping the façade and rolling my eyes at myself.

The elevator dings again, saving me from whatever she's about to say. The cardiac care unit is laid out in front of us, a large nurses' desk surrounded by small glass rooms, each one with a patient hooked up to all kinds of machines, whirring and beeping, keeping them monitored and alive.

That panic from earlier – that faded when Sullivan said that Stew was alright – is back and it's solidified into a hard knot in my stomach: small, but present, and making itself known. I take a deep breath and let it out slowly as I follow Sullivan past one patient and then another before we arrive at Stew's room.

One of the nurses nods at us. "You'll be Ms Sullivan and Mr Avery?" she asks, checking a clipboard.

It's definitely past visiting hours. There's no one else there. Clearly an exception is being made, so I make sure to be as polite as possible. "Yes, ma'am, that's us."

"You have ten minutes," she warns, before waving us in.

Stew's awake, hooked up to various machines, one probably monitoring his heart, another looks like maybe oxygen levels and there are tubes in his nose probably helping with his breathing post-surgery.

"Hey Skip," I manage to say, even though now it feels like there's an actual rock in my gut.

"Figured you'd be out of it a little longer," Sullivan chimes in, but her voice is soft, way softer than I've ever heard it before. She approaches his bedside and reaches for his hand, taking it in hers, careful not to disturb the IV.

I stand behind her, my back to the glass wall. The room is small, barely big enough for the two of us to crowd beside his bed.

"No rest for the wicked," Stew rasps, and lets out a slow breath before answering the question neither of us asked. "Triple bypass. Lucky to be alive, apparently. Don't feel that lucky right now. They split me open like a chicken."

Sullivan cringes, but I force myself to laugh, knowing that's what Stew wants, and the grin that lights up his face lets me know I read it right.

"I . . . we . . ." she starts and stops. "I'm sorry we were so . . ."

"You didn't clog my arteries, Frankie," he cuts her off gently. "Smoking for twenty years and forty years on the road eating terrible food did that just fine. Though I wouldn't mind if you two could refrain from the bickering around me."

"Done," she agrees.

"You got it," I confirm.

"Good," he says, nods firmly and then winces.

"What was so urgent you need to see us tonight?" Frankie asks, her voice still soft.

"I'm gonna take a leave of absence. Doctor's orders. Nothing stressful for at least a few months while I recover, and apparently my job is stressful."

"Okay, so what's the plan?" I ask, crossing my arms over my chest, leaning harder into the glass wall.

"You're taking over."

He's not talking to me, though.

He's talking to Sullivan, looking right at her.

"Interim General Manager, until I get back."

Sullivan backs up a step and then another until she's barely an inch away from me and that soft scent invades my senses when I inhale. It takes a lot of self-control to not reach out and put a steadying hand on her shoulder. I've never seen her so thrown before. It's so stunning that the creeping panic I was feeling in this godawful place melts away.

"Stew, you can't just . . . there are other guys who have been . . ." she stutters, but he shakes his head.

"There's no one else. I know you have what it takes to run this team and you're going to prove me right. Okay?"

"Okay," she agrees.

"And you," he says, his eyes flickering over her shoulder to me, as she finally realizes just how close we are. She steps away quickly, glancing back at me as she does. Her eyes are still wide in shock and I'm not sure if she's actually taken a breath. "You're going to help her."

"Stew, I'm no GM."

"No, you're not. You don't have the head for it. But the organization is going to need to know you have my back re this decision."

"Done," I agree.

"Good," he affirms, and lets out a heavy breath, his eyes flickering closed. "You can kick them out now."

I don't realize who he's talking to at first, but then a voice calls from the doorway.

"Your ten minutes was up ten minutes ago," the nurse from earlier says. "I'm going to have to ask you to leave."

Sullivan leans over and presses a kiss to Stew's forehead. He waves her away. Then I approach and press my hand to his forearm. He's warm to the touch and that's a relief. I somehow thought he'd be freezing cold, but, no, he's warm and alive and he's going to be okay.

"I mean it. You're going to help her," he whispers, his eyes still closed. I'm sure Sullivan doesn't hear it.

"I promise."

Then he pats my hand and, with a final squeeze of his arm, I follow Sullivan out the door and back to the elevator.

It's empty this time.

"You don't have to help me," she says, as the doors close, turning to me and looking me dead in the eye.

"Skip asked, so I will."

"Then I need one thing from you."

"What's that?"

"The best way you can help me is to stay out of my way."

"What? No, that's not . . ."

"You and I don't see eye to eye on what makes a great base-ball team. We never have. Do I have that right?"

"You do."

"Stew entrusted me with the team in his absence and he wants you to help. So I'm asking you not to interfere with my decisions. I have a plan for this team. It's why they hired me and it's why Stew asked me to take over. If you want to help, you can stand there and look pretty and agree with everything I say when I pitch to ownership on a decision."

"I don't think that's what Stew meant when he asked me to help you."

"What was with you back there, anyway?" she asks, and I nearly get whiplash at the change of subject.

"What?"

"The arms crossed and the 'get as far away from Stew as you could' stance."

Ding!

We're at the ground floor.

I stride past her out of the elevator, but she keeps pace easily enough even in those heels that bring her forehead right to my nose.

"I don't like hospitals," I say, as we finally escape out into the Brooklyn night and I pull in a deep breath of crisp air, only slightly tainted by the exhaust from the ambulances idling at the curb.

"Fair enough," she says, wrapping her arms around herself and rubbing them up and down against the chill. "Where's the car? He said he'd be right around."

"So that's it?" I ask.

"What's it?"

"You're just letting it go? Me helping you?"

"Yeah."

"Why?"

"You know how Stew said that you don't have the head for being a GM?" she says, as the car pulls into the driveway and comes to a stop right in front of us. She opens the door for herself and then turns back to me.

"Yeah?" I ask, stepping closer and getting another hit of that fucking incredible scent as her eyes flash at me, the streetlights making them sparkle.

"Well, I do."

The implication is clear. She'll allow me to be there because she knows she can run circles around me.

I should be insulted.

I should be furious.

And I'd have time to be either of those things if I wasn't so fucking turned on by it.

Chapter 5

FRANCESCA

Interim General Manager.

This is what I've always wanted.

Almost.

One day that *interim* qualifier won't be there. But for now it's time to get to work.

Russell Field is nearly empty when I arrive, just a few security guards and Gregory, Stew's assistant, who is faithfully at his desk every day by seven.

It seems that won't change even with Stew in the hospital.

"I'm going to swap desks to sit over here while you're filling in. He left his notes from his call with Dan Wilson for you," Gregory says from my office doorway, a stack of paperwork in his arms. "And his notes on the pitch presentation you sent him about Nakamura. I'm going to head over to the hospital in a few if you have anything for him."

"I don't right now," I say, taking the files from him. "Go and make sure he's resting as much as possible and then I'm going to need you back here. I won't be able to do this without you."

"Really?" Gregory asks, clear surprise playing across his face.

Did he think I was just going to take over?

Do everything myself?

Probably.

But I won't.

I can't do this entirely by myself.

He's a kid just out of city college, not the usual Ivy League graduate that gets an opportunity at baseball operations for a major league club. He grew up just a few blocks from where we stand right now. This is his dream as much as its mine. Plus, he's phenomenal at his job. He loves the game and he knows his stuff.

"Really," I reassure him, and he lets out a heavy sigh, but doesn't make a move to leave. "Now, what's on your mind?"

"There are some rumblings," he starts, but I don't need to hear more.

"Out of Richard and Harry's office?"

Gregory's silence is enough of an answer.

Richard Dobbins and Harry Turner, assistant general managers just like me: one for major league scouting, the other for player development. Both have been with the Eagles longer than I have, both kept on from the previous administration before Stew moved from the dugout to the front office.

Both probably think they should have gotten the nod in Stew's absence.

"If it means anything, I think you're the right person for the job."

"I appreciate that."

"And Stew wouldn't just give it to you because . . ."

"Because I'm a woman?"

He blinks at me and then says, "I was gonna say because

he likes you better, but, yeah, that might be why they're extra pissed now that I think about it."

"Yeah," I say, grinning at the young man who is so kind he'd never assume someone was being sexist. "Do me a favor before you go, and get me Dan Wilson on the phone and hang out for a minute. I have an offer for him he's going to want to hear."

I loathe agents like Dan Wilson. I can respect an agent who goes hard for his clients, who does everything they can to get the highest bid for the most number of years. What I don't respect is the shady strategies he uses, sending "anonymous" tips to reporters, inventing phantom interest in his clients to stir up enthusiasm around the league and overvaluing his players to such an extent that many of them end up missing out on weeks or even months of a season while they wait for offers that aren't coming. He built his reputation more than a decade ago on deals that taught teams to be wary of his clients. Dan makes it about *him*, not about his players or about the game.

My desk phone rings. It's Gregory.

"I have Dan Wilson on the line."

I sit up at my desk, straightening my shoulders and lifting my chin, as if the man will be right across from me. Okay. I've got this.

"Thanks, Greg," I say and he disconnects and then transfers the call.

"Dan Wilson here. What can I do for you, Miss Sullivan?"

"Just calling to introduce myself. It hasn't hit the papers yet, but with Stew out on medical leave, I'll be serving as interim and I have full organizational authority to handle negotiations."

"I was sorry to hear about Stew. How's the prognosis?"

"I'll leave it to Stew to decide how much he wants out there, but when I saw him, he looked good."

"Glad to hear that."

"I thought you would be. Well, just wanted to touch base. You have a good one, Dan. Hope to talk to you soon. I'll have my assistant get you my cell number in case you want to talk anything through."

I disconnect the call and wait a second and then another until I'm sure he's not on the other end.

"Greg," I call out, and he wheels his chair over to my open office door. "Send Dan's assistant my cell number."

He'll call back. I know he will.

The Eagles are a major part of the leverage he wants to use for Ethan Quicke's negotiations. If we're not involved, other teams will wonder what we know about him that they don't. A nagging injury? Toxic personality? Problems off the field? Women? Alcohol? Drugs? Could be anything. Could be nothing. But if we're out of touch with him after he opted out, everyone will assume it was *something*.

My phone buzzes on my desk.

Dan Wilson.

And then another text.

—*We'll be setting up meetings for Ethan Quicke tomorrow. In person. Have your assistant reach out for details.*

In person? Wait . . . doesn't Ethan Quicke live in . . .

—*Enjoy Montana, Miss Sullivan.*

Damn it.

I played him.

He played me right back.

Okay, then.

I guess I'm going to Montana.

The boarding area near my gate is completely packed, which feels odd for a flight to Bozeman from New York. Well, New Jersey, actually. The only non-stop today is out of Newark and since it's literally my first day on the job, I wasn't going to ask ownership to use the private jet.

I'm gonna save that one for another trip to Japan if I need to. Once Nakamura gets posted and I need to emphasize, once again, just how committed we are to signing him.

But I'm not looking forward to sitting in a coach seat surrounded by what looks like a gathering of every Montana transplant in the tri-state area, almost all of them wearing something that declares them a loyalist of either the Montana State Bobcats or the Montana Grizzlies.

Ah.

College football.

How did I forget about college football?

A quick search on my phone confirms it. Montana State at home against Montana.

That's gotta be a big rivalry.

It does not bode well for Gregory finding me a hotel room, but if anyone can do it, it's him.

A woman from the airline arrives at the boarding gate and starts her announcements, so I head straight for the line. I might be in coach, but I have priority boarding with every major airline in the US. Sometimes working for a baseball team feels more like being a professional airline passenger.

"Phew, thought I wasn't gonna make it."

"What are you doing here?" I ask, not even turning to look at Charlie Avery. I can *feel* him there just fine, the clean scent of his cologne, with just a hint of spice and citrus to it, lingering ever so slightly in the air after her slid in line behind me. He always smells like he just stepped out of the best shower of his life.

It's a vast improvement from the usual heavy colognes and body sprays ballplayers tend to soak themselves in.

"I was at the hospital when Gregory was booking your flight. Told him to book two seats."

"That part I figured out. I mean *why* are you here?"

"You're going to Montana to talk to Ethan Quicke, right?"

"And if I am?"

"Stew said I should go too."

"Stew's on leave. He doesn't get a say."

"You want me to call him up in the CCU and tell him you said that?"

I ignore him. "Don't you have better things to do than fly to Bozeman? Like putting together a coaching staff?"

"I've got Javy for the pitchers. I want to take my time with the others."

The two passengers ahead of us start moving and I follow, trying not to look left toward first class when they turn that way as we board the airplane. I make a right and check my ticket.

"Keep on going," Charlie says behind me. "Gregory said we're in the last row."

"Together?"

"They were the only seats left. It was this or flying to Houston with a seven-hour layover before connecting."

"Last row it is."

The rows are three across and our seats are pressed up against the back of the plane, unable to recline, with a toilet just to our right.

Lovely.

"Been a minute since I've flown like this," Charlie mutters as he settles into the aisle seat after I move into mine beside the window. My knees are *nearly* pressed into the seatback in front of me. Charlie's even worse off: his frame both too long and too wide for the narrow space.

And so we wait with growing trepidation as the rest of the flight boards. If we got the last two seats, that means the one between us is taken, but maybe whoever it is didn't make it to the airport? A missed connection or, I don't know, *something* that'll make this trip fractionally more pleasant.

But then it happens. A tall young man, probably the same height as Charlie, lists side to side as he walks down the aisle, stumbling just slightly as he comes to a stop at the row ahead of us and then squints up at the numbers listed.

Great.

"I'm here, fucking middle seat," he slurs lightly at Charlie, and points to the open seat, but then his vision focuses on me and his eyes widen, a slow smirk lifting. "And lucky me."

I'm annoyed at the gate agent for letting him on the plane when he's *clearly* drunk, but mostly I'm pissed at myself for getting outmaneuvered by Dan Wilson. This is my punishment. Four hours and change trapped next to this overgrown cowboy playing city slicker as he flies home for a football game.

"Nah, man," Charlie says, standing up, blocking me from the guy's view. "I'm middle. You get the aisle. More leg room."

He claps the guy on the shoulder and then folds himself, somehow, into the middle seat beside me.

"You didn't have to . . ." I whisper, but he cuts me off.

"Yeah, I did," he says, yanking his seatbelt on, shifting against the straight back of the seat before crossing his arms over his chest and letting his eyes fall shut. "Wake me when we land."

"Will do."

As soon as we take off, I pull my laptop out and get to work. Charlie's deep even breathing is as constant as the absolute leaf-blower snores emanating from the drunk guy he gave up his seat to. Every now and then the man jerks awake and disappears into the bathroom, where the sliding pocket door does absolutely nothing to disguise the noises he makes in there.

Somewhere over South Dakota – according to the flight tracker on the seat back – our row buddy tosses himself back into his seat, his elbow jutting hard and fast into Charlie's side. It jostles him, not enough to wake him up, not entirely, but enough to have him shift with a light groan.

His arms unfold and his shoulders slump before his head slides down against the back wall at what has to be a terrible angle. He must realize it, even in his sleep, because he shifts his body until he's curled almost entirely to one side and his head lands gently on my shoulder. Or rather his chin does, his forehead cushioned lightly in my hair, his nose nudging at the sensitive spot just below my ear.

His contented exhale sends a soft breath against my skin, his lips nearly grazing my neck. A gentle quaking shiver slides through my body, radiating down to the tips of my toes and back up again before settling in a swirling rush of heat deep inside of me.

I let out a shaky breath, biting hard into my bottom lip to hold back a moan as he buries his face into the curve of my shoulder and rasps out a gravely "Francesca" into my over-heated skin.

No one calls me that.

I haven't gone by Francesca since the nuns in elementary school insisted on using my full name. It was so infuriating.

It's still infuriating, but this is a different kind all together.

It's infuriatingly hot.

Trying desperately to get some relief, I pull in a deep breath and let it out slowly, but then his mouth moves again, his lips brushing my pulse point and it's all I can do to keep a sharp keen from echoing at the back of my throat. I grip the edge of my tray table as my thighs unconsciously rub together beneath the soft but constraining material of my skirt. It's not enough.

I would probably be able to hold it together if I didn't already know what it feels like to have his lips pressed against mine, to know just how his tongue would nudge against my lower lip to ask permission, to already understand just how thoroughly his mouth would set the rest of my body alight, stoking a passion that's been missing in my life for far too long.

Then, with annoyingly perfect timing, our friend in the aisle seat reaffirms his calling as a landscaping crew sound machine and the burst of noise is enough to jolt Charlie awake.

"Shit," he groans and even *that's* hot, because his voice is still rough with sleep, but he moves away almost instantly. "Sorry. You should have just elbowed me. It's what my ex used to do when I got too clingy."

He says it all in a mumbled whisper and I have no idea if he even meant to say any of it. Probably not. He's still half asleep, but it takes everything in me not to call his ex a complete idiot. Who the hell elbows away a man who can make you feel like this?

I don't even particularly like him and I didn't have it in me.

Actually, maybe I should call her and ask for some tips.

Charlie shakes his head and then rakes a hand through his shaggy hair and, in the dim glow of the reading light above us, I catch a few silvers threaded through the light brown. He's not even forty, but somehow they suit him.

"What?" he asks, and I realize I must have stared for a moment too long.

"Did you get your beauty sleep?" I say, and it works, as he sends me a light eye roll.

"Never pass up a meal or a chance to sleep," he counters.

"Fair enough."

"What are you working on?"

"An offer for Quicke based on Stew's notes."

"And what are we offering him?"

I shift my laptop so he can see my screen and his eyes flicker over what I've put together.

It's four years, with a vesting option for a fifth year if he pitches more than two hundred innings in the final year. A couple of bonuses for innings thresholds beyond that, one for a CY Young award, but I doubt he'll get to that level again, post-season contributions, etc. Also, we axe the no trade clause from his last contract. Twenty-two million average annual value.

He lets out a low whistle at the number and I turn to him, one eyebrow raised. I know exactly how much he got paid for his last contract and it was nearly double what I plan on presenting to Quicke.

"What?" he asks.

"Nothing."

"C'mon, it's something. I can tell."

"Just . . ." I trail off, hesitating. "I'm still not sure what you're doing here."

"Like I said . . . "

"No, I get why you're coming to Montana, but what are you doing *here,* in the last row of a regional commercial jet."

"What can I say? I'm . . . eccentric."

"You're *something*," I shoot back, but he just smiles, this time giving the megawatt grin that made hearts flutter every day back in LA, and shrugs helplessly.

"Did you know that most professional athletes end up bankrupt after they retire?"

"I did, actually."

"I swore to my parents that if I skipped college to go pro out of high school that I would be smart with money."

"And you kept your word."

"I did. So, when I'm flying, I mostly fly coach, business class if it's a long flight." He gestures to his long legs. "When I'm looking for a place in a new city, I stay with friends instead of a hotel."

"And when you retire, you come back a year later as a manager."

"That isn't so much about the money."

"Then what?"

But before he can answer, an absolutely wretched noise comes from the end of our row as the Montana bro vomits all over himself.

The flight attendants are sympathetic and bring wipes and some air freshener, but there isn't much to be done except wait it out and try not to breathe too deeply.

The first burst of fresh air when we deplane in the spacious Bozeman airport, with its vaulted ceilings lined with wooden beams, is more than welcome. The views of the mountains in the distance as soon as we make it outside is such a stark contrast to being outside arrivals at JFK that I can't help but laugh.

Gregory, as usual, can be counted on. There's a driver waiting for us near baggage claim and he already knows to take us straight to the Kimpton Armory Hotel.

"Best hotel in Bozeman," the driver says, not seeming to recognize either of us. "You two in town for the game?"

"Of course," Charlie says. "Go Cats Go!"

I blink at him, wondering what the hell he's talking about when the driver laughs.

"I'd say what I usually say about the Grizz, but there's a lady present."

Charlie laughs with him. "Oh, she's heard worse."

"Just about fifteen minutes out. Any stops along the way?"

"No, straight to the hotel, thanks," I chime in, a little more annoyed than I probably should be at being left out of the conversation.

The ride is as quick as the driver promised and the hotel driveway is bustling. I see several of the people from our flight, though thankfully not a particular row mate. I turn back to tip our driver, but Charlie's already sliding the man a hundred-dollar bill.

"I thought you promised your parents you'd be smart with money?" I ask, but he just grins and shrugs as we take our bags and head inside the hotel. It sits large and majestic on what is otherwise a pretty nondescript street in the middle of an unremarkable neighborhood.

The air might be fresh, but the city itself doesn't do much for me.

There's a short line to check in and, when we get to the desk, a woman about my height with a bright white smile usually seen on the streets of Los Angeles greets us.

"Welcome to the Kimpton Armory Hotel, Bozeman," she says, through the grin, and though I'm the one standing in front of her, she directs the words to Charlie.

"Thank you," I say, leaning into her line of sight. "We're checking in. Two rooms, and should be under Sullivan, Francesca."

She clicks at her computer for a moment and then another. "There's just one room under Sullivan, ma'am. Could the other room be under a different name?"

Her voice is hopeful and I have to contain a snort. "Charles Avery?" I say, failing to keep her attention on me as Charlie steps up and shows me his phone.

It's a text from Gregory.

—*Was only able to secure one room. The hotel is booked solid. Sorry!*

"It's just the one room," Charlie says, as I let out a heavy sigh.

"Can you check and see if there are any other rooms that have become available? I'd really appreciate it."

The woman, Kayla on her name tag, looks at me like I've sprouted another head, but she checks and then shakes her head.

"I'm sorry. There's just the one room. How many keys will you need?"

"Two's perfect, Kayla. Thank you," Charlie says.

In the middle of nowhere Montana with Charlie Avery surrounded by literally thousands of people about to be punch drunk about their state's biggest college football rivalry and there's only one room at the inn.

Great. That's just great.

Chapter 6

CHARLIE

There's only one bed.

Technically.

There's a sofa that I'm pretty sure will pull out into a bed if I look. And I will since I'll obviously be camping out there tonight.

I toss my bag onto a luggage rack built into the wall and admire the view: not the tree-lined streets with the shadowy outlines of mountains in the distance, as nothing in the Bozeman skyline is high enough to obscure them. No, the view I mean is Sullivan, leaning up against the door jamb that leads to the suite's bedroom, pulling one high pump and then the other off her feet with a breathy sigh of relief that sends a visceral jolt through me.

She pads into the room, walking back and forth with her eyes closed, taking deep breaths, scrunching her feet as she does. Her toenails are painted a neutral color.

"What are you doing?"

"Making fists with my toes."

That's . . . not what I expected.

"Fists with your toes?"

One stormy blue eye opens and studies me, the other still shut. "Haven't you ever seen *Die Hard*?"

"I have," I admit. "I just . . ."

"Didn't think *I* would have?"

"Doesn't seem like your style."

"Yeah, and what's my style?"

"*Moneyball*?"

She smiles and I know I'm right as she quotes, "How can you not be romantic about baseball?"

I roll my eyes, hearing Brad Pitt as Billy Beane's voice in my head over hers. "I can be plenty romantic about baseball. I have a hard time being romantic about a team that never actually won anything getting lionized like it has. I think it's been bad for the game."

"Here we go," she groans.

And she's not wrong. I have *opinions* about that movie.

"They had Hudson, Zito and Mulder at the top of their rotation that year and you're gonna tell me that Scott Hatteburg's on-base percentage was why they won a hundred and three games?"

"I'm not telling you anything. Analytics were a thing before *Moneyball*, they were a thing before the book came out, before the movie came out and before you ever got to the big leagues. And I'm not going round and round with you about it. That bathroom has one of the biggest bathtubs I've ever seen, so, if you don't mind, I'm gonna go soak it in for a while before I have to deal with Ethan Quicke's massive ego."

And that's a visual that I absolutely will never get out of my head. A tub full of steamy water, a smattering of bubbles, her hair up at the top of her head, a few strands falling down, stuck against the damp, glowing skin of her cheek and her neck, her toes peeking up out of the water at the edge of the tub. Before my fantasy can travel up the length of her legs to where fuller, curvier parts of her would rise up out of the water, the click of the bathroom door closing behind the fantasy's real-life counterpart pulls me back to the present.

The sound of water filling the tub escapes through the small gap at the bottom of the bathroom door, and while I can't hear the sound of fabric hitting the floor, my imagination is good enough to know I probably should get the fuck out of this room before I spontaneously combust.

I know I have Quicke's number somewhere in my phone. We were at an All-Star Game together a few years ago. Feels like a lifetime ago now.

—*Just landed in Bozeman. You wanna grab a drink?*

—*Sure. You at the Armory?*

—*Yeah.*

—*There's a bar on the roof. Meet you in ten.*

The response is instant. Like he was waiting for someone to reach out. Huh. Now that's interesting. I wonder how many teams are actually going through with this dog-and-pony show Dan Wilson set up. Probably not that many. The market for starting pitchers is pretty light this season and none of the major contenders will likely make any moves until Nakamura is off the board.

So maybe we can get a deal done here.

I snag a little notepad and pen from the desk, jotting down a deal just a shade under the specs Sullivan laid out for me.

The view from the rooftop bar is marginally better than the one from the hotel room, but oddly familiar to me. Without the mountains in the distance, it could almost look like back home: wide expanses of flat land dotted with small cities laid in a grid pattern and small pockets of development popping up. One day they'd be populated by families that all look as vaguely the same as the houses themselves.

I don't see Quicke anywhere, so I find a seat in the far corner and wait, ordering an Old Fashioned from the bartender. My expectations aren't high, but the drink is strong, the tang of the orange sitting pleasantly on my tongue.

When Ethan Quicke appears, it takes him a little while to make his way across the bar, stopping at every other table to shake hands and take selfies. Hometown boy makes good. I know the feeling. Montana isn't exactly known for producing major league talent.

When he finally reaches me I've finished my drink and called the bartender over.

"Another Old Fashioned?" he asks, and I nod and then he looks to Quicke.

"Just a beer for me, whatever's on tap."

Once we have our drinks, I sit back with mine in hand and nod out toward the crowd where people are still buzzing about his entrance.

"Your adoring public."

"Eh, the price I pay for coming home." He takes a sip from his beer and then sets it in front of him, leaning in, elbows on his knees. "It was nice of you to make the trip. I didn't expect it."

"My team now. I want to have a say in who's on it."

"I was surprised when you took the gig. Always thought you'd ride off into the sunset and never be heard from again."

"I have my reasons," I say, but he waits me out and I give in. "A championship."

Ethan considers that and nods. "And you think the Eagles can get you that?"

"With the right pieces in place, sure. I think that's true of any organization."

"And I'm one of those pieces?"

"That remains to be seen."

"I was sorry to hear about Stew," he says, changing the subject.

"He'll be okay."

"You and Frankie Sullivan are holding down the fort until he gets back?"

"That's the idea. More Sullivan than me."

"Then why are we sitting here?"

"I thought I'd see if we could work this out." I lean forward in my seat and take a sip. "I've been in your shoes, on the down swing, one last contract before you hang 'em up. I get it."

"Okay, so you're good cop and she comes in later as bad cop if I don't take whatever you're offering. Not a bad strategy. Dan thought that's what you'd do."

"Yeah, where is Dan?"

"Japan. Apparently Nakamura's looking for an American agent."

"He left you to negotiate your own deal?"

"I know what I want."

"How's this?" I slide the folded-up piece of hotel room note-paper across the table to him and wait, finishing my drink and gazing out into the Montana landscape.

There's a grunt of what sounds like approval from Quicke and then the click of a pen and the scratch of it against paper.

He slides it back across the table.

Same specs, but one extra year.

It'll make him thirty-nine at the end of the deal.

The same age I am now.

But he's a pitcher with a rubber arm and he's a lefty.

"Welcome back to the Brooklyn Eagles, Ethan," I extend a hand to him, but he takes another sip of his beer and grins.

"One more thing and we have a deal."

"What's that?"

"I want to start Opening Day."

"Don't push it."

He laughs and then reaches for my hand to shake it firmly. Done and dusted.

That's one of those cowboy sayings, right? If not, it sounds like it.

This almost makes that godawful flight stuck between a drunk asshole and a woman who I desperately want to touch even though I know that way absolute madness lies. She'll be happy, though, and now maybe she'll understand that I'm here and I'm not going anywhere.

"Do you have tickets to the game?" Quicke asks, as he stands.

I stand too and toss a few bills down on the table for the server. "Nah, not really my thing."

"You should come. Both of you. I have a suite. I assume she's waiting back in her room for word on whether or not she needs to come up here guns blazing to play the heavy?"

"Yeah, okay," I agree, suddenly a little bit chagrined that I won't get to see her in action. "Text me the details."

My phone dings once and then again as I'm headed back down to the room, both messages from Quicke. The first is the info about the suite. The second is a link to his Instagram, where it's a simple dark blue background with an NY. The caption is simple: *Always home.*

That was quick. Too quick and the feeling of victory I had all the way down from the roof crumbles and, before I can reach for my room key, the door flies open.

Her hair is thrown up into a riot of a messy bun and she's wearing a tank top and cotton shorts with a light cotton robe over the top, just an inch or so longer than the shorts. She looks fucking amazing and absolutely furious.

"What the hell did you do?"

"What do you mean?" I ask, buying some time because I obviously know exactly what she's talking about.

I manage to inch past her and she lets the hotel room door shut behind me before wheeling around, hands on her hips, clearly even more pissed at my evasion.

"Save it." She follows me deeper into the room, nearly bumping her chest against mine as she pushes up onto her toes to make sure she's looking me dead in the eye as she says, "I already got a text from Dan Wilson. You negotiated a deal with Ethan Quicke and you didn't think I needed to be there when you did?"

"Stew told me to help you. I'm helping. I got him at the number you wanted and no no-trade clause."

"I didn't want him."

"What?"

"I. Didn't. Want. Him. I wanted him to *think* we wanted him. I wanted him to turn us down and then I wanted to leak to the press that he turned down a fantastic offer. It would send a sign to Nakamura that we have the money, we need to sign him *and* that we're committed to winning. Ethan Quicke is an asshole prima donna whose best years are behind him. We'd get one, *maybe* two more good years out of him before that contract will be an absolute bust."

"What? Then why the hell didn't you tell me that?"

"Because it's not your job. It's mine. You were here to do one thing and one thing only: make everyone believe that we pushed as hard we could to get Quicke, but that *he* was being unreasonable. He *is* being unreasonable. Or at least he was. How did you get him to agree?"

"I gave him an extra year without the vesting option. Lower AAV."

"You gave him an extra year. He'll be nearly *forty* at the end of the contract. He doesn't need a no-trade clause, because no one is going to want him. This is a nightmare. I'm in a nightmare."

"If you had just told me what you were doing this wouldn't be a problem. Jesus, why don't you trust me?"

"Why the hell would I trust you? The only thing you've ever done is fight me. Every game analysis. Every scouting report. Every damn day back in LA, it's all you ever did."

"It's because I respect you."

That stops her.

"You fought with me because you *respect* me?"

"I don't know if you realize this, Sullivan, but despite fighting you every damn day, I pretty much followed your gameplans to the letter."

"No, you didn't."

"Unless game conditions changed, which even you have to admit happens once in a while. It's why we play them and don't just let the computer run simulations every day. I fought you because I needed to make sure the person giving us those plans, the person doing the analysis, really believed in them."

"Are you saying you made me literally want to tear my hair out every day we worked together because of some sort of test?"

"No, yes . . . not, not a test. I've been in baseball long enough to have worked with enough guys who think they know their shit, but didn't. The only thing I ever cared about was winning and I had to be sure that I was doing everything possible to make that happen. Lot of good it did me."

Something flickers in her eyes, an understanding even if that fury is still there. It's in the rapid rise and fall of her chest that is *barely* being contained by that tank top and I lift my gaze up and away from it as quickly as I can, but probably too late for her not to have noticed.

"Listen, I'm sorry if I made you feel like I didn't respect you, but you gotta know that, if I didn't respect you, I wouldn't have talked to you at all. That's why they hired you, you know, because the guy before you was actually a hack and I told them I wouldn't work with him anymore."

"Then they hired me."

"They did."

"And how much say did you have in that?"

"None. They told me that they were going to promote the best analyst they had in the minors and, if I had a problem with that one . . . how did they put it, *an aging catcher with a bad knee doesn't dictate how the organization runs.*"

Most of her ire seems to slip away at that.

"Ouch."

"Yeah, but they were right, you know."

"You played for five years after that and your last year was actually the best of them. You had another year or two left in you."

It's nice of her to say, but it's not true.

"You saw my medicals, didn't you?"

"You could have moved to DH, got out from behind the plate, just focused on hitting."

"Nah, I'd done my twenty. I would have driven everyone crazy only playing half the game, hanging out in the dugout, not being able to control what was going on out on the field, and they had that kid Díaz coming up behind me. It wouldn't have been fair to him."

She tilts her head in silent agreement, but then she levels me with a serious stare. "We got interrupted back on the plane and you never answered my question. Why are you back?"

"To get the one thing I never had as a player."

"A ring," she answers for me.

"A ring. You told me once that's what you wanted too."

"I did. I do."

"And here we are on the same team, again, and we both want the same thing."

"So what are you saying?"

"What if we call a truce on . . ." I wave vaguely at the space between us, "this and focus on that. What if we trusted each other, like Stew wants, and build this team together."

"If I agree to this, I need a clear chain of command. Stew named me his interim. I'm ultimately the one responsible for making a call. I had to deal with you ignoring my analysis when – what did you say? – conditions changed on the field, but now you're going to have to deal with me telling you no. This is my world, not yours."

"You'll listen to me? You'll hear me out?"

"I will," she says, firmly, her eyes blue steel. She means it.

"Okay, Sullivan," I say, extending my hand to her. "Let's do this." Her hand slides into mine, cool to the touch, her handshake firm, strong even, stronger than I expected, but soft too.

"For the ring?"

"For the ring."

Then she tugs on my hand, using it as leverage to pull herself almost entirely against me.

"But if you ever pull another stunt like you did today again, you're done, understood?"

I hum a yes as my eyes are drawn down toward her mouth

and, just as I make up my mind to lean in and fuck the consequences, she nods firmly and drops back a step.

My hand doesn't release hers, though, and I can't quite convince myself to let go. But she's not letting go either and her eyes lift to mine, a question in them.

Is she remembering too?

Because every one of my senses is on high alert, instant recall back to a parking lot in LA where I was emotionally wrecked and physically exhausted and didn't have the energy to fight against the rising need to pull her in and find out if that mouth of hers wasn't just talented with verbal slings that always hit their mark.

It would be so easy, just a quick tug and she'd be back in my arms. I wouldn't even have to bend that far down, as she's tall enough that I could kiss her all day long and avoid an aching neck.

Shit like that matters when you're pushing forty.

But I shouldn't and, to be perfectly honest, I'm not sure if she'd kiss me back or haul my ass to HR for sexual harassment. I'd say it's a coin flip.

Finally, she's the one that pulls away and I let her go as she steps back and then worries her bottom lip with her teeth.

Fuck, I didn't need to add that expression to the catalog of things I can fantasize about.

Distraction. I need one. Badly.

"Quicke invited us to the game."

She wrinkles her nose. "Do you want to go?"

"Nothing else to do. Everyone's in town for it and rivalries are always fun."

"Are you a football fan?" she asks.

"It's fine. Not my favorite."

"Me neither. Except maybe basketball. There's enough scoring in basketball that a clock feels necessary. The other clock sports, football especially, just feel . . . empty, like there's a false momentum to them without enough scoring to make up for it."

"I never thought about it that way. I don't know if *anyone* has ever thought about it that way."

She shrugs. "It's just how my brain works. Always has. It's why baseball appealed to me as a kid. You have to earn it. If you don't, the game just *never* ends."

Now *that* I've thought about before and suddenly I don't want to go hang out in a suite with Ethan Quicke and his high-school and college buddy entourage and eat cold appetizers while we watch two teams I couldn't give two shits about.

I don't care what we do, I just want to do it with her.

"Fuck the game."

"Really? Didn't you just say there's nothing else to do," she asks. "You okay, Avery?"

"I'm great. C'mon, let's go."

"Go where?"

"We haven't eaten anything all day aside from airplane peanuts. Let's get some food, a couple of drinks, and I want you to walk me through your plan for the forty-man roster one spot at a time."

"Seriously?"

"Why? You got anything better to do?"

"Absolutely not. Let's go."

She spins away from me and I have to lean back to avoid getting whipped in the face by a rogue lock of blonde hair. That scent trails behind her. I'm momentarily swept away by it again, by *her* again. By the rage and the righteous indignation that melted away at my confession.

I only manage to regain my focus in time to catch sight of her robe falling from her shoulders to the floor of the bedroom and her lifting that tank top up and over her head, just as the door closes.

And I collapse down onto the couch, letting out a shaky breath.

A truce.

An agreement to work together.

This is what I wanted.

So why do I feel like she just owned me entirely?

And why do I like it so fucking much?

Chapter 7

FRANCESCA

The bar is somehow exactly what I imagined: reflecting the city we're in, an odd mismatch of what Montana used to be and what it is now. Like a layer of old west nostalgia slapped on top of an attempt at industrial chic.

Even in just dark jeans and a black wrap top, a black leather jacket and black pumps, I feel wildly out of place. The dress code matches the décor: urban cowboy or cowgirl, as it were. I very much look like I just hopped off a plane from the East Coast.

Charlie blends a bit better, his jeans well broken in, his heather-blue t-shirt just on the other side of washed enough to hug his large frame just right.

"Fake-ass cowboy shit," Charlie mutters from my side.

I laugh. "Exactly! I was trying to figure out what felt so wrong. It's trying too hard."

The bar is as packed as the rest of the town – overflow fans who don't have tickets to the game but who want to watch it with a crowd.

"C'mon, let's find a table," he says, shouldering through groups of people scattered through the room, reaching for my hand. I hesitate for a second, flashing back to the hotel, the feeling of connection so unexpected and intense that it feels like I shouldn't want to feel it again. Like it's dangerous.

It is dangerous.

But I've never played it safe in my entire life.

So I take his hand and let that feeling wash over me again.

There's a freedom here that I wouldn't feel if we were back in New York, an anonymity that makes it okay when the bodies surge around us and I have to step even closer, our arms entwined as I press into his side.

And there's something about that contact, the solid muscle of his bicep, the warmth of his body, the way he maneuvers me through the space, anticipating collisions and avoiding them, putting himself between me and the rest of the room.

That doesn't keep me from nearly getting decapitated by a guy throwing his arm out wide to gesture the size of something as we pass, though. I brace for impact, but Charlie must have seen it coming because he yanks me closer and I fall into him, so the guy's hand only hits air.

"You good?" he murmurs into my ear, his breath ghosting across my skin and making me shiver despite the heat created by the crowd. It's so easy to imagine him asking that in a different context, his body wrapped around mine, his hands everywhere, pushing inside of me, his mouth at my ear, trailing down to my neck, his teeth sinking into the curve where it meets my shoulder just firmly enough to leave a mark.

"Yeah," I manage to breathe out, despite the images whirling around in my mind, disappearing as quickly as they arrived.

I half want to spin around and tell the guy off, but that would require pushing away and breaking this odd little bubble we've

created as we make our way to the one open table at the far end
of the room.

Instead I lean in closer and, while Charlie doesn't pull away,
I can feel the surprise as he looks down at me as he gives me a
slight squeeze.

What am I doing?

It's just been so long since I've felt this way.

Protected. Sheltered. And, if the way he's looking at me is
any indication, wanted.

Is he feeling this too?

There's always been tension between us, but it was easy
enough to explain away. Our jobs are pressurized, the stakes
were high and both of us are incredibly competitive. But this? It
was never like this, not until that last night at Dodger Stadium.

And now, apparently.

No.

This cannot happen.

When we get to the table, I slide away from him, planting
myself firmly in the center of one side of the booth while he
takes the seat opposite mine.

"Are you hungry?" I ask, knowing my tone is too bright, too
high pitched, too everything.

And he's not an idiot. He knows what I'm doing. I'm sure
of it, but he allows it, easily, and as if nothing just happened
between us.

What am I saying?

Nothing happened.

And nothing is going to happen.

So, it's fine. I'm fine. He's fine. We're both just fine.

"Yeah, I can eat," he says, but then he cringes, the double
entendre too much for the both of us.

I bet he can, is the only response that pops into my head,

and even though I don't say it out loud, I know my face absolutely gives me away. He sends me a withering look, but he breaks almost immediately, his grin slow, but growing wide. And I can't help it, despite biting my lip to hold it back. I let out a slightly hysterical giggle and, once it escapes, there's nothing I can do to stop myself.

I dissolve into laughter so hard and so long that my eyes start tearing. And he's laughing too, a pleasant gravely sound that comes from his chest. Somehow, that's also incredibly hot.

God, this is just a vicious cycle. Is there anything he can do right now that won't turn me on?

I try to take a deep breath, reaching for a napkin from the holder at the edge of our table to dab the tears away from my eyes, grateful that a bunch of mascara doesn't come away as I do. This is good. Laughing is good. Laughing together is even better. We can just move on now, talk about the plan for the off season and how we're going to win a championship.

A waitress comes over to the table, a timely distraction.

"What can I get you?" she asks.

"Beer for me," he says, and I just shake my head. I cannot drink alcohol when I'm like this. Alcohol and this feeling? That's a terrible combination.

"Just a Diet Coke, thanks," I order. "We should get food."

I deliberately phrase it that way and he sends me a knowing look, but nods.

"Burgers?"

Perfect. Burgers are maybe the least sexy thing in the world to eat.

"That sounds good. Cheddar on mine, medium rare," I say.

"The same for me, with bacon too. Fries to split?"

I nod and the waitress jots it all down and scampers away through the ever-growing sea of people.

"Okay, lay it out for me," he says, leaning forward in his seat, resting his forearms on the table. "Nakamura is the main target, but this team needs more than just an A1 guy behind him."

"You're right. The original plan wasn't to have Quicke in the rotation, but here we are," I say, sending him one final short glare before moving on. "But he'll be a decent contributor."

"What about behind the plate?"

"You noticed that, huh?"

"That Gibbons had elbow surgery and will be out for a year, maybe more, maybe forever, depending upon his recovery? Yeah. I noticed."

"We've got a kid in the minors, young, a little bit raw."

"What does Stew think about him?"

"He thinks he's got the makings of an All Star."

"What do you think about him?"

"I think, with the right coaching, he's got the makings of a Hall of Famer."

"Sullivan, is the reason you didn't give Stew a harder time about hiring me because you think I can help this kid – what's his name?"

"Cole Davis."

"Okay, and who else will Cole Davis be catching this season?"

"We've got Huff for the third spot and Verdasco in the four."

"And your fifth starter?"

"Another kid, Archie Esposito. He's been lights out at every level."

"What's the catch?"

"We kept him down at Double A last year. Player development thought he needed more time. He's a little bit off center. You know, typical lefty, but they wanted him to have a couple more starts down there. He didn't get any time at Triple A let alone with us at the big club, but I think he's ready and I think he'll start the season as our five and be our two or three by the September."

His eyes widen. "Really?"

"Really. He's got great stuff. Fastball tops out at 103, but he's more effective at 98 or 99. He can spot his changeup and he's got a knuckler."

"You mean a knuckle curve?"

"No, I mean a knuckleball. He'll throw it in any count, totally unafraid. But he confuses people."

"Why would you throw a knuckleball if you can throw 103?"

"Exactly, but I think he's special."

"When we get down to Florida, I'll catch some of his sessions myself. I'd like to see that."

"I think you'll like him, once you get used to him."

"An acquired taste?"

"For sure. Harmless, sweet, even, but like I said, a little bit odd."

Our drinks and food come out at the same time, a testament to the bar's service given the absolute crush of a rivalry football crowd. And I didn't realize just how hungry I was until I took a massive bite of my cheeseburger.

I close my eyes and groan a little bit around the first bite. "God, that's good," I mumble, as I swallow down some perfectly cooked greasy, cheesy mess.

When I open my eyes he's staring at me from across the table a little slack jawed, his own burger only halfway to his mouth.

"What?"

"Nothing, I just . . ."

"What?"

"I can't remember the last time I sat down with a woman and had a meal."

"Seriously?"

"Is that so hard to believe?"

"I mean kind of. I guess I always assumed you'd retire and get remarried, have a couple of kids. That's usually what guys who skipped out on that during their careers do."

"Nah, I think I always knew I'd be back. Unfinished business, plus I never really thought you could have both and do both right."

"You don't wish you had a kid who'd remember you playing?"

"No sense in wishing for things that can't happen."

It must be nice to really feel that way, to look back and truly feel content with the choices you made. I don't have regrets per se, but I do wonder what my life would look like now if I hadn't wasted so much time with Shane. If instead I'd walked away before he had a chance to hurt me as much as he did.

But then I wouldn't be here right now and, at this moment, there's no place I'd rather be.

"No regrets," I say, with a grin. "That's rare."

"We don't have time for regrets. We have a championship to win, right?" Charlie says, and then refocuses. "Okay, last but not least: centerfield."

Right, back to work.

"There's another kid. Xander Greene. Lanky, gap-to-gap hitter, can run like the wind."

"Three rookies?"

"It's, in theory, how we pay for Nakamura . . ."

"How old are they?" he asks, taking another sip of his beer.

"Twenty-one."

He nearly spits out the beer, coughing as he manages to wheeze, "What, all of them? Three rookies and Nakamura? It sounds like a mediocre eighties movie."

She ignores my stray thought. "Like I said, it's how we pay for Nakamura. They'll all be making the minimum. It cuts more than fifty million off our books right away."

"So you want to win a World Series starting two rookies every day at two of the premier positions on the field, one of which is going to have to learn an entirely new pitching staff and adjust to the major leagues. That pitching staff will have one rookie and one import from Japan who'll also be making that adjustment five thousand miles away from home."

"Yes."

"Fuck. I'm gonna need something stronger than beer."

"Stew knows about it. He's on board. Hell, half of it was his idea."

"Which half?"

"The half that has you managing them and Javy coming on to work with Nakamura and Esposito."

"No other major changes?"

"No, nothing major. So, what do you think?"

"I think it's insane. What did your computer spit out?"

"The margins are . . . tight. I've run a ton of simulations and most of them are inconclusive, but the ceiling is high. More than a significant percentage have resulted in optimal outcomes."

"In English?"

"Most of the time it thinks we win, a lot."

"How much is most?"

"Forty-two percent

"Pretty sure forty-two isn't most of anything."

"It's the plurality of the result . . . the largest percentage. Twenty-seven percent of the time it has us out of the postseason entirely. The rest of the time it has us doing well, but not ultimately coming out on top, but I'm skeptical of post-season predictive analytics."

"You think your own computer is wrong?"

"I think, on the day to day, it's more right than not, but once the season shortens to just winning the game in front of you and worrying about tomorrow, tomorrow, that's when it gets fuzzier."

"Stew didn't mention any of this when he brought me in."

"Stew doesn't show his entire hand to anyone, let alone someone he isn't sure is actually sticking around. And then, before he got the chance, he ended up in the CCU. Besides, none of this is your job – you've just decided to make it that way."

"I guess I did."

"Do you think you can bring Davis along?"

"This is the first I'm hearing about the kid. Do you have a scouting report?"

I tilt my head at him in mock offense and scoff. "Who exactly do you think you're talking to?" I ask, and then lowering the pitch of my voice as much as I can in a terrible imitation of him, "Do I have a scouting report?"

Pulling it up on my phone, I show him a video our player development people pulled together, which Charlie watches carefully, brow furrowed thoughtfully as he zooms in and then slows the video down before starting it from the beginning again.

"How many strike outs did he have last season?"

"Thirty-three in over five hundred plate appearances, most of which were at the beginning of the season."

"Shit," he says, sitting back in his seat with a heavy breath. "That's . . ."

"It's some kind of ghost of Tony Gwynn stuff."

"And his power numbers?"

"OPS of 1.245."

"You're right. He's ready. There's some stuff we can work on with his pitch framing, but he's ready. How does he handle a staff?"

"He can handle Esposito and, like I said, Esposito's . . . quirky, to say the least. I think he'll be okay, but you'll be there to help him."

"Yeah, yeah, I will. Kid's young enough to be my kid. All of them are."

"You would have been a *very* young dad to Nakamura."

"We still haven't signed him and, even if we do, you know what they're going to say, right? Relying on four kids barely old enough to buy a beer."

"I don't care what they say."

"What, really?"

"You think I managed to become one of the few female executives in this game by caring what unqualified men have to say about me?"

"Actually, I think that's exactly how you did it. Baseball's a game of perception, especially in the front office. You had to make them believe in you to get where you are."

I just stare at him, more annoyed than I should be by how insightful that particular thought is.

"What? Nothing to say to that?"

"Sometimes I forget you're not just a dumb jock with a pretty face."

"You think I'm pretty?"

"I think you know very well exactly what you look like," I say, half wishing now I'd ordered something with alcohol in it to take the edge off. It's hard to keep my focus when he's looking at me like that, like he knows exactly where my mind really is.

"You grew up a Dodgers fan, right?"

"Yeah, why?"

"And you're what? Twenty-eight, twenty-nine?"

"Thirty-four."

"Really? Huh, you look younger."

"Where is this going, exactly?"

"Just trying to do some math. You're five years younger than me."

"Well done," I quip, but he ignores me.

"Did you have a poster of me on your wall, Sullivan?"

Damn it.

"I did not have your poster on my wall," I hedge, and distract myself by taking a long sip from my soda.

It was on the back of my door: Charlie standing tall in his Dodger uniform, hair tousled after throwing off his catcher's mask to grab a foul ball, eye black streaked attractively across his cheekbones, a bit of stubble lining his jaw. I can see it like it's in front of me right now. It stayed up for years, ever after I left for college. My parents eventually converted my bedroom to a yoga studio and I'm not sure what became of the poster version of Charlie Avery, but he still lives in my mind clearly enough.

He hums in response, but his eyes are twinkling at me, like he sees right through my almost lie, but he must decide to let it go as his attention is drawn over my shoulder.

"Do you wanna dance?"

"What?"

He nods behind me and I turn in my seat to see a bunch of couples out on the dance floor at the back of the bar, a band nestled in the corner playing some country music that I wouldn't be able to identify with a gun to my head.

"*You* want to dance?" I ask, turning back to him, but he's out of his booth, holding a hand out to me.

"It looks like fun."

"I thought we were here to work."

"We did work and neither one of us has anywhere else to be until tomorrow morning. Unless you want to take up Ethan Quicke's offer of the suite."

"Absolutely not."

"Then come on, dance with me."

"Do you think it's a good idea?"

"Are you worried you won't be able to control yourself around me, Sullivan?"

"Do you really want to talk about who does and doesn't have self-control?"

He clicks his tongue, acknowledging the hit, but he doesn't retract his hand.

"I don't bite," he assures me.

"Don't you?"

I *distinctly* remember the nip of his teeth against my bottom lip that night back in LA. And he must too, because even in the dim lighting of the bar, there's an actual flush rising beneath the stubble on his cheeks.

"Which one of us can't control themselves again?" he deflects.

Fuck it.

I slide out of the booth and head straight for the dance floor without looking back. I don't have to. I know he's behind me. There are a few couples in well-worn cowboy boots doing some kind of two step that I wouldn't be able to recreate even after a month of dance lessons, but when I turn, Charlie's there and, with no hesitation, one hand finds my waist while the other takes my hand in his. And I have no choice except to follow his steps that somehow match the beat of the twanging country song and which looks an awful lot like what the other dancers are doing.

"You can dance?" I marvel, looking up at him in surprise before panicking and refocusing on my feet.

"Do you think I would have asked you if I couldn't? Don't bother looking at your feet, Sullivan. I got you. Look at me."

I look up into his eyes and try to keep my gaze there, but it's hard to not look down, to not check to make sure I don't step on his toes.

"I have to know," I begin, trying to relax into the steps and let him lead, but I have no idea what I'm doing, "where did you learn this?"

"Iowa isn't exactly a place that shuns country music."

"That's right. You're a Midwest boy."

"Way more time out of it than in now, but, yeah, it was home."

"You never went back?"

A lot of guys make their off season home back wherever they're from, finding comfort in the familiar.

"As soon as I got to LA, I never wanted to be anywhere else."

"Until now?"

"It stopped feeling like home after . . ." he trails off. "I love that city, and it'll always be special, but one season without going to the ballpark every day was plenty. Watching the game move on without me, it was . . ."

"Impossible," I finish for him, because I know that feeling all too well. "Like you've lost a part of yourself and nothing will ever fill the hole it left behind."

He misses a step and his foot catches mine as I trip into him. He catches me easily, hands steady at my hips, drawing me into him to keep me from crashing to the dance floor.

"How could you possibly know that?"

Chapter 8

CHARLIE

"What do you mean?" she asks, stepping further away from me, her face suddenly clouded over with an emotion that I don't recognize, pulling free from my grasp and my hands flex into fists, instantly missing the feel of her warmth against them.

I shrug, trying clear my mind, trying to rid it of the need to reach out for her. "Look at you, you're living your dream, how do you know what it feels like to lose it?"

"How do I . . . are you serious right now?"

Shit. That look I know well. Furrowed brow, hands on her hips, eyes narrowed dangerously. What the hell did I just say? I can't even remember.

"I . . ." I try to gather my thoughts again, something about dreams and, yeah, that's it, she understood, she gets me and it's confusing as fuck that, somehow, she's mad about it?

Then she's gone, pushing past me off the dance floor ,weaving her way through the crowd that's still locked on the Montana vs Montana State showdown, and I try to follow her path with my eyes, but then it hits me that we didn't pay yet for our meals. The last thing I need is some hit job in the press that I skip out on my meals in the middle of Small Town USA. I go back to the table to toss some bills on it before racing out into the night.

I have no idea what I did to set her off, but clearly I hit a nerve.

I follow as fast as I can. The hotel is only down the street from and, with the game going on, there's barely anyone blocking my view. If my knee wasn't held together with spit and a prayer, I'd try to sprint down the sidewalk and catch up with her. But it is, so instead I set a steady pace, keeping her in my line of sight as she stalks into the hotel.

I make my way into the lobby just in time to see the elevator doors close with her behind them, so I call for another one and wait.

What the hell did I say? I was caught up in the moment, marveling at the way she understood me so well and then . . . she was gone.

Thankfully I have a room key in my wallet, sparing me the indignity of knocking on the door until she deigned to open it.

She's standing in the center of the room, her back to me, staring out that window, the view even more nondescript now that it's too dark out to see the mountain range coloring the horizon.

"Look, I'm sorry," I begin, but she cuts me off, raising a hand and stepping right up to me, nearly chest to chest.

"Don't, it's not . . . I'm not mad at you."

"You're not?"

Shrugging, she throws her hands up in frustration. "Not entirely, I just . . . you really don't get it, do you?"

"Get what? Frankie, talk to me."

"Do you know how many dreams I've lost?"

Her voice is soft, like she doesn't want to give voice to whatever she's about to tell me. She doesn't let me answer, not that I have any idea what to say.

"When I was a little girl all I ever wanted to do was play baseball. And I was so good at it. You know that feeling? When you're a kid and you're better than everyone else on the field. It just hits you one day, right? That they're all here," she holds a hand up, "and you're here" and lifts the other one a foot above it.

I nod.

"Of course you do. I was so good, Charlie, *so good*, but when I was twelve, and still better than every boy in my class, they told me that my dream was impossible, that girls don't play baseball and they certainly don't play it in the major leagues. That coach said it right to my face, in front of the other players, like he wasn't absolutely crushing my soul with every word. So I went home and cried my little pre-teen heart out about it and then asked my parents to sign me up for softball. I remember my dad asking me if I was sure, as he knew how much I loved it, and I said that I was, that I knew it was where I belonged. I was lying, but I wanted so badly for it to be the truth that I made it so. I got a new dream and I learned to love that game. They told me that, if I worked hard, I could play in college and, at the end of that rainbow, if managed to be better than all the other little girls, there could be an Olympic gold medal waiting for me. So I went for it. I put my entire heart into it. And I got good at it. I got so good at it schools across the country wanted me to come play for them, wanted me to lead their team to the Women's College World Series. You know what that's like, right? When the college coaches come calling?"

I nod again. They'd come calling, but I hadn't listened. I'd gone right to the minor leagues, a chance she never had, a choice that just wasn't available to her. The puzzle pieces start to click into place.

"And off I went and, while I was there, absolutely dominating and dreaming dreams of Olympic gold, another bomb gets dropped. Sorry, softball's out of the Olympics. You're just going to have to find another dream . . . again. But I was smart this time. I knew better than to put my entire heart and soul into one dream."

Another luxury I didn't even know I had.

"Fool me once, shame on you, fool me twice and all that," she says, rolling her eyes, maybe at me, maybe at society. I don't know, but I don't blame her either way. "I had a backup plan this time. I majored in data analysis and focused on predictive models. I was going to show that coach who told me girls don't make it to the major leagues. I was going to make it. And you know what happened?"

It's probably a rhetorical question, but I answer it anyway. "You did it."

"I did it. I fought tooth and nail to get my foot in the door, had to prove myself and be twice as good as everyone else out there, but I did it. I lost my dreams at twelve and at twenty and, if someone takes *this* dream from me, so help me God, I'll find another one."

"Sullivan, I didn't mean . . ." I start, but she's not having it.

"Of course you didn't," she says, throwing her hands up before letting them fall to her sides and shaking her head. "You didn't know. How could you know? Why would you ever think that we had the same dream? I don't even know why I'm telling you any of this."

Her voice fades and we're surrounded by the complete silence in the room, as there's no noise from the city, such as it is, out that stupid window.

"I know why."

That stops her.

"You do?"

"Because if we're going to do this, I needed to know."

"What?"

Something tightens in my chest at her question, and for a moment she's that twelve-year-old girl she spoke about, her dream dead before it ever really had a chance to live.

"I needed to know just how much you have to lose . . . again. If this doesn't work, our truce I mean, I can keep going, but you . . . you only get . . ."

"I only get one shot," she finishes for me. "Especially now."

Now it's my turn to be confused.

"General manager was what I've been working toward, but I didn't expect it to happen so soon. I thought I'd have more time to build up my reputation, to make myself hirable no matter how things ended with the Eagles."

I blink at her. "What are you talking about?"

"Haven't you ever heard that old saying about working in baseball? "If you don't win, you're going to be fired. If you do win, you've only put off the day you're going to be fired." It's what happens to us, all of us. But there's a weird space where you might get fired, but other teams will still want you. I wanted to make sure I was firmly in that category before . . ."

"Before you were ultimately responsible for the result."

She hums her agreement. "Do you know how long a GM usually lasts in a job?"

"No."

"It's actually just a little shorter than the average playing career. Five and a half years."

"That's . . . not very long."

"No, it isn't. But assistant GMs? They tend to stick around longer – thirteen years, actually."

"Of course you ran the numbers," I say, trying to break the odd sort of tension between us, and it works. She lets out a shaky breath and a laugh.

"Of course I did," she agrees. "I was hoping to stick it out as an assistant for a little longer, build a reputation as someone valuable to an organization so that, once this ends, there'd be a relatively soft landing, but here I am, so I need to make sure . . ."

"That you succeed."

"Exactly, so I guess I just needed you to understand that I have a lot to lose here and not just a ring this year, but my chance at ever getting one."

I step closer and all I want is to pull her into my arms and hold her to my chest and tell her it's going to be okay, even though I'm pretty sure that's the last thing a woman like Francesca Sullivan wants.

"Then that's what we'll do," I say, and brave another step toward her and reach out, lifting a hand to her face, but hesitating, giving her a moment and then another to pull away before I brush my thumb along the line of her jaw. I'm watching in wonder as it makes her lips part and she pulls in a soft gasp at the contact.

I want to draw that sound from her again. My fingers curl around the back of her neck and there's no gasp this time, but a long, deep breath, and I'm so close now I feel the rise and fall of her breasts against my chest, the fabric of my t-shirt sliding against my chest in a whisper of what it would be like to feel skin against skin.

"Can I . . ." I begin to ask, just like I did two years ago in that parking lot with my world crashing down around me and her the only thing that seemed to tether me in place, but this time she shakes her head, a hand at my chest, gently, but firmly pushing me away.

"No," she whispers, and then her shoulders straighten and I let my hand drop. "We can't."

She slips away, shaky for a moment on those heels she's always balancing on before she spins on her toe. The bedroom door is nearly closed behind her when she looks back, holding my eyes with hers, and I think I see regret there just before she closes it. When it clicks into place, I finally release my breath, my chest rattling and hollow.

With a hand as shaky as her legs were a moment ago, I run it through my hair and then over my face, muffling a heavy groan the best I can.

I'm hard as a fucking rock and we didn't even kiss.

I grab the bag of toiletries I managed to cobble together in my mad dash to the airport and lock myself in the bathroom, getting the shower as hot as humanly possible before shucking off my shirt, the rest of my clothes following before I douse myself under the shockingly good water pressure.

There's no temptation to even attempt to talk myself out of it. I'm too worked up, too desperate.

For her.

Leaning up against the tiles I let the hot water sluice down my back, the steam curling up into the air and it's easy to imagine that the heat in the air is her body beneath mine, limbs entwined, wrapping around me.

I could lift her up against me, let those long legs cross behind my back, her smooth skin cool to the touch but warming with every second she's in my arms. She'd call my name. *Charlie*, she'd murmur in my ear, as my mouth works against the silky skin at her neck, down to the generous rise of her breasts.

Grasping myself tightly, hard and heavy in my hand, I imagine sliding inside of her slowly. I chuckle at the idea that I'd have any kind of restraint at this point, but fuck it, it's a fantasy and that's what I'd want to do – take her in long, deliberate strokes, building her pleasure with mine, making her writhe against me, our bodies dancing into the sweetest friction despite the water cascading over us. I'd bring her to the edge and then pull back and then do it again until she rakes her nails down my back, maybe leaving a mark or two along the way, a signal that she's had enough of my teasing. But I'd draw it out still, waiting until she begs me because I need her to want me as much as I want her.

Outside of this shower that feels impossible, but right here, right now, I can make myself believe it, just for a few more seconds, just a few more strokes before my hips break the rhythm I set and rut forward, harder and faster of their own volition, a desperate pounding that leaves me gasping for breath against the steam and choking out a strangled "Francesca" that I can only hope is drowned out by the steady beat of the water against the tiles.

Relief. Sweet relief. Thank fuck.

I didn't realize just how worked up I was until this moment, the water washing away any damning evidence of the last few minutes, as I catch my breath. I should have known, though. It's not that I haven't had opportunities recently, I have, and I've taken advantage of them. Consenting adults, no strings, quick and easy, both of us knowing it wasn't anything more than that.

But that kind of connection started to feel hollow a long time ago. Come to think of it, it started feeling that way during my last year, as it became clearer and clearer that it was time to call it quits.

Shutting off the water, I wrap a towel around my waist, the hotel nice enough that the towels are soft and large enough to actually serve their purpose. Wiping away the fog that has steamed up the mirrors against the wall, I lean on the bathroom vanity and stare my reflection. Older than I picture in my head, but I recognize the look in my own eyes: it's how I used to feel before a big game, before going out to do the only thing I ever loved. I haven't seen that look in a long time, not for years. The last time I saw it was reflected in the windows of her car that night in the parking lot.

I think that's why I wanted to kiss her then, when it was all over, to see if I could feel that *thing* again, to feel alive, to know it was possible after walking away from the game.

So I did and it was. But now I wonder if that was just her.

Maybe it was. Maybe it still is.

And if that's true, if she's the thing that makes me feel this way, then I need to do everything I can to hang on to her.

I'm too old not to sleep on anything other than a bed.

The nearly five-hour flight crushed into the middle seat is followed by a night trying to fold all six feet four of me onto this sorry excuse for a couch.

Of course, I could have actually unfolded the mattress below the cushions that did a piss poor job of supporting my back all night.

But that would have required not just throwing myself onto the nearest flat surface and trying desperately to fall asleep and not think about the woman just beyond the bedroom door.

That last look she gave me just before she closed the door, her gaze soft and longing. I've never seen her look at me like that before. That first kiss, I took her by surprise. I know I did. Hell, I took myself by surprise, but afterwards it made a lot of sense. There was always a tension between us, always a lit fuse headed toward dynamite, always on the verge of exploding, but never quite fully detonating. That spark is still there, obviously.

The last remnants of sleep shake away when the bedroom door opens and she steps into the room pulling her suitcase behind her.

"Aren't you up yet?" she asks, her expression completely devoid of any emotion, like last night never happened. Either she's an amazing actress or she wasn't nearly as affected as I was. I almost want to hate her for it.

"Kind of," I manage to croak out, as I sit up and stretch my neck back and forth, a sharp pain slicing through me with the motion. "What's going on?"

"I need to get to the airport."

"What? I thought our flight wasn't until later tonight?"

"Yours is, I switched mine."

"Seriously?"

Was she so put off by what happened last night that she doesn't even want to be on a plane with me back to New York?

"Listen, I'm sorry if I made you uncomfortable. I swear I thought . . ."

"It isn't that. I'm not going back to New York. I want to fly into Phoenix and do some more recent scouting on the guys I told you about last night. They're a major part of my pitch to ownership on Nakamura and I need to have the most up-to-date information."

"And I'm not invited?"

"What? No, I just thought . . . I figured after last night you wouldn't want to . . ."

Ah, so maybe not unaffected, maybe just hiding it really, really well. Until now.

And I kind of want to hate her for that too. I've never been able to hide my emotions if they were strong enough, not on the field and not off it. "Didn't we decide that we were going to do what we had to do to get that ring?"

"Yeah, but . . ."

"No buts," I cut her off again, and I grin at the way she purses her lips at me. Good, she's annoyed at me, which means she'll be distracted enough to not think about what almost happened last night. "Besides, there's no way there's a direct flight from Bozeman to Phoenix, and I'm not sitting in another stupid small seat with a layover."

"What are you talking about?"

"I told you I was smart with my money, but desperate times. I have a share in a charter company. We're flying private."

I expect her to protest, but no, she just shrugs and gestures at me. "Well, don't you have to make a call or something to get that to happen?"

"Right," I say, tossing the blanket I'd burrowed under last night aside and standing up, reaching for my phone where I'd plugged it in to charge.

"Oh."

"What?" I ask, turning to her, but her eyes don't meet mine, they're focused just a little lower, where I'm only wearing a pair of boxer briefs. The heat had been pumping against the chilly Montana autumn air last night and I've always run hot when I sleep.

"Sorry," she mumbles, turning around and fussing with her luggage.

"Nothing you haven't seen before," I say with a chuckle, rummaging in my bag for a pair of sweatpants and a t-shirt. "You were always in the clubhouse; I'm sure guys were way more naked than this."

"I always tried to avoid it. Some guys thought it was funny to just, you know, wander around naked when there were women there, but I couldn't escape it completely. So, no, it . . . you, at least, aren't something I've seen before."

I definitely played with dickheads like that, who thought it was hilarious to make the women we worked with as uncomfortable as possible. I quickly pull on my clothes and then say, "All done."

She clears her throat before turning back around, but still doesn't quite meet my eye. Is she embarrassed? It's . . . sweet. "Are you sure you want to come with me?" she asks, and her flush deepens as the double meaning of her words hits her.

"I'm sure," I answer simply, letting the innuendo slide past us, and her shoulders drop in clear relief. "Let's go."

Chapter 9

FRANCESCA

Arizona was not on the agenda when I left New York to clean up the mess with Ethan Quicke. But I'm here now and, in that brief moment between stepping out of the recirculated cool air of the plane and the air conditioning pumping through the airport, the dry heat leaking through from the tarmac reminds me that I did not pack for the desert.

"Wait," I say, glancing into one of the few shops at the tiny airport our chartered flight landed in, though I don't really feel like donning anything that proclaims ARIZONA across my boobs. I mentally run through what I have in my bag, but it's basically pajamas, the one suit I wore on the way in and the clothes I wore last night: jeans and long sleeves. There's a pair of cotton shorts in there that could pass, but nothing on top that wouldn't be wildly inappropriate.

It's going to be at least ninety degrees out there today and I'll be spending it out in the blazing sun.

"What is it?" Charlie asks.

"Do you have a shirt I can borrow?"

"Uh," he hesitates, looking me up and down quickly, but the speed doesn't stop a soft jolt going through me. "I don't think anything I own will fit you."

"A t-shirt? I can tie it up." He pauses and for a second his eyes go a little unfocused. "You know what, forget it. We can just stop at a store on the way."

"No," he assures me. "I have something. Hang on."

He squats down and I'm hit with an extremely odd sense of deja vu. He was a catcher and he probably spent more time squatting than some human beings spend standing. He pulls a folded bit of navy-blue cotton from his bag and hands it to me. As he stands, he lets out a muffled groan and the click in his knee is so loud I think it echoes up into the rafters of the terminal.

"I wore it, but it wasn't like we ran a marathon. It should be pretty clean."

"Thanks," I say, taking it and disappearing into the bathroom.

One of the major demands of my job is the sheer amount of travel, sometimes to places no one has ever heard of before crisscrossing the country to see in person if my analyses prove true, to see if the players can live up or down to what the algorithm says. I've changed in more than one airport bathroom in my life, though admittedly this bathroom that serves passengers that just flew a chartered flight is one of the nicer ones I've ever been in. Even still, it's a public restroom. Not exactly the height of luxury or cleanliness. But as I pull his shirt over my head, I do what normally would feel absolutely insane. I inhale. It's the same shirt he wore last night, a faded Brooklyn Eagles logo printed on soft cotton that still smells vaguely like laundry detergent, but also clearly tinged with the lingering scent of him.

I lift my hair out of the collar, letting it fall down my back, and then tie the bottom of the shirt into a tight knot just above the small of my back and fold the sleeves up enough so they're not hanging down to my elbows. Paired with the sneakers I brought along just in case I got up the motivation to go for a run while I was away and it's not a bad look for a minor league ballpark.

Okay, good to go.

"Huh," Charlie grunts, when I rejoin him.

"What?"

"I don't think I've ever seen you dressed so casual for work."

"I was pretty casual last night."

I flinch. Again with the double entendre. It's like I'm incapable of speaking around him without making it sound like I want to bang him.

Which, if I'm being honest, isn't that far from the truth.

At least it wasn't last night, just after telling him that I couldn't go there with him, not again, closing the door behind me and immediately diving under the covers to try and get some relief. I was embarrassingly wet when I shed my jeans and panties, it barely took anything at all, just a few flicks of my fingers, even though they felt too soft and too small. So, I imagined his hands, warm, the way they were holding me while we danced ,and large, the way his palm and fingers were able to completely wrap around me, thumb pressing gently into the space just below my hip bone. It wasn't hard to imagine the same pressure between my legs, the callouses made permanent by the bat and ball over a lifetime sending me over the edge. It was a quiet, shuddering release and I'm not exactly proud of it, but I didn't know what else to do.

Just like he has before, though, he lets it go, though I can see amusement dancing merrily in his eyes.

"C'mon," I say, pushing past the awkwardness coursing through me, "we're going straight to the field. The game is at one."

"Aye, aye, captain," he says, tapping two fingers to his forehead in a salute before falling into step with me. "So, one more time, we're here to look at . . ."

I pick up where he trails off. "Cole Davis, catcher. Archie Esposito, lefty pitcher – he's getting the start today – and Xander Greene, centerfield."

"And you really think you can convince ownership that they should go with them to start the season?"

"I wasn't sure," I admit, but then make sure I stare straight ahead, determined not to look at him when I say, "but with your backing and Stew's, I know I can. It won't take long before they prove themselves out on the field."

"Three rookies: feels like one of those things your computer would say is too risky. Not enough data to form a conclusion? Does not compute," he finishes, in an awful robot voice.

"You haven't met them yet. They're special and they're mostly special because of each other."

"What?"

"You don't recognize the names?"

"Should I?"

"They're sort of famous. All from the same town, played in the Little League World Series together, won it together and then won the California high-school state championship together. So, we drafted them *together*. Figured, what could it hurt, maybe they'll be able to recreate some magic at the pro level. And they did, won the rookie ball championship two years ago. Davis and Greene were a little further along in their development than Esposito, and he struggled without them, but once we promoted him to Double A, it was like someone flicked a switch, gave up five total runs in his final fifty innings pitched of the season."

He lets out a low whistle, like he's impressed. He should be.

"Like I said, they're special – the whole greater than the sum of its parts, and the parts are pretty damn good."

"And you really think it translates to the major league level?"

"I know it does. The skill sets are there, but I want you to see for yourself and, if you think I'm right, then we fly back to New York tonight and, first thing Monday morning, I go in and pitch it. Nakamura's going to post soon and I can't waste any more time. Our focus has to be on signing him and making his transition to the States as smooth as humanly possible."

"Okay then," he says, as we step out into a dry but blistering Arizona morning, "let's go take a look at the kids."

The ballpark is small, but intimate, in the way that minor league stadiums tend to be, with local sponsors splashed along the outfield walls, scoreboards from twenty years ago or more with lightbulbs still serving to indicate balls and strikes instead of the flashy screens you see in the majors. There's no upper deck, just one level lined with concessions up behind the seats on the concourse.

There's a charm to it, almost like going back in time.

Actually, for me and definitely for Charlie, it does feel like we've stepped into the past. Camelback Ranch is *also* the spring training home for the Dodgers, once they moved their off-season operations from Florida to Arizona. It's a state-of-the-art facility where every winter dozens of ballplayers converge to prepare for the major league season ahead.

The teams are already on the field doing their last preparations before the game begins, playing catch, stretching out, waiting for the umpires to emerge from their changing room and start it up.

"Being back here is weird," I say, giving Charlie an opening and he takes it.

"Fucking surreal is more like it," he says. "Never thought I'd be back, honestly."

"You didn't think about coaching for the Dodgers?"

"Nah, I would have been a distraction for the current guys for sure. Besides, I needed to get out of LA. It was . . . time."

"You needed to get out of the city that adores you?"

"It's complicated. Why did you leave? Hometown girl and all that."

"Stew made me an offer I couldn't refuse."

"Bull, they would have matched it. They loved you over there."

"It's complicated," I hedge, not really feeling the need to unload my stupid divorce sob story in the middle of a ballpark.

It's late in the fall league's schedule and with a win today, their temporary team, the Glendale Desert Dogs, will be headed to a short playoff round.

"Do you want to talk to them beforehand?" I ask. "I can get a message down to the dugout if you want."

Charlie shakes his head almost immediately. "Nah, I'd rather they didn't know I was here. Let's grab seats down at baseline and we'll," he stops at a vendor and points to a Desert Dogs hat, black and orange with a howling dog at the center, motioning that he'll take two, "go incognito."

"I don't think we have to worry about anyone recognizing me," I say with a laugh, but I pull my hair up into a ponytail and slide it through the back of the hat so it sits comfortably on my head.

He clicks his tongue like he disagrees as we find our section, up the third base line, a few rows above the dugout with a perfect view inside the first-base dugout. That's where our boys will emerge from in a few minutes. It'll give us a chance to see how they interact with each other and with their teammates during the game.

"This field isn't that big," he says, as he allows me to precede him into the row, settling down beside me and gesturing around us.

"So, that means fewer people to notice," I counter.

"No, I mean, they'll be able to see into the stands from the dugout."

"I doubt they'll be worrying about some random woman in the stands. They've got a game to play."

"I promise you, the boys in that dugout are gonna notice you, anyone who looks in this general direction is gonna notice you. You gotta know that, right?"

Rolling my eyes at him, I say, "I don't know any such thing."

Charlie shifts in his seat, angling his shoulders as much as he can in the tight seat, not nearly as roomy as the cushioned luxury we enjoyed on the flight down. He has to lift his elbow onto the plastic edge of the seat back to turn and face me. Blue eyes steady and warm as his forearm brushes my shoulder just slightly.

"I don't know how to say this, because I can't imagine you don't already know it, Sullivan, but you're the most beautiful woman in every room you walk into."

I want to say something clever, something flippant, about how we're not even in a room, and how beauty is subjective – *anything* that doesn't require me to actually deal with the way he's looking at me and the words he just said. The only words I can manage are a murmured "Thank you."

It's odd. I've never wanted to be judged by how I look, but it's been a while since a man offered a compliment that sincere. Because he meant it. I can tell by the warmth in his eyes and the nod he gives me when I don't protest. Though it seems like maybe he doesn't know what to say now and it's so odd to see him tongue tied that I determinedly break the silence.

"I'm at a ballpark to watch a baseball game. I need a hot dog and a beer," I say, reaching into my bag and pulling out my card, waving it at him. "I buy, you fly?"

"Put the card away, Frankie," he insists, before sliding from his seat and jogging back up the steps to the concourse to grab us food.

He's gone before I can react to him actually using my name. I don't think I've ever heard him say it before, at least not while he was conscious. Then again, on the plane it was *Francesca*. That was indescribably hot, but this, just a casual Frankie, there was something more to that, something simple and easy about it, like he knows me.

And maybe he does, or at least maybe he's starting to.

I busy myself with my phone, trying not to think too hard about what just happened, scrolling through messages, ignoring most of them and then my emails – nothing urgent there either. What good is having a high-pressure job if it isn't there to distract you from the extremely hot ex-major league star who just called you beautiful?

Something in my chest flutters pleasantly at the thought.

No. I decided last night that this couldn't happen. Actually, I decided a long time ago. You don't smash glass ceilings in professional sports by fantasizing about your colleagues. And that's what he is. He's a colleague. We basically have the exact same level of authority within the organization.

Clearly, it's something that concerns him also. He said as much that last night in LA, that we didn't work together anymore, and then he kissed me. So clearly that's a line for him too.

We're both adults. We're both capable of controlling ourselves. And we're here to do a job, because *this* is our job, even if right now we just look like two people out for a date night at the ballpark.

Even more so when he comes back a minute later laden down with a box of food, balancing two beers and a scorebook underneath it all. Oh, I should have told him to get me one too. Keeping score is an art form all its own and it's been so long since I've been able to do it just for fun.

"I didn't know what you liked on your hot dog," he says, handing one off to me and then digging into his pocket for a fist full of packets. Mustard, ketchup, mayo, relish, and a little plastic cup of jalapeños. "LA girls like a little kick, right?"

"We do," I agree, trying desperately to keep the resolve I'd just managed to build up less than a minute ago.

Handsome. Confident. Thoughtful.

A far cry from the arrogant prick I faced down every day back in LA, even if he thought it was a sign of respect.

Retirement has been good for him.

"Can I ask you something?" I squeeze some deli mustard onto my hot dog, licking a bit off my fingers when I'm done.

He clears his throat and blinks at me, expression blank. "What?"

I don't repeat myself, sure that he heard me. "Is it just for a championship?"

"What?"

"Are you only back for a championship? If we win it all this season, are you one and done?"

"I . . ." he starts, but then stops. "I hadn't thought about it."

"You signed a five-year contract."

He shrugs. "It's what my agent negotiated. As you've been more than happy to point out, I don't need the money."

"And so I ask again, are you just here for the ring? And then that's it, back to retirement?"

"Maybe," he says. "I'm not sure I really know."

"Okay."

I let it go, not sure if that should bother me or not. If I should want him to stay and keep doing this with me or if these ridiculous butterflies that have followed us from Brooklyn to Bozeman and now Glendale could be unleashed if he called it quits after a year and we'd be free to explore what that might mean.

"Okay?" he asks. "Nothing else to say?"

"Not really anything else *to* say."

"Unlike you," he mutters, and I'm saved from having to come up with a zinger of my own when the public address announcer calls us all to our feet and asks us to remove our hats for a local kid singing the national anthem.

And when we do, both of us generally standing taller than the rest of the crowd, it's easy to see the three kids in Brooklyn Eagles uniforms standing just outside the dugout steps beside each other, all three of their gazes locked directly on us.

Yeah, we've been spotted.

"Told you so," Charlie mutters, out of the corner of his mouth, and I'm not mature enough to keep myself from elbowing his side sharply, grinning at the wheeze he lets out at the contact.

"I think they're looking at *you*," I shoot back, and get a glare from two extremely patriotic looking older men in front of us as the kid wraps up with a slightly off-key and warbling *and the home of the braaaaveeeeee.*

He makes that sound again, that half tsk, half grunt, but I let it go this time because I'm still thinking about that question he didn't answer. Is this it for him? I'm trying to build something that lasts, a team that won't just win one championship, but contend every year. And somehow, in the last two weeks, Charlie Avery has become a part of that plan.

And maybe it's too soon to worry about it, too early to let it take up even the smallest bit of space in my mind, but it's there now and it's too late to forget it.

I busy myself arranging the jalapeños on my hot dog and then dousing it with some more deli mustard, a combination that feels like an odd convergence of the old and new in my life, LA heat and New York spice. Half Dodger Dog, half Eagle Weiner.

I take a bite and feel the heat spark against my tongue. Nice. Then I look to my left and Charlie's spreading ketchup across his hot dog.

"What are you doing?"

He stops and looks over at me. "Eating?"

"No, with that ketchup, and what is that, mayonnaise?"

"I'm putting it on my hot dog?"

"That hot dog is a travesty."

"It's how I've always had them."

"You can take the Midwest out of the boy . . ."

"Okay, coastal elite snob," he teases. "Don't knock it until you try it."

"That will not be anywhere near my mouth. I have standards."

He lifts an eyebrow at me and I can actually feel the pink in my cheeks as I flush, and it only grows when his eyes flick down to my lips.

I release a shaky breath, but he clearly doesn't care one bit for my sanity as he flicks his tongue against his bottom lip, still staring at mine.

I reach for my beer to take a long sip and keep my stupid mouth from talking me right into another awkward innuendo.

Oh thank God, warmups are done and Archie Esposito stands on the mound ready to throw the first pitch and get this game going.

"Here," he says, reaching down to his feet and handing me the scorebook and a pen tucked inside the spiral binding.

"It's for me?"

"I remember you used to keep a book during spring training."

"You do?"

"You were always in the stands, even during the split squads, exhibitions, whatever. Hard not to notice."

"It was my job."

"No, it wasn't. You had all the video and biometrics stuff recording. It wasn't your job to sit there and keep score of a game that didn't even count."

"No, it wasn't," I agree, finally, not even sure why I didn't want to admit it. "It makes me feel like I made it."

He doesn't seem to understand.

"When I was five, my dad taught me how to keep score sitting in front of the TV. And when I do it now, it's like I'm talking to that little girl, telling her we made it."

The umpire signals play ball.

Yeah, I made it.

Chapter 10

CHARLIE

The ballpark isn't crowded and, while it's warm and sunny, there are enough clouds and an occasional breeze to make it the perfect afternoon for a baseball game. The last time I watched a game from the stands was earlier this year. The Dodgers retired my number 8, but I could barely bring myself to watch the game from up in the suite they gave me for the day. It was all still too fresh and I still resented the hell out of not being out there on the field.

This feels completely different.

Just a few yards away from the action and, for a bunch of kids out there, the dream is still very much alive and close enough for them to touch it. Teams generally send their best prospects to the Arizona Fall League and most of these kids have a real shot at making it to the Bigs.

And three of those kids are definitely the ones we're here to watch. After Archie Esposito set down the other team one, two, three in the top of the first inning, Xander Greene led off with a single and promptly stole second base. The next kid, one of the Red Sox prospects, flew out to center and the Phillies future second baseman struck out, and now Cole Davis is at the plate, two outs, runner in scoring position, and the pitcher, a fireballer that might make a great pitcher one day, as soon as he can control exactly where his 101-mph fastball will end up when he lets it go.

The first pitch is high and tight, sending Davis sprawling backward into the dirt as he just barely avoids taking one to the head.

Standing up, the kid replaces the batting helmet that went flying to the ground when he took cover.

The sparse crowd gasps and some even boo.

"Control your stuff or get off the mound," Frankie mutters from beside me.

"Restraining yourself?" I ask. I can feel her vibrating beside me, like she wants to leap to her feet and shout at the kid out on the field instead of composing herself.

"I'm a professional," she grinds out.

"Are you?"

"Barely. There's a reason I watch most of the games from my office. No one can hear me losing it," she says, as she carefully marks a ball into the little box for Davis's at bat on her score sheet.

"I didn't know that. You ever get this heated for me?"

Fuck. Her talent for innuendo is apparently contagious.

She just snorts, though, her attention still mostly on the game in front of her. "All the time."

"Really?"

"I know you thought I hated you, but you were one of my guys. All I wanted was for you to succeed."

I want to respond, but I have no idea what to say to that.

Thankfully she doesn't seem to need a response.

"C'mon, Davis," she says, only a little bit louder than her heckling.

I join her. "Let's go, kid. Get one to drive." I clap a bit, like I would if I were standing in the dugout right now and I'd penciled him into the cleanup spot myself.

The next pitch is pure heat like the last, but instead of at Davis's ear, it's belt high on the inner half.

With what seems like just a quick shift of his weight and a snap of his wrists, the bat glides through the strike zone and barrel meets ball.

And then the ball whistles in a low rising drive what has to be four hundred and fifty feet to dead centerfield.

My eyes flash to the scoreboard to see the pitch speed. 101mph. I don't even want to hazard a guess at its exit velocity.

Fuck.

The kid can hit.

I can almost feel it in my hands, the sheer power of that moment when a round ball hits a round bat squarely, the hardest thing to do in professional sports. It happened in my very last at bat. We were already down 9-0 in the bottom of the 9th inning and there wasn't anyone on base. A meaningless home run that made the score 9-1 when the Yankees won the World Series. Five minutes later the game was over, the season was over and my career was over.

But for Cole Davis, it's all just beginning.

Hell, he probably wasn't even out of diapers during my rookie season.

He rounds third and heads for home and, just as he crosses home plate, he turns toward us, looks me dead in the eye and points.

The little fuck.

Yeah, I want to manage this kid.

I lean toward Frankie and say, "He reminds me of me."

"Yeah, except he's a switch hitter."

"Show off."

She laughs and her shoulder bumps into mine as the next batter makes the final out of the inning and she finishes up her scoring.

"What do you think so far?"

"Can't tell a lot in one half inning."

"You know a lot of kids that can take 101 to dead center from the left side?"

"Fair point."

"Anyway, the homer was impressive, but I think his work behind the plate is even more valuable. Look at his framing, it's so subtle," she says, her chin brushing against the top of my shoulder as she does, nodding out to the field where Esposito is set to pitch. "He can turn a ball into a strike with just the slightest movement of his wrist. Fools the umpire almost every time."

"Yeah," I say, holding a hand out in front of me like I'm about to catch a ball, demonstrating the twist of my wrist in a motion that mimics how I used to create the visual illusion for the umpire that a borderline pitch was actually a strike, giving my pitcher the advantage. It's a dying art, one that will probably go away entirely once they have cameras calling balls and strikes instead.

"When I got to college, I had a coach that insisted that just yanking it back into the strike zone was better," she says, rolling her eyes. "I literally had to do a video presentation to show him."

"Don't even get me started on that bullshit. Are the umpires fooled by it? Sometimes, but if you're consistently framing it right, the amount of calls you'll get the benefit of the doubt on are so much higher."

Davis receives another pitch from Esposito framing it, but it's a little too obvious. Ball four and the batter can take first. I click my tongue. "That wasn't bad, but he'd do better to just gently lift with the wrist. Once they see your elbow is moving, you're toast."

She mimics me, left hand out, "Show me?"

I reach for it, covering it with my own. My hand fully encases hers, guiding her wrist in the subtle turn that served me well behind the plate, but when my thumb brushes against the inside of her wrist and her breathing hitches, a soft little gasp that draws my gaze from our hands to her face, searching there for what she might be thinking.

Last night she said no and I respect that, even if I slipped a bit earlier by calling her beautiful, but she asked me to touch her just now and now all I can envision is sitting back against my headboard, Frankie resting against my chest, my body curved around her, my hand guiding hers down between her legs before begging her to show me exactly how she likes to be touched, snaking an arm around her waist to hold her to me while I watch her get herself off.

Crack!

The unmistakable sound of ball hitting bat jolts us both back to reality and I'm a little stunned at just how close we'd gotten, her nose brushing mine as she pulls away and my gaze follows hers out to the outfield, where a ball bounces off the wall in center.

One of the kids we're here to look at, Xander Greene, fields it cleanly and fires it back in toward the infield.

"He can throw," I mutter, standing with the rest of the crowd as the ball comes in to home, Esposito, the pitcher ,backing up the plate, but Davis receives it, shifts his weight and tags the runner smoothly. He's out, but the play doesn't stop there; the guy who hit it is trying to motor into second base, but Davis doesn't hesitate, sending a missile to second to nail the runner there.

Inning over in impressive as all fuck fashion.

"Just the way you drew it up," Frankie says with a laugh, clapping at their efforts as Davis and Esposito wait for Greene to come in from the outfield and high five him before they all disappear back into the dugout. She quickly updates her scorebook, biting her lip to tamp down her smile.

"You might be right about these kids."

Her head lifts and her face lights up so thoroughly at that, I'm confused. Tell her she's the most beautiful woman in any room she walks into and I get a simple thank you. Tell her she's right about three minor leaguers' potential to break into the big leagues next season and her smile is brighter than the shine on any World Series ring.

It's confusing as hell. Not that I don't approve of her priorities.

It's just normally, if I can't get a woman out of my head, I make a move, but that isn't an option here.

"It'll be a learning curve, but I think this plan of yours, it might actually work. Should we tell them the good news?"

"We'll take them to dinner after the game," she says. "We'll let them know they're going to have an opportunity this spring, no guarantees."

The Desert Dogs are up by a run going into the late innings of the game and Esposito is cruising along.

"This kid's stuff is fire."

Frankie clicks her tongue. "It is, but they should pull him."

"What? Why?"

She shows me her phone where real time game analytics are

being spit out onto her screen. It feels just like it used to back when I was playing, my instincts screaming one thing at me while her data said something else.

"Spin rate is down on his slider – it's a sign of fatigue. I don't have access to our biometric data in the stands, but I bet his shoulder is dropping down just a little too."

"They still aren't making hard contact and—" I start to say that Esposito's making the other team look silly when . . .

Crack!

The next pitch is launched deep to centerfield. Greene gets a great read on it and makes the catch, nearly crashing into the wall as he does.

"Shit," I mutter.

"Yeah, I know, it's really annoying," she says, and I can hear the smile in her voice as she says it, "how I'm always right."

"Incredibly annoying, but I know when I'm beat. We'll do it your way, Sullivan."

"I appreciate that, but make sure you keep pushing back, okay?"

"What ,do you like fighting with me or something?" I ask, turning to look down at her just in time to see a flush spreading across her cheeks.

"The human element is important too. There are things numbers can't tell you and, if I'm going to trust anyone's instincts, I guess yours are pretty good."

"High praise," I quip, fighting down the urge to say it with my lips brushing her ear before trailing the kiss down to the underside of her jaw to see if I can make that soft blush deepen.

I snap myself out of it just in time to focus my gaze back onto the field when she turns toward me.

"Don't get used to it," she mutters, but that smile is definitely still there.

The Desert Dogs end up losing the game, but it doesn't matter, not really. It's an exhibition league, at its best, but looking at the three young men we're here to see, you'd have no idea that the game didn't even count.

"Sorry we couldn't win one for you," Davis says, freshly showered, his mop of brown hair still wet and falling into his eyes when he, Greene and Esposito meet us outside the clubhouse post-game.

I don't blow it off, though. I like that he cares. "You kept fighting," I say, offering him a hand to shake. "That rally was almost enough in the 9th."

"Almost," he says, shaking his head in real disappointment. "It's nice to meet you, Mr Avery."

"Skip'll do," I correct him, and nod to the other boys. "Good game, gentlemen. Very good." They beam at me, a little less likely to take the loss as hard as their teammate. That's good, it'll keep him grounded. "You all know Francesca Sullivan, I imagine?"

"It's good to see you all again," she says, at my side. "Can we buy you boys dinner?"

Despite what I'm sure was a decent spread in the clubhouse after the game, their nods are emphatic and immediate.

"Fantastic," I say, "I know just the place."

It's one of my favorite spots in Glendale, La Bonita Cantina, which sounds kind of cheesy and looks worse, being stuck in the middle of a nondescript shopping center, but the food is always fresh and tastes incredible and they're not stingy with the drinks.

The sheer amount of food three twenty-one-year-old boys can pack away at a good Mexican restaurant is honestly impressive. I was cooked after nursing one beer for a couple of hours and my third enchilada, but they're still going strong.

Archie Esposito, dark haired and dark eyed, almost shy compared to the other two, can't quite take his eyes off Frankie while she praises their efforts on the field today. I know a crush when I see one and, honestly, I can only hope that I don't look like that when I stare at her.

Is that what I have? A crush? Maybe. It's been so long since I've felt *anything* for a woman beyond a physical pull that I don't really recognize that a feeling beyond that exists.

"We'll work on an analysis for you on how often that knuckler should be brought out, though your catcher does a pretty good job at mixing it in," Frankie says to Archie, and then lets her eyes twinkle across the table at his teammate.

"Yeah, Cole and I have been working on that," Archie says, his heart eyes not going anywhere.

"It's important for him to throw it," Cole says, "or he'll lose the feel, but not so much that it gets predictable and they expect it. Not that they can handle it when he does throw it, but we want it to always be in the back of their head. It gets us some cheap strikes on fastballs when they think there's a chance for the junk."

"That was some impressive hitting today," I say to Cole.

"Xander got on and then got over to second. He was worried about him moving over to third and left one where I could get it."

I tip my beer bottle toward Xander and nod. "Can't drive in runners that aren't on base causing havoc."

The centerfielder actually blushes, a red flush climbing up into his light blond hair, neatly swooped to the side, a clear effort made versus the other two, who seem happy enough with the just-out-of-the-shower look.

"Exactly," Cole agrees, and whacks his teammate roughly on the shoulder, almost hard enough to knock the drink out of his hand. "Just doing my job."

These are good answers. Answers that will play well with the New York media. Factually correct, deflective of praise and, yeah, mostly boring, but that's the point. He's not just good on the field, he'll be good off it.

You need to have that thing in that city, that thing that Jeter and Judge and Brunson and Manning all have in common. I'm ahead of myself, so far ahead that I honestly can't even believe it, but I can see it clear as day, this kid, captain of the Brooklyn Eagles, his best friends on the field with him, a decade of success and a ring or two or maybe three, four if I'm being greedy.

These are my guys.

I glance over at Frankie, a satisfied smile playing across her mouth while she lifts her drink for a slow sip. She's right there with me. Hell, she was there before me. Of course she was.

"What are your off-season plans?" she asks them, finishing off her second margarita.

"Back home for a little bit, but then we're all gonna grab a place in Clearwater together, get down there early."

"I think that's a very good idea," I say.

"It's actually saves us from having to suggest it. We want all of you to have a good holiday season, focus on spending time with your families and then prioritize getting ready for Spring Training. You'll all be at big league camp and obviously it'll be up to you to show us that you're ready."

"Fuck," Archie blurts out.

"Dude," Xander shoots at him.

Cole is silent, his mouth open, blinking in clear stupefaction before he gives himself a little shake and says, "I'm sorry, could you . . . could you repeat that?"

"You'll be in the big-league camp this spring and, if we see what we think we'll see, I'd say you three have a shot at coming north with us."

He takes one final swig from his beer and then nods. "Excuse me for a second," he says, pushing away from the table, standing and weaving his way through the restaurant back toward the bathroom.

Xander stands to follow him, while Archie just looks confused, but I shake my head. "I'll go."

I find him in the bathroom, splashing water on his face, getting a little down the front of his shirt in the process, but he doesn't seem to notice.

"You okay, kid?"

"Were you okay, when they told you?"

"Nearly shit myself."

"Yeah, that's . . . I might do that later."

"Fair enough."

"You mean it, though? That I . . . we . . ."

"Yeah, we mean it. Well, she does. She's the one calling the shots when it comes to this stuff, at least until we get out on the field."

He nods and then takes a deep steadying breath. "Fuck, I must seem like such a dickhead right now. It's just . . . I gave up a lot to sign out of high school. We all did. Scholarships and shit. My parents are *still* pissed about it."

"Well, give it a couple of months, work your ass off, stay healthy and you'll be having one hell of a *I told you so* conversation with them."

"Claudia's gonna freak out when I tell her."

Ah, there's a girl. Of course there is.

"How long have you been with her?"

"Oh, I'm not, we're not, she's my best friend, other than the boys. She's Archie's sister."

I don't quite believe him about the *not* part of it, but don't push it. "Good, that's good. She's from before . . . what's about to happen."

He nods and then a question appears in his eyes and I wonder if he's ballsy enough to ask it. I know I would have been when I was twenty-one.

"What about you and . . ." he trails off for a beat, and then gathers his courage, "you and her." He motions with his chin back behind me through the door where we left Frankie with his buddies.

"What about us?"

"We were watching you the whole game, wondering what the fuck you guys were doing here, but I have eyes, Skip, and you two seemed . . . cozy."

"Kid, I'm gonna teach you your first big league lesson right now."

"Mind my own fucking business?" His smile is wide and entirely shit eating.

I snort. "Yeah, you're gonna be fine. C'mon, let's go back there before Esposito faints if she smiles at him too big."

He's clearly holding back another comment and I add it to the list of captain-like qualities: knowing when to shut the hell up in front of the grown-ups.

I slid the waiter my card when we got here and Frankie rolls her eyes when he brings it back, check already paid, muttering about being able to expense it to the club, and we walk the boys back to the parking lot.

"You coming to the game tomorrow?"

My eyes flick to Frankie for an answer. It's her call.

"No, we have to get back to New York. Winter meetings are coming up in a few weeks and we still have some moves we want to make."

"Thanks for this, Ms Sullivan, Skip. We really appreciate it." Davis says, clearly speaking for all of them.

"Yeah, our meal money doesn't really cover this," Esposito pipes up.

"We'll see you in Florida?" Greene asks, like he's still unsure any of this was real.

"We'll see you in Florida," Frankie confirms, and we wave them off as our Uber pulls up.

"Wait, did you make a hotel reservation?" she asks, brow furrowed as I hold open the door to the backseat for her.

"I have a condo here."

"You do? Wait, of course you do."

It's only about a ten-minute drive from the restaurant to my place. It's been a minute since I've been there, though a cleaning crew comes in every couple of weeks to keep the dust from piling up. I should probably sell it now that I'm with a team that hosts spring training in Florida. No sense in holding on to a property I'm never going to use.

Ugh, Florida. Humidity and rain instead of Arizona's brutal but dry heat.

That I'm not looking forward to at all.

But it'll be better than January through March in New York, with slush in the streets and bitter cold air biting at your skin every time you go outside.

"This is . . ." she trails off, "very clean."

"You don't have to be polite. It was basically a crash pad for spring training every year. I didn't need much."

She's trying to be nice, but her face gives it away, a nose wrinkle. I bought it a couple of years into my career, a simple one-bedroom condo within five minutes of the Camelback Ranch complex. All the walls are painted white with a ceramic white-tile floor. A large gray area rug with a black leather sectional defines the living room space, with the kitchen on the other side, also white, the only thing breaking that up is the dark countertops.

Gemma always hated it. Called it my bachelor pad and that we should upgrade it to something nicer.

Huh.

That's interesting.

I haven't thought about Gemma for days. Weeks even. Not since . . .

Not since I landed in New York.

And the reason why laughs at me. "You have a couch, a TV mounted on the wall and two bar stools in your kitchen. Did you have some kind of spartan philosophy about depriving yourself during training or something?"

"There's a bed at least."

"Well, I'm thrilled to know that you weren't crashing on a couch all those years. It does look pretty comfortable, though."

"No way, you're taking the bed," I insist.

She shakes her head. "You didn't fit on the couch in Bozeman and there's no way you're not still sore. I saw the way you stood up at the airport this morning. Your knee is acting up."

"Knee's fine."

"It's not fine. The couch is massive. I'll be good out here."

"My mother would actually kill me if I let you sleep on the couch. She'd come back from the dead and murder me."

"That's not fair."

"What?"

"Using chivalry isn't dead and your mom's beyond-the-grave disappointment in combination."

"Who ever said I play fair?"

"Didn't you win an award for it at some point?"

"The Roberto Clemente Award for the player who best

exemplifies the game of baseball, sportsmanship, community involvement and the individual's contribution to his team."

"That's the one."

"I've got news for you about that guy."

"Yeah, what's that?"

"He retired."

Chapter 11

FRANCESCA

"You say retired like you mean dead," I say, shaking my head at him as I leave my luggage next to the couch and toeing off my sneakers. If I just make sure to fall asleep there, I'll win without having to fight him on it more.

"Felt like it at the time," he admits, turning into his kitchen. "I . . . there was nothing after baseball."

Opening the fridge, there's an extremely organized selection of beverages lined up on the glass shelves. He grabs himself a beer and then turns to me, a question in his eyes. I nod and he grabs one for me too, a Modelo, like he was drinking at the restaurant.

"So you came back, for the ring, like you said," I continue, as he pops the tops off both of them and settles on one side of the long peninsula in the kitchen, dark quartz a contrast against the shiny white cabinets.

"Yeah, for the ring, but what you asked me, about whether that was the only reason? No, it wasn't. This is where I've always belonged. Ring or not, I'm in it for the long haul."

"You haven't even managed one game. Maybe see how you like it first," I caution. "It's different. The first time I watched a game I'd analyzed and I couldn't be out there to do it myself, it was hard."

"Oh, I'm sure that part will drive me nuts," he admits, taking a quick sip. "But kids like that? And a talent like Nakamura and, hell, even an ego-driven dick like Ethan Quicke. I love that shit, getting your chess pieces together and figuring out the best way to deploy them, getting the best out of them. I'm excited, for the first time in a long time."

"About baseball?"

"About anything," he says, with a half a shrug and a self-deprecating grin, not entirely unlike the smile Cole Davis wore today when we were singing his praises.

"That's . . ." I trail off.

"Sad?" he finishes for me.

"No," I insist, but when he sends me a disbelieving look, I change my mind. "Well, maybe, but I was going to say familiar."

"Really?" he asks, in clear surprise.

"Do you know why I was, what did you call it, jacking your ride when we ran into each other at the airport?"

"No," he says simply, waiting for me to elaborate, but it's not that easy.

Taking a deep breath, I let it out slowly, wondering if I'm really going to share this with him. I barely talked about it with Bianca and she knew the whole sordid story. Finally, I give in, just a little bit. "I'd given up my ride to a family I knew."

"That was nice of you," he says, though it's clear he's confused.

"No, it wasn't, it was . . . I don't know exactly what it was, but it wasn't nice. The family, it was my ex-husband's family,

his new wife, their baby, and I saw them and I just thought . . .
I don't know what I thought."

"I take it it wasn't an amicable divorce?" he asks, probably
already knowing the answer.

"It was not. He cheated on me. With her. They got married
like a couple of weeks after our divorce was finalized, and she
was already pregnant. He quit his job in finance, the job he
claimed to love, and they're, I don't know exactly what to call
it, but influencers, I guess? I don't know exactly what they do,
as my best friend blocked all their accounts for me."

"That's a good friend. I unfollowed my ex, but we grew up
together, same small town, same childhood friends, so people
think it's fun to tag us in the same stuff. Sometimes I see her on
a friend's post, and she remarried Vaughn Keegan, you know
the linebacker from the Rams? And fans will randomly post
about her too."

"Are you kidding me?"

"Price of fame."

"No, that's ridiculous," I argue. "People are the worst."

"It's fine. I barely go on that stuff anyway."

"Still, you shouldn't have to see that," I say, reaching out and
covering Charlie's hand with mine, and his eyes flicker down
to stare at how we're now touching. Suddenly an air of tension
simmers between us, settling gently where my pale fingers lay
over the perpetually tan back of his hand. I try to break it with
a question. "It was an amicable split?"

"It was, as much as it could be. She wanted to start a family
and I knew that I couldn't do that while I was playing. I was too
selfish, too focused. I don't know how some guys did it. They
made it look easy too. Javy just always had his family around
and Maria had her own company and that seemed impossible
to me."

"I'm sorry," I say, though I don't know why I'm apologizing.

"Nah, I'm sorry your ex was such a shithead. And who the hell would cheat on you? Fucking idiot."

"I don't think it was about me, really."

"It wasn't, but still," he insists. "You don't cheat. That's just rule number one. You want out? You say something, you don't cheat. Ever."

"A pro athlete who thinks cheating isn't okay: are you some kind of unicorn?"

"There are more of us than you'd think," he says, and his hand shifts beneath mine, a shiver sliding through me when his calloused fingertips brush against the inside of my wrist, just like he did back at the ballpark.

"You . . ." I start and then stop when he does it again. "Fuck."

"Do you want me to stop?"

"No," I whisper, and his touch disappears and I nearly whimper at the loss of contact.

"No, you don't want me to stop or . . . just no?" he asks.

"Don't stop," I clarify, finding my voice, trying desperately to ignore just how good his touch is making me feel, how incredibly aroused I am by the briefest contact, by the tenor of his voice, "but this . . . it can't . . . we can't *really* do this. It wouldn't work. We're . . . we . . ."

"What happened in LA stayed in LA," he says. "What happens in Arizona can stay right here."

"Yeah?" I ask, cringing inwardly at how desperate and breathy the word sounded.

"If that's what you want. That's what we'll do."

"Okay."

"Okay, yes? I need to hear you say it, no confusion, no misinterpretation. Do you want this, Francesca?"

Fuck.

"You called me that before," I say, avoiding the question, buying time, trying to let the rational side of my brain, whatever's left of it, talk me out of this.

"Did I?" he asks, setting aside his beer and mine before coming around the counter to stand in front of me, his hands reaching out as he steps ever closer.

My hands find his and he takes them, before lifting one to his mouth, his lips caressing the skin his fingers found just a moment ago and a jolt goes through me, a heady surge of pure lust.

"On the plane to Bozeman," I manage to say, as one of his hands lifts to cup my cheek, his body close enough now to brush against mine, like when we danced in that ridiculous bar in Montana. "You fell asleep and I heard you say it."

"That makes sense," he admits. "I've only ever called you that in my head."

"You've thought about me?" I ask, as his head bends toward where he'd buried his face while we were on the plane.

"I have."

"Since we kissed."

"Since the first time I saw you."

It breaks the mood, just ever so slightly.

I pull back to look up into his eyes. "That's . . . you never . . ."

"We worked together," he explains, lifting one shoulder.

"We work together now."

"Not like this. Not like . . ." he trails off, one hand leaving me to run through his hair. "I was the captain of the team, a perennial All Star, future Hall of Fame. I was in the middle of a ten-year contract worth nearly three hundred million dollars. You worked in the analytics department. If things went bad, who do you think would have taken the fall?"

"So you didn't . . ." I trail off, not sure how that question would have ended. He didn't make a move? Seduce me? Make my place of work wildly uncomfortable? I was married at the time. So was he. An absolute recipe for disaster. Chivalry isn't dead. Its name is Charlie Avery.

"I didn't," he confirms.

"And now?"

"Now *you* outrank me," he says, and I open my mouth, my head full of comebacks, but he keeps going, "technically, and just barely, *and* I'm still a future Hall of Famer. All things considered, I'd call us relatively equal."

"Is that what you'd call us?"

"Equally desperate maybe."

"Desperate?"

"I told you, I've wanted you since that first day. What was that? Five years ago? Six? That's a long time to want someone."

It is.

Did I want him back then? Oh, probably, if I'd allowed myself even a second to think about why we were constantly at each other's throats, a series of daily throwdowns that could have just as easily have been resolved by finding the nearest flat surface and relieving that tension in the best possible way.

I've been quiet too long, thinking too deeply, because he steps away fully and I'm suddenly bereft at the loss of contact.

"Don't," I say, reaching out, my fingers wrapping gently around his wrist and watch, fascinated as goosebumps appear at my touch.

And just like that, the spark between us flares to life again. It's a dangerous thing, to know that with one simple touch I can feel this way, electricity dancing in my veins and across my skin, a slow simmer that could easily turn into a fully-fledged inferno.

He stands still. So incredibly still, like a marble statue as I reach up to run my fingertips along the sharp cut of his jawline, his eyes wary and careful when I move even closer, our bodies nearly brushing.

"Do you want me?" I ask. I need to hear it again. He was right. I am desperate.

"You know I do," he answers in a soft whisper, his breath ghosting over my lips before inhaling deeply, his chest rising and falling while his teeth dig into his bottom lip.

Holding himself back?

It's hot as hell.

Pushing up on my toes, I let my hand slide up into his hair, feeling the silky strands slip through my fingers as I finally close the distance between us, just a brush of my lips against his. I pull away, just for a second, getting my bearings and now waiting for him. He has my permission; I've opened the door and now he needs to kick it open.

He does.

His mouth is almost violent against mine, one hand at my hip, puling me into him, the other at my neck, his thumb pressing into my pulse point, his large palm moving me *just so* to get the angle right as his mouth seals over mine, an all-consuming kiss, flashes of light dancing behind my closed eyes as my arms wrap around his shoulders, desperate for some leverage to give as good as I'm getting.

It's a wild frenzied connection, hot opened-mouthed kisses and hands everywhere, bodies colliding as his teeth nip at my bottom lip before diving down over my jaw to my neck as he spins us around and backs us up, one stumbling step and then another until my hip collides with the countertop.

His hands slide around to my ass, pulling me against him, holding my hips to his as he presses forward, a mockery of what my body is truly craving, but the friction of his jeans and my cotton shorts is enough to have me pulling away gasping. He takes that as his cue to lift me up onto the countertop and step between my legs, immediately going straight back to work at my neck, his hands running up and down my thighs before settling his hands around them, his thumbs working gently inward as they caress my skin.

I can't believe I'm doing this. Or, actually, I can. What I can't believe is that I held out this long. Which is kind of pathetic because *this long* isn't that long at all. Though right now I'm pretty pissed at myself that two years ago I didn't grab him by the shirt, push him into the back seat of my car and ride him until dawn in the shadow of Dodger Stadium.

But there's no going back and I'm here now with his mouth nipping at my throat, his fingertips inching ever closer to exactly where I want him to go, but then, instead, he pulls away, staring down at me for a moment and then another, our ragged breath the only sound in the sad, nondescript condo.

He lifts one hand to my breast, his thumb coaxing the peak into an aching pebble, desperate for more, for his tongue and his lips and maybe just a little bit of his teeth.

"Fuck me," I choke out when those teeth graze a sensitive spot just below my ear and his responding grunt answers while his mouth latches on, marking my skin with the force of his kiss.

"That's the idea," he mumbles against my neck.

I yank away from him and nearly whimper at the loss of contact, but I need more than this, I need to feel him on my skin. Pulling his borrowed t-shirt up over my head, I toss it behind me and sit back, watching him watch me.

"Fuck," he breathes out, and I almost want to roll my eyes because I'm wearing a pretty normal bra, just some white satin and a bit of lace around the back.

"It's nothing special," I insist, running a thumb under the strap over one shoulder. It's cold in the apartment, the AC working overtime, and a shiver runs through me, goosebumps appearing over my skin.

He looks down at me, a lock of his brown hair falling down over his forehead. "You think I give a shit about the bra? Just fucking look at you, Sullivan."

"Back to Sullivan, huh?"

"When you're being obtuse about how fucking sexy you are, damn right."

Lifting a leg, I settle my heel into the small of his back, drawing him closer to me, pulling his body flush with mine. "Charlie?"

"Yeah?" he chokes out, his hands falling to my hips, one finger dipping briefly beneath the waistband, making me shiver against more than just the cold, before he grips it tightly, keeping our bodies pressed together.

"Touch me."

I don't have to ask twice. He ducks his head, his nose tracing the edge of my bra before diving between my breasts, inhaling deeply before pressing a warm, lingering kiss in the valley between them. Then he looks up, his eyes holding mine for a second and then another. "So soft," he whispers against my skin, and then he closes his eyes, as his mouth slides up and over the steep rise.

One hand slips up over my ribcage, his thumb tracing the underside of my other breast before he weighs it in his palm. Gasping, I don't know what I want more, his hands or his mouth, but he doesn't make me choose. With a sharp yank, he pulls the fabric down, the cold air only hitting me for a split second before his hand covers one tightening nipple and his mouth falls to the other.

I tighten my legs around him, pulling myself up as close as I can, desperate to create as much sweet friction as possible between us, my hips moving in time with the absolute filthy sounds he's making as his mouth explores one breast and then the other. Burying a hand in his hair, the other holding his shoulder for dear life, I can't help but fall back onto the counter, taking him with me as his lips start a trail down over the planes of my stomach, stopping for an agonizing detour at my belly button, circling it gently with his tongue before resting his cheek against the jut of my hip bone.

His fingers play with the fabric strings tied into a neat bow at the waist of my shorts. "Can I?" he asks.

"Yes," I say, wondering idly if later on I'll be embarrassed at how quickly I agreed for him to completely expose me when he's still fully clothed, but right now I don't care at all. I need more of him, more of his mouth, more of his fingers.

"So fucking pretty," he mutters, when he pulls the cotton free of my feet, taking my socks along with them. "And so fucking ready."

His thumb presses against the silken fabric of my panties.

"You look pretty ready too," I shoot back, my gaze flickering to the substantial bulge against the zipper of his jeans.

He reaches down to adjust himself. "That's for later," he promises. "Right now, all I want is to do is . . ." he hesitates for a second, like maybe he's not sure I want to hear it.

"Tell me," I beg.

"I want to suck on your clit until your thighs are shaking around my ears and your voice goes hoarse from screaming my name."

"Oh my God," I manage to mumble, when he leans over me again, pressing a kiss to my lips, gentle and sweet, the exact opposite of the words he just uttered.

"Can I?" he asks, his fingertips smoothly running up my thighs before gripping them firmly while he takes a quick nip at my breast.

The answer is yes. Obviously. I open my mouth to tell him, but across the room, on top of my luggage, my phone dings once, twice, three and, no, four, five times in a row.

There's only a handful of numbers that are set to break through my do not disturb features.

I push up to my elbows and, in the process, brush against the front of his jeans, eliciting a choked groan.

"I need to . . ." I trail off, just as the phone starts to ring.

Yeah, I definitely need to get that.

"I got it," he says, stepping away, running a hand through his hair, and the view is almost as good from the back as he goes to grab my phone.

I slide off the countertop, adjusting my bra so I'm covered at least a little and grab my shorts, pulling them on with shaking hands, trying and failing to tie the string again.

"It's Stew," Charlie says, as he walks back to me with my phone held out for me.

Stew? Why the hell is he calling right now? Or at all. He's supposed to be on leave.

"Hello?" I gasp into the phone, knowing I sound like I just finished a dozen wind sprints. I try to take a deep, even breath, but it's not easy.

"Frankie?" Stew's voice is on the other end of the line, clear as a bell.

"What's . . . what's up? What time is it there? Aren't you still in the hospital?"

Charlie steps into my line of sight, holding my shirt out for me and I try to grin at him as I take it, as there's no way to put it on with the phone to my ear.

"They discharged me this morning. Good behavior."

"Is that a thing?"

"No, Frankie, it means I could walk around the room a couple of laps and I took a shit to the doctor's satisfaction."

"Lovely."

"You asked."

I didn't, actually, but I move on. "What's up?"

"You and Avery, I need you back in New York ASAP."

"Stew, you can't go back to work yet."

"I'm not, but just because I'm on leave doesn't mean I can't take a couple of phone calls and, if my source is right, Ethan Quicke just used whatever the fuck he agreed to in Montana as leverage to sign with the Dodgers."

"We look like we don't know what we're doing."

"We really do," Stew agrees. "I gotta go. Rita thinks I'm getting a glass of water and she's gonna come in here soon and start yelling, but get your ass back here. You gotta fix this shit before . . ."

"Before?"

"Before my source publishes."

Damn it.

A reporter and one Stew clearly has a relationship with, giving him a heads up instead of just leaking it.

"But that's not the worst part."

"It gets worse?"

"Hannah Vinch knows too."

Fuck. Hannah is one of the ownership group's chief representatives from the board. She generally stays out of our business and lets Stew run the day-to-day operations, but when she does make her presence known, it's either really good or really, really bad.

This definitely qualifies as really bad.

"Yeah, and they're *pissed*. She's holding them off for a bit because I promised her that we have a plan, with or without Quicke, but she wants to hear it from you, since I'm technically on leave."

"You're not *technically* on leave, Stew. You need to be resting. Go back to bed. I got this. I'll grab the next flight I can and I'll stop by to see you tomorrow morning before I go into the office."

"Good, and Frankie?"

"Yeah?"

"How'd the kids look?"

"How did you know we're in Arizona?"

"I have eyes everywhere, kiddo. So, how'd they look?"

"They look great and it seems like they've already imprinted on Charlie, so it should make for an interesting spring training."

"He's Charlie now?"

"That's his name, isn't it?"

"Sure is," he agrees, "just not used to you calling him that." Then he's laughing, and the laugh turns into a cough and then a muffled curse. "Okay, I gotta go. Rita's found me, and if you could see her face right now, you'd be running for the hills."

"Go, get some rest," I insist, and with a quick goodbye, the line goes dead. As soon as I hang up, I pull the shirt back over my head. Only to immediately realize it's on backwards and I have to pull my arms in and twist it around.

When I brush my hair out of my face, Charlie is already on his phone. "There's a flight back at nine tomorrow morning. Or I could call up my charter company and get you out of here tonight . . ." he trails off.

And leaves it up to me.

Take the flight tomorrow morning and we can pick up right where we left off, finally give in to this *thing* between us.

Or I could call an Uber right now, be on a plane back to New York, grab a shower and a fresh outfit, and be back in the office tomorrow morning to deal with the crap headed our way.

It's not even a hard decision. I wish it was, though.

"I'm gonna call an Uber," I say, and to his credit, his expression doesn't change at all. In fact, other than the ungodly mess that I made of his hair, you'd never know that he just had me laid out on his kitchen counter top practically begging him to fuck me.

All he does is start dialing a number and lifts the phone to his ear when it connects.

Chapter 12

CHARLIE

I focus on the phone call. That's all I can do. That's safe and simple and very unsexy.

"Express Charters, this is Bernice. How can I help you?"

Her accent is thick and southern and her voice high-pitched and very much the opposite of Frankie's.

It helps.

"Hi, this is Charlie Avery."

"Mr Avery," Bernice says. "How was your flight to Phoenix?"

"It was great, as always. That's one of the reasons I'm calling, actually. I'm going to need a flight out of Phoenix into New York as soon as practicable."

"New York. It'll be hard to get into JFK or LaGuardia at this hour. Can you do Teterboro?"

I want to ask Frankie if the smaller airport in New Jersey works for her, but she's focused on her phone, tapping away, probably calling for a car. I allow my eyes to just take her in, from the wreck of a messy ponytail pushed off to the side now to the soft flush still painting the apples of her cheeks. It might be from sitting out in the unforgiving desert sun this afternoon, but I choose to believe she's still feeling what I'm feeling, the hum of arousal still coursing through her veins. My shirt, which is now not tied up or tucked into her shorts, is actually longer than her shorts. It looks like maybe she just threw on the shirt after leaving my bed, something to wear when we made breakfast in the kitchen tomorrow morning and let the eggs burn while I put her back up on the counter and make good on my promise from just a minute ago.

"Sir?" Bernice asks.

I clear my throat and, with it, the fantasy. "Teterboro is fine, but then I'll need a car for one passenger back into Brooklyn."

"For just you? Is it the usual address? Mr Vasquez's residence?"

"No, no, I won't be on the flight. It'll be for a Ms Francesca Sullivan."

"The same Ms Sullivan from the previous flight?"

"That's the one. She'll give the driver her address when she arrives."

"Okay, it'll be an hour or two, but as soon as I have this confirmed, I'll get the flight information to you. It will be out of Phoenix Sky Harbor."

"Perfect. Thanks, Bernice."

"Thank you, Mr Avery. You have a good night."

When I end the call, I turn back to her and she's looking at me again.

"You're not coming back?" she asks, and I can't catch her tone. I don't know if she's disappointed or relieved or, maybe, somewhere in-between.

"No, it sounds like you've got enough on your plate. I'll stick around, go to the boys' game tomorrow and then maybe hop over to LA. I need to get my house on the market and pack up my stuff."

It's an excuse and not even a very good one. She knows it and so do I, but the relief is real when she lets it go and focuses on her phone. If what just happened between us here is going to stay here, there's no way I can get on the plane with her. I need some space to get my head right.

"The Uber is two minutes away," she says.

"I'll walk you out."

"No!" She nearly shouts it, and then shakes her head and says, softer this time, "No, that's okay. I'll be . . . it's better if we . . . say goodbye here."

"Okay then. I'll see you back in New York," I say, having no idea what else to do. Do I kiss her? Hug her? Just stand here feeling like a massive dick?

She sends me a tight smile and then grabs at the handle of her suitcase, but she misjudges it and sends the purse she'd balanced on top crashing to the floor.

"Crap."

Bending down into a crouch, she sits in a squat to gather the scattered debris, her wallet, several tubes of make-up, a little emergency kit with Band-Aids and wipes and a stain stick and a couple of tampons. I reach down and grab it as she stands up.

"Here," I say, holding it out to her and, when she takes it, her fingertips brush against mine, sending not just a shiver, but a lightning bolt of energy through me.

Fuck, I want her.

And now that I almost had her, I'm not sure that want is ever going to go away.

She makes to step back, but I circle her wrist, lightly. She could easily pull away from the bracelet of my fingers. She doesn't, though, just stares at my hand and then looks up into my eyes. I can feel her pulse thrumming against my fingertips.

So I take a chance, just like I did back in Bozeman.

"Stay," I rasp, so low, she doesn't answer, and I wonder if she heard me. I open my mouth to say it again, but that's when she pulls away, slowly, and shakes her head.

"I can't. You know I can't."

And I do know that. Women who sleep with men in this industry are shunned.

She's worked too hard and too long.

Doesn't stop me from wishing it was different, though.

I watch her leave and, once the door clicks shut behind her, I spin in place and head straight for the kitchen to grab another beer. I don't look at the counter, just march into the bedroom and shut the door behind me.

I need to sleep this off. Sleep her off, praying to any higher power out there that might exist that I don't dream about her.

But first a shower.

A cold one.

Ice cold.

The first thing I see when I get out of the shower, towel wrapped around my waist, is a missed call lighting up my phone screen from my nightstand. I nearly trip over my discarded clothes trying to get to it, but when I sit on the edge of my bed it's not the name I hoped for on the notification.

Ethan Quicke.

Taking a long slug from the beer I got from the fridge, I call him back.

"Charlie!" he says, like he's greeting an old friend, "how's it going?"

"Really?" I shoot back. "How's it going? Shitty, it's going fucking shitty."

"Oh, I guess you heard," he says. "I wanted to talk to you before it leaked."

"Yeah, I heard. What the fuck are you doing? We shook hands. That means something where I come from. I thought it did where you come from too."

"You know how it is. Dan was upset that I shook on a deal that he didn't approve, so I let him go to other teams with the chance to counteroffer. I didn't expect anyone to top what we agreed to, but the Dodgers did and I need to do what's best for me and my family."

"And that extra couple of million will really make a difference."

It sounds insane – millions of dollars do matter, but at a certain point, how much is too much? When does it become Monopoly money?

He scoffs. "Like you wouldn't have done the same thing."

"Newsflash, asshole, I didn't do the same thing. You think that contract I signed with the Dodgers was the most money I could get? I wanted to play there. I wanted to win a championship with the only organization I ever played for. That's what you said you wanted too. And it was all bullshit."

"Yeah, well, it's not my fault you were a weak negotiator then and naive about that shit now. This is a business and I don't owe the Eagles any fucking thing, especially when they want to replace me with some import who's never thrown a goddamn pitch in the major leagues."

"You know what? Fuck you. I'll see you in October, motherfucker."

"Yeah, you wish, asshole."

The line goes dead.

Fuck.

I shouldn't have done that, even if it felt good.

But I realize I meant every word. And it's because of her. Frankie. She has me believing, really believing in this absolutely batshit plan of hers.

I toss myself back onto the mattress, trying not to think about the plans I had for it less than an hour ago, yanking the sheets up over my body and flicking off the lights.

Sleep.

Go to sleep.

Don't dream.

Wake up to an empty bed and move the fuck on.

Win a bunch of baseball games.

Face the Dodgers in October and take Ethan Quicke deep.

Fuck, wait, no I won't be out on the field.

I might be a little bit drunk.

Okay, not me. But I can make sure that kid, the Davis kid, knows exactly what's coming, I'll have Frankie run her computer a billion times to make sure and then let the kid take him deep.

Yes. Good.

But first, sleep.

And, thank God, I'm out as soon as my head hits the pillow.

"You okay, Skip?" Cole Davis asks me, all suited up for the game ahead of him while we stand on the field less than an hour before first pitch.

My flight's not until later tonight, commercial (my budget *does* have limits), but business class so I actually fit in the damn seat, and I figured it wouldn't hurt to take in one more Desert Dog game before I head back to New York.

"Hungover," I admit.

The beers at dinner and then the two once I got home were a

little too much for my metabolism to handle anymore. Getting old sucks. I used to be able to go out with the boys at night, have a couple of drinks to unwind and then wake up the next day and go four for four with a homer and two doubles before doing it all over again that night.

"I don't get those," he says, a wide grin playing across his features.

He's a good-looking kid. Gonna be a star in New York if we bring him along right, but that comes with a whole other host of issues. That's a problem for April, though, not right now.

"Where's Ms Sullivan?" he asks.

"Back in Brooklyn," I grumble out.

Cole clicks his tongue, but like last night, knows to mostly keep his trap shut. "so, it's just you today."

"Just me, kid, is that okay? Do you need more of an audience?"

He laughs and claps me on the shoulder. "Nah, we'll put on a show for you."

"No show necessary. Just play your game. That's more than enough, got it?"

"Got it."

"Hey, Mr Avery," Archie Esposito says, darting out of the dugout, bouncing like he didn't throw eight shutout innings the day before. Oh, to be twenty-one again. "You're back! Where's . . ." he's cut off by Davis's elbow to his gut. "Ouch, what the hell, Cole?"

"Shut up," Cole mumbles, and I ignore their interplay.

"You boys have a good game and, when I see you after the holidays, be ready to work, and Davis, when you wrap things up here, the first thing I want you to do is study the staff."

"Homework, Skip?"

"Consider it your final exam before graduation. I want a full scouting report on everyone on our staff and a complete write up on Nakamura."

His eyes light up at the prospect of catching one of the best pitchers in the world. "We got a shot at getting him?"

"If Frankie has anything to say about it, we do."

"Then it's in the bag."

She does inspire that kind of confidence.

"You just focus on making the team. No guarantees. Let me and Frankie take care of the rest."

I'm way more anonymous in the stands without a gorgeous blonde sitting next to me biting her lip as she carefully keeps score, drawing extra attention with her on-the-money insights that the dudes sitting around us don't expect from her. I like it that way. I can just watch the game, watch as Davis launches another homer and as Greene makes a diving catch in center before legging out a triple in the next inning.

These kids. They're really something.

I leave before the game is over, a car picking me up just outside the ballpark, and everything about the flight home is better, that business-class seat without anyone next to me, the plane's bathrooms nowhere near my row. Hell, there's even complimentary alcohol and some decent food, but, shit, if I don't miss that crappy coach seat with Frankie pressed up against me.

And that thought alone is enough to have me redirecting the driver that meets me at the airport from Javy's address to Russell Field instead.

She's there, exactly where I thought she'd be, at her desk, long after she should be gone for the day already, the sun setting across the window that overlooks the field.

Her office door is open, so I knock on the frame and lean against it when she raises a finger, eyes still focused on the computer screen in front of her while she furiously types away at the keyboard.

"Just let me . . ." she trails off, before finishing up and then sitting back in her chair and turning toward me.

Clearly, I wasn't who she expected to be standing there. Her posture immediately straightens and she reaches up to fix the clear plastic glasses she's got perched on her nose.

"I didn't know you wore glasses."

"Oh," she says, touching them again. "Blue light glasses. For the screen glare. I was getting headaches."

"They suit you," I say, like I'm someone's mother, and try not to actually cringe.

"You're back," she says.

"I'm back. Went to another Desert Dogs game to watch the kids. They looked good."

"Yeah, I, uh, caught the live stream of it while I was working."

"Of course you did."

"What?"

"Nothing, I just . . . I think we need to clear the air."

She looks at me intently before nodding. "I agree."

"You do?"

Not gonna lie, I kind of thought she'd be cool with just ignoring what happened and continue pretending like nothing happened for the rest of our lives.

"Yeah, I think we might have gotten our wires crossed, when we called a truce."

"I don't recall any wires, but go on."

"Charlie . . ." she trails off, a desperate note in her voice. My own name suddenly feels like a gut punch. It doesn't sound like it did the other night in Arizona. There's no yearning for my mouth or my fingers or my dick. She just wants me to stop.

"Sorry, you were saying – crossed wires?"

"I think, well, no, I *know* that there's always been some tension between us and it hasn't always been good, but when we decided to actually work together, I feel like maybe that tension had nowhere to go, so it found a different outlet."

She's making it sound like the tension had a mind of its own. Like neither one of us were there, making choices, deciding that we wanted each other. But it's a decent enough cop out, and lets us both off the hook, so I go with it.

"That's as good an explanation as any."

"Right." She nods to herself. "We just have to make sure that we direct our energy into something productive. Building this team, getting ready for next season, making sure our roster is as strong as it can be. Do you agree?"

She hasn't left me much choice, even if she's not completely wrong. "I do."

"Okay, good." And then she moves on instantly, like we weren't just talking about how yesterday I was this close to fucking her against my bedroom wall. "The Winter Meetings are right after Thanksgiving. Rumor has it that Nakamura is going be posted around the same time."

"I thought ownership was out on Nakamura."

"I talked them around."

"You did?"

"I will. I have a meeting with Hannah Vinch tomorrow morning. I'll get her to agree that if we can get Nakamura to defer a ton of money after the end of his contract. It'll free us up to sign more players now and give the team a better chance of winning."

"How much money?"

"Almost all of it."

"Do you think he'll take it? Guys have done stuff like that

before, but usually because they want to play for a specific team."

"I'll . . . think of something. Being in New York helps: a massive and enthusiastic Asian population, major endorsement opportunities. But we'll be competing with the Yankees, and if they're feeling up to it, the Mets, with those same attractions."

"What do you need from me?"

"I think we'll probably need you in Nashville during the Winter Meetings."

"Then I'm there."

"Great."

"Separate hotel rooms this time, though."

And, thank fuck, she laughs.

"Separate hotel rooms," she agrees. "I'll be in touch soon."

"But no touching."

"Charlie . . ." she says again, but this time it's affectionate exasperation. "Get out of my office."

"Yes, ma'am."

Stepping out of the stadium into the evening, I hunch my shoulders against the November chill. The World Series ended a little more than a week ago and with it the last vestiges of summer. I'm still dressed for Arizona, so I hunch my shoulders against the wind as I make the relatively short walk from the ballpark toward Javy's house.

The neighborhood is bustling.

It was clearly built around the stadium, with restaurants and bars lining the streets in the immediate surrounding blocks. They're buzzing with activity, though during the season it's probably jam packed with fans, like it has been since back before the Eagles, when the Dodgers called it home.

It's easy to imagine the old world underneath and propping

up the new. A working- to middle-class neighborhood on real estate that became more and more valuable as the years went along, pushing out the families that were there back in the day for the people that were pushed out of Manhattan when those rents got out of control.

But I'll give this neighborhood one thing: they kept the charm.

The mostly original architecture once you crossover into a more residential area, the brownstones lining the streets, trees sprouting out of the sidewalks, families out and about taking an after-dinner stroll and runners with earbuds in weaving around them while the weather is still okay and there's still some sunlight this late.

When I get back to Javy's they saved me a plate from the absolute feast their chef made for dinner that night.

"When I move into my own place, you need to give me the woman's name. If I don't have someone making my meals, I'm going to end up eating out every night and I'll become one of those guys who *looks* retired."

Maria rolls her eyes as she offers me seconds. "Most women don't like the starved scarecrow look."

I'm definitely not skinny by anyone's definition except hers.

Javy pats his belly, which is definitely thicker than back in our playing days. "I earned every inch of this while we were playing."

"I bet Frankie Sullivan won't mind a few extra pounds," Maria adds in, still dishing more pasta with some of the spiciest fra diavolo sauce I've ever had onto my plate.

"Who said anything about Frankie Sullivan?" I ask, glaring at Javy.

"I didn't say anything," Javy insists, raising his hands in innocence.

"He didn't have to," Maria teases. "I remember back when you were both with the Dodgers – you complained about her almost nonstop. There's not a man in the world that talks about a woman that much unless he's interested."

I can feel the color rising at the back of my neck and she pounces.

"Oh my God, did something happen in Montana? Or, wait, you went to Arizona after too! Are you two . . ."

"We're not. We're very much not. We work together."

"Well, the only person I was ever worried about Javy cheating on me with was you, and you two worked together for fifteen years."

"I would never cheat on you, and he's not my type," Javy insists.

"Please, your bromance was legendary. They used to do fan art of you two."

Javy groans. "Oh God, and the writing. Do you remember? That one website with the stories?"

"Ha!" Maria laughs. "A couple of the other WAGs loved to send me links to those."

"Aww, babe, were you really jealous?"

"I'm always jealous, *mi amor*," she says, coming up behind him to kiss his cheek, and when Javy reaches up to pull her into his lap, I push my plate away and stand.

"And that's my cue," I say, slapping a hand over my eyes like a traumatized child as I leave the kitchen. "Tomorrow I start looking for a place to live."

"You're welcome to stay here with us as long as you need," Javy calls back, with Maria's giggles punctuating every word.

"Nah, I want to get out of your hair. I'll find a place up here and then I need to get a spot in Clearwater. It's not the Pacific, but the Gulf views aren't bad either. Good night, you two. Don't defile that table. Your children eat there."

There's no response, just more giggling and the echoing sound of a plate crashing to the floor as I climb the stairs as fast as my stupid knee will let me.

Chapter 13

FRANCESCA

I've only ever been to Hannah Vinch's office by myself once. It was on my first day, when she summoned me upstairs to the office suite that overlooks the ballpark from just below the upper deck. It's right behind home plate, prime real estate for ticket sales, and would fit a few luxury suites that would bring in thousands every game, but the ownership group decided to keep it intact so they'd be able to observe the team from on high whenever it struck their fancy.

The views, even from the waiting area, just beyond the large double doors, are stunning. It's up high enough to see Prospect Park laid out in front of me with lower Manhattan in the distance, a sea of muted greens and browns, oranges and yellows and an outline of shadowy skyscrapers beyond.

Nancy, the assistant who runs the office even in Hannah's almost continual absence, greets me with a smile and gestures to a chair set up against the dark wood-paneled walls, but I prefer the view. It already feels enough like I'm being called to the principal's office, about to be reprimanded for something that, while it isn't exactly my fault, was still my responsibility. Sitting down will just make it worse.

I was supposed to bring Ethan Quicke back into the fold or let him go on our terms. I wanted the latter, but thought I had done the former, even if Charlie was the one to get the deal done.

The last time I was here alone she called me in to congratulate me, talked about how there aren't enough women at the top in baseball and that she was thrilled to give me this opportunity. But she made it clear that's what it was, a chance. No guarantees.

I wonder if this means my chance is up.

"She'll see you now," Nancy says, standing up to open the office door for me, though I have no idea how she knows Hannah is ready to see me. "Ms Vinch, as requested, Francesca Sullivan is here to see you."

There's my full name again, though it obviously doesn't sound nearly as good as when Charlie says it, and now it really feels like I'm in trouble.

"Frankie," Hannah says, standing up and coming around her desk. Older than me by ten years or maybe a few more, but at least a foot shorter even in the towering heels she's wearing, Louboutins if my instincts are right (and they usually are about shoes). "Come in, come in. I had Nancy bring us some tea for our meeting."

"Tea?" I ask, as she leads me to the couch in the corner of her office, overlooking the field, somehow an even better view than in the waiting area since it's centered right above home plate.

"Yes," she says. "Tea. Why, do you prefer coffee?"

I do, but it doesn't matter. "No, I just . . ."

Hannah smiles widely, teeth bright white and perfectly

straight, which makes sense for a billionaire with controlling interest in a Major League Baseball organization. "Did you think I brought you here to scold you?"

"Honestly? Yes."

"Pssh. No, not at all. Let's sit. You make me nervous standing there, all six foot whatever of you. We have some things to discuss."

I make her nervous? Sounds fake, but okay.

"Five ten," I say, as I smooth my skirt beneath me and prop myself at the end of the rounded couch while she sits opposite me and pours out two cups of tea. "Without the heels."

She makes a disgruntled noise from the back of her throat and then says "Sugar? Milk?"

"Sugar," I say, and she adds two actual lumps from a bowl, no sweetener packets to be found.

"Okay," she says, once she's prepared her own cup. "Tell me what happened with Charlie Avery."

The tea is hot. And I nearly spit it out all over her cream velvet couch at her very casual request, images of that last night in Arizona flickering through my mind like a slide show: his mouth, his hands, me splayed out nearly naked on his kitchen counter.

She can't possibly mean that.

One neatly manicured eyebrow rises at my lack of response while I swallow my sip of tea and cough a bit, to try and buy time.

"With Ethan Quicke," I say, finally, and she nods. "It was a miscalculation," I admit. "Charlie Avery is the kind of guy whose word is as good as his bond. Quicke isn't. I'd much rather have the former on my side than the latter."

Hannah hums and then nods again. "Agreed."

Okay, so . . . I'm definitely not in trouble and I'm not

exactly one to just let things go. "So, why exactly did you want to see me?"

She takes a small sip of her tea and replaces the cup on its saucer. "Stew mentioned you've been wanting to pitch me on Kai Nakamura."

"I do."

"Okay, so let's hear it."

"Oh, I have an entire presentation prepared with documentation and I assumed we'd be meeting with the guys from player development and scouting."

Hannah waves a dismissive hand. "I've heard from them." She has? "Most of them believe he's not worth the price. It's the posting fee, plus his contract, in excess of three hundred and fifty million dollars, but what I want to know is why you want him."

"He's a generational talent. There is no pitcher in the major leagues or coming up from the minors that will be able to compete with his stuff: velocity, control, wicked spin rate and . . ." I trail off, not sure if this part matters, though it feels like it might matter more than anything. ". . . all he wants to do is win and that's what we want to do here, right?"

It's something that the ownership group insists upon over and over again whenever they release a statement, that our mission is to win, but fans, rightly, have pointed out over the years that their actions don't match their words, their commitment to trading for or signing the best players never seems to come to fruition in favor of budget cuts and building for a fictional next year that doesn't materialize.

"In theory, yes."

"What if it wasn't just a theory? What if I tell you that we can cut payroll next year and still sign Nakamura and have a real chance to win?"

"I'd say you're insane."

"Well, that's part of why you hired me, isn't it?"

Hannah snorts and then picks up her teacup again. "Okay, Frankie. Explain."

"I've used my algorithm to predict performance while also investing wisely in a handful of star players whose contributions can't be duplicated through multiple players. We utilize the resources we already have from within the organization to make up the difference."

"Is that why you and our new manager went to Arizona?"

"It was," I say, trying not to betray my surprise that she knew where we were. "There are three kids playing out there that both Charlie and I have assessed. We think they're ready to contribute at the major league level."

"Three players, all barely twenty-one, with little if any experience above Double A starting at three premiere positions next season and we can win with that?"

"We can, with Nakamura to lead the rotation and Esposito slotting into that fifth start position, our second, third and fourth guys were three of the best in the league last year, keeping us in games, not taxing the bullpen too much."

"And both Stew and Avery are on board with this?"

"They are."

She takes one final long sip from her teacup and finishes it off, holding my eyes with hers firmly. "I'll go back to the board with it, no guarantees, but for now I can authorize you at least putting us forward when he's posted. We'll see how negotiations go from there."

"Seriously? That's . . . you're agreeing?"

"I am," Hannah says, smiling at me. "But a word of caution."

"Of course."

"This is on your head. I know you believe in this plan and

you have Stew and Avery's backing, but this is ultimately your recommendation and its success or its failure will be pinned to you. No one is going to fire Stew or Avery over an off season move like this, not with Stew's health or with Avery's reputation. A first-time female interim general manager who got in over her head trying to play with the big boys? It'll be you."

"I know."

"I thought you would. Good luck, Frankie. You're going to need it."

Then I'm shuffled out of the office by Nancy, who appears out of nowhere again, holding the door open for me with a smile and then shutting it firmly behind us.

Shaking my head, having no idea whether to be thrilled or petrified by what just went down, I start to head downstairs, back to my office ,when Nancy gently clears her throat.

"She wants you to succeed," the gray-haired secretary says. "Desperately wants it. She loves baseball, has since she was a little girl. She wants to win the World Series and she wants you to build the team that does it."

"She made that clear."

"Then why are you still standing here?" Nancy asks, clearly exasperated with me. "Go do it."

I'm halfway to the elevator, staring out at that view of the park and Manhattan, millions of people going about their day and none of them have any idea.

The Brooklyn Eagles want a championship and I'm the one that's going to bring it home.

But first *I* need to go home, unpack, and get myself together before it all begins again. We don't just need Nakamura; we need to make sure he's surrounded by the best possible team. Cole, Archie and Xander are the start of that, but not the end.

When I landed back in NY I dropped my stuff and went

straight into the office, but now I need to unpack, and get cleaned up before heading back in to work.

My car can't quite pull up to the front of my place because there's a massive moving truck double parked and blocking most of the street.

"I'll get out here," I say, and send him on his way, but as I approach the house, I catch sight of a familiar form. One I can't quite believe I'm seeing and, when he sees me, his surprise is just as extreme.

Shane gapes at me, mouth open, staring unblinking before he finally says, "What are you doing here?"

"What . . . I live here," I respond, trying desperately to come up with another reason for why he might be standing here with a moving truck.

"You live here?"

"Yes, I live here. The second and third floor."

"You live on the second and third floor of this house."

"Yeah, and if you don't mind, I'd like to get to my apartment?"

"Your apartment."

"In this building."

"Shane, I really don't have time for this, so if you could . . ."

That's when it clicks. The apartment on the ground level has been vacant for a little while. Ursula, a sweet Dominican lady, had moved to assisted living a few months ago and her kids had refurbished it before putting it up for sale.

"You're moving in."

"We signed the paperwork this morning. They said the upstairs neighbor was quiet, travels a lot for work, that we'll barely hear her."

"Yes, well, I'm her."

"Shane, can you help me with this?" a female voice calls

from the other side of the truck. "I want to make sure we get a before shot of all the boxes in the truck and then some progress shots of everything moving where it belongs . . . oh, hi."

"Hi," I say, trying to wrap my head around this.

"Frankie."

"No, no, you need to move somewhere else. Eight million people live in this huge city and you managed to find your-selves *here*? How did this even happen?"

Then it occurs to me, a sinking feeling in my stomach that's confirmed the longer I stare at him in silence. He was never able to hide anything from me for long, not when we were mar-ried (I figured out he was cheating within a couple of weeks) and he definitely can't fool me now.

This is not a coincidence.

This is very, very, very much on purpose.

The perfect wrench to throw into their perfect influencer lives. The perfect thing to hook people with on their videos: "we live downstairs from his ex-wife . . ." on every video, get-ting those likes and views and followers, and the sponsorships and paid promotions that follow.

"Frankie."

"No, absolutely not. You need to back out of the deal."

"We're not doing that."

"Then you need to rent it and move somewhere else. You can't do this."

"You're being unreasonable."

"*I'm* being unreasonable?"

I can feel myself boiling over, all the pressure and the tension and the roller-coaster emotions of the last few days coalescing into what will for sure be a viral meltdown of epic proportions, the kind that makes it from TikTok to Instagram and, a couple of days later, to Facebook then to Page 6 and then, finally, to

Hannah Vinch's radar. Where it could cost me everything I've ever worked for.

And sure enough, Jessie has her phone out, ready to record. Fuck. That.

I close my mouth, shaking my head, and sprint up the stairs, hopefully out of sight before she can press that red button and get a shot of my retreating ass.

As soon as the door is closed behind me, I whip out my phone and dial Bianca, kicking off my heels and falling back against the door.

"Hey, what's up?" she answers, right away.

Thank God for my best friend.

Moving into my apartment, I toss my bag onto the couch and let my hair down, sighing as the weight releases at the back of my head. "I need you to check Jessie's feed right now."

"What? Why?"

Making my way into my bedroom, I switch her to speaker phone and slide out of my work clothes, adding the pieces to the pile for dry cleaning and pulling on a pair of cotton shorts and that t-shirt I borrowed from Charlie, the cotton still holding on to that clean scent of his, mixing just a little with my own perfume and shampoo.

Yeah, I don't want to think too hard about the implications of why breathing it in makes my shoulders relax and simultaneously sends a zing of lightning over my skin.

"Just look and tell me what you see."

"Moving to New York, but we knew that . . ." she trails off. "There's a 'Stay with us while we find our new home' post. There's . . . okay, it looks like they found a house. Uh, I'm sorry . . . is that your street?"

"Not just my street. Downstairs. Literally below my feet right now, moving in."

"You're kidding me?"

"I very much am *not* kidding you. They're moving in."

"Shit. There's nothing you can do?"

"What can I do? Call the co-op board and say what? They don't care. And besides that, there is no way this is a coincidence. They would have had to apply for the space months ago. This was planned, from start to finish. Hell, I half think they staged running into me at the airport."

"That's some real psychopath behavior," she says. "Sounds like Shane. What are you gonna do?"

"I . . . I don't . . ." I trail off. "I don't know."

"Well, there are two choices right now: stay or go?"

That's Bianca, always getting right to the heart of a problem and, even if she doesn't have a solution for you, helping you get there on your own.

And leaving? That sounds kind of nice right now.

"I could go to Florida, work from there for a while."

I have a condo down there, that oddly reminds me of the one Charlie has in Arizona, a lot of tile and white paint and bland furniture that's just a place to crash after long days at the ballpark. Though it does have the added bonus of being at the beach.

There's a lot of appeal to the idea.

"You could," Bianca says, but even though her tone is absolutely neutral, I know exactly what my best friend since childhood is thinking because it's exactly what I'm thinking too.

"Wouldn't that be running away?"

"Maybe a little bit," she allows, "but you work from down there after the holidays anyway. You'd just be moving it up a little."

That's true, but that's when everyone from the organization

starts to shift down to our spring training home, when the early bird players start showing up, when our efforts this time of year start to become real. But it's not time for that yet. There's still work to be done up north.

"But no, I can't. Stew's here and recovering. I don't know when or if he's going to be able to make the trip down. And then, when they post Nakamura, I want to be here to roll out the red carpet, I don't want to be scrambling back to Brooklyn and . . ."

"And you don't want to run away."

"I don't."

"Well, then you won't, but you'll still come out for Thanksgiving, right? Xavier and I would love to have you. The family is going all out."

Thanksgiving in LA, with my best friend. Sounds perfect.

"I'm there."

"And if that guy you keep jet setting across the country with on his *private jet* doesn't have anywhere to go, let him know he's welcome too."

"B!"

"What?"

"Stop it."

"No, I don't think I will."

"I'm hanging up now."

"Bye, best friend."

"Bye, best friend."

Almost as soon as I hang up, my phone rings again.

"Did some inappropriate innuendo about private jets just occur to you?"

"What?"

That's . . . not Bianca's voice.

I slap a hand against my forehead. "Sorry, I was just . . ." I trail off, trying to recover, but there's nothing I can say to Charlie right now that will convince him that I *wasn't* just talking about him.

"You got a thing for my private jet?" he asks, but I can hear the real humor in his voice. Now that I know how he sounds when he's actually being suggestive, it's easy to tell the difference. I ignore the question.

"What's up?" I ask, climbing onto my bed and leaning back against the pillows, trying and failing to resist the urge to recline completely against them.

Laying down while talking to him feels like a bad idea, like tempting fate or toeing a line or, I don't know, a special form of masochism.

"I need a real estate agent. Two, actually, one here and one in LA."

That was not what I was expecting, but the words real estate just sit there in my brain, dancing around, teasing me with the idea that *he* could have moved in downstairs instead of Shane and his little family.

Hell, maybe *I* need a real estate agent. Maybe I should just move? That would solve the problem for sure.

"Frankie?" he asks, when I'm silent too long.

"Yeah, sorry. The team has a few we work with. I can have Gregory hook you up with one tomorrow. Things getting a little crowded at Javy's?"

He chuckles roughly. "I might be barricaded in the guest room while I try very, very hard not to hear anything happening in the rest of the house."

"Don't they have kids?"

"Their kids sleep like rocks, just like Javy."

"If it makes you feel any better, I'm in the same boat. Worse, actually."

"How is that possible?"

"My ex-husband and his wife and kid are moving in downstairs."

"The ex you gave your car to at the airport?"

"How many ex-husbands do you think I have?"

"Fair. That's . . . it has to be on purpose, right?"

"I think so. No way to prove it, though. I'm just dreading becoming the star of their 'we live downstairs from his ex-wife and look how amazing we are for it' social media bait."

"I could . . ."

"You will not."

"You didn't even know what I was going to say."

"Doesn't matter. I don't need a guy to fight my battles for me."

"I didn't say you did."

"Then there's no reason for you to go all macho and go over there and . . ."

"I wasn't going to do that. I was going to call my lawyer and see if there's anything you can do to make sure that doesn't happen. A restraining order or, I don't know, at least a 'you're on notice, don't fuck around and find out' letter."

"Is that an official legal action?"

"Hell if I know, I'm just a dumb jock."

I laugh and then let out a heavy sigh, but he doesn't let the conversation lag.

"How did it go with Mrs Vinch?"

"You knew about that?"

"I went to visit Stew today, and he told me."

"I should do that."

"He'd love to see you, but, first, what happened? Did she give you the go ahead on Nakamura?"

"She did."

"Sullivan, that's awesome. Why aren't you out celebrating?"

"Jet lag finally got me," I admit. It's been a long week and I'm exhausted. "I'm just gonna crash tonight."

"Look at us, party animals. It's barely nine and I'm already in sweatpants."

"I'm about to be, but I'm still a little bit wired. I need to chill out before I'll be able to sleep."

"Okay," he says. "tell me about the meeting."

"She's terrifying," I say, with a laugh, "and gorgeous. I feel like if you're a billionaire and part of a major league ownership group you shouldn't be allowed to also be hot?"

"Says the woman breaking a similar rule."

"What rule is that?"

"Knowing as much about baseball as I do and also being hot."

"I don't think that's a rule."

"It should be," he says, and then immediately pivots. "So, a full green light on Nakamura."

"As good as one. I'm sure there's a level that they won't go to, so our pitch is going to have to do a little more heavy lifting, but I mean . . . there's something to be said for coming to play where Jackie Robinson broke the color barrier, where you can be *the guy* that leads an organization to its first championship since the middle of the twentieth century, to own this city in a way no other player ever has before, to give the most loyal fan-base this side of Chicago 2016 a championship, to make next year into *this year*."

Chapter 14

CHARLIE

Resting back against the leather headboard in Javy's guest room, her voice is clear and warm through the phone. The way she talks about baseball, the way she sells it, it has me ready to suit up and get back behind the plate, even with just one working knee.

And when she finally takes a breath, it's accompanied with a soft self-deprecating laugh. "That's the idea anyway."

"It's a great pitch."

"But will it be enough?" she asks, and I glance down at the space beside me, empty, the sheets and blankets still smooth the way Javy's housekeeper left them before I arrived. I can imagine her there, next to me. She'd be sitting up, those glasses perched on her nose to help with the glare of the laptop while I do my best to distract her from whatever numbers are flashing on the screen. I'd close the laptop and place it aside gently before pulling her into my lap, her long legs winding around me and holding tight before she flips us over, letting me press her into the mattress and lift up my t-shirt, which she routinely wears to bed.

"Charlie?"

Her voice draws me back and I wonder about that t-shirt. I never did get it back from her and I'm definitely not going to ask for it.

"Yeah, Sullivan?"

"Thanks."

"For what?"

"For offering to kick his ass."

"I never said that."

"You didn't have to."

And she's right. I would have gone down there and, well, maybe not have kicked her ex's ass, but made it crystal clear that his camera should never, ever be pointed in her direction. That's what finally gets me, what makes it absolutely crystal clear that I need to hang up the phone right now, go to LA, like I originally planned, sell my house and get away before there's no going back for me.

If I don't get some distance now, I'll be too far gone on her to ever get over it.

"I'm gonna let you go," I say, and she hums agreement with a mumbled good night, and when the call goes dead instead of hurling my phone across the room, I use it to book a flight back out to LA tomorrow morning.

In the short time I was in New York, I've half fallen in love with the city, but waking up in my own bed after living out of a suitcase for the better part of three weeks felt good. I took in the familiar ocean views spanning the floor-to-ceiling windows in my bedroom and remembered exactly what I loved about living here for the better part of twenty years.

I probably should have sold this house a long time ago. After the divorce, I needed a place to live and a couple of

teammates insisted that, if I was going to be a single professional athlete in LA, I needed to live somewhere that matched
that persona.

Which is how I ended up with a beach house up in Malibu
with a panorama of the Pacific and a commute way longer than
it could have been if I'd bought in Burbank or the Valley.

Except I never actually lived that life. No late-night parties.
No groupies. Just a couple of relationships that went nowhere.
My focus solely on the game, never able to really stop long
enough to find someone willing to put up with that kind of
single-mindedness.

Still, it's a gorgeous place, Spanish style and set into the cliff
side, which made it a pain in the ass for my lawyers to insure,
but money wasn't really a concern back then.

It's not really a concern now, though I'm keenly aware that
my biggest paydays are behind me.

The amount of money we're talking about throwing at
Nakamura soon is probably going to be double what I earned
in my entire career, which is why this house has to go before I
buy something in New York, probably near Javy, which is *only*
so I can live near my best friend and pitching coach and be able
to walk to the ballpark and has nothing to do with who else
lives in that neighborhood.

Shit.

Three thousand miles and she's still the only thing on
my mind.

She's like the game, in my blood, maybe woven into my
soul now.

And just like the game, I don't want to let her go.

At least I have the real estate agent to distract me. Gregory
made an appointment for one to come and look at the house
and, when there's a buzz from the gate, I don't hesitate to just

let the car through, pulling on t-shirt and basketball shorts, before heading straight for the door.

At first, it feels like maybe I'm hallucinating, that early morning cross-country flight catching up with me, but no, there she is, full armor – skirt suit, hair in an updo, dark red lipstick and aviator sunglasses the only nod to it still feeling like summer here in mid-November.

"They posted Nakamura," she says, walking right by me into the house. "He's taking meetings in LA. Why didn't you pick up your phone? Also, there's some woman right behind me and she didn't look like a stalker, so I let her follow me through the gate."

I want to ask what a stalker looks like and what she would have done if she thought one was trying to get to me, but she's silent now and staring.

"Holy shit," she mumbles under her breath, then she turns looking at me, almost accusatory. "Sometimes I forget you're rich."

"The percentage in a private jet didn't give it away?"

"That felt less . . . tangible," she says, shaking her head.

"Soon it won't be. I'm selling."

"Glad to hear that," a new voice joins us. The real estate agent is an older woman with her silver hair pinned back, sensible slacks and a blouse, sedate and professional, but all clearly expensive.

"I'll get out of your way," Frankie says. "We're going to get a block of suites to set up shop."

"And you came to me first because . . ." I stop myself and cringe when she flinches.

"I don't . . . I don't know why I . . . sorry, I can go . . . I can't check into the hotel for a couple of hours and I figured I'd pick you up first. I'll go."

"No!" And now it's my turn to flinch at the absolute maniac I sound like, shouting like that. "I mean, it's great . . . good that you're here."

"Yeah?" she asks, and there's something in her voice, a little bit fragile, that has me stepping closer, just barely stopping myself for reaching out for her.

"If this isn't a good time, I can come back?" the realtor asks from the doorway.

We both freeze and turn back to her. Her eyes are flicking between us with a tiny smirk.

"No, no, it's fine," I say, beckoning the woman further into the house. "I can show you around and then," I turn back to Frankie, "lunch?"

All traces of uneasiness are gone from her face. "Lunch is good."

"Not breakfast?" The realtor suggests, checking her watch.

"She's on New York time."

"I'm on New York time."

Our words jumble together and the realtor's smirk becomes a smile. "Okay, let's get started so you two can go get your lunch."

Frankie settles down in the living room while I take the realtor, Greta, around the property. The tour doesn't take long, as the house was always more about the location than sheer size: three bedrooms, three baths, along with the mostly open concept main living area, whitewashed walls lined with wooden beams across the ceiling, a pool out back, and the view, obviously, which Greta dutifully documents with her phone.

"We have an office in New York and a colleague of mine will be in touch when you're ready to return to Brooklyn. There are several options we've already curated for you that fit within your budget."

How exactly she got my budget when even I'm not sure what I want to spend, I have no idea, though Gregory's sheer efficiency isn't exactly a surprise.

"Appreciate you taking the time."

"It was my pleasure, Mr. Avery. We'll get back to you with more information and a suggested range based on the current comps by the end of the day and, with your permission, we'll do some preview showings in the next week or so to drum up interest before we go to market."

"Sounds good. Thanks for coming out."

I walk her to the door and turn to see Frankie curled up in a corner of my couch, her laptop open, her fingers still on the keys, but her head lolling against the back cushions. I don't know what time she got the news about Nakamura's posting, but the odds are that she hasn't slept since. Her breathing is deep and steady, her face totally relaxed, peaceful. But, shit, that position can't be comfortable and if she's sleeping that way, it's because she's bone tired.

Yeah, there's no way she slept at all.

And now I've got a problem. Do I leave her there, neck at an awkward angle, one foot still in those heels she insists on wearing or . . . . do I get her somewhere she can actually sleep?

Easy enough. I'll ask her.

Crouching down, using the overstuffed arm of the couch to keep my balance and take some of the weight off my knees, I whisper, "Sullivan, you want to sleep here or in a bed?"

She sighs a little bit, shifting against the cushions and my reflexes are still good enough to catch her computer before it slides off her lap and crashes to the floor.

Carefully, I make sure to not touch any keys, or I'd probably inadvertently send an email to trade half the roster in the process. I slide it onto the coffee table and then shift my weight again, trying to stay in that crouch.

"Here or bed?" I ask again, just a little louder, and that seems to break through to her subconscious.

"Bed," she finally mumbles.

Yeah, that's good enough for me. Pushing up off the couch, I lean in and slide an arm under her knees and guide her arms around my neck. And the way she responds to my touch, just a brush of my fingers against the skin inside her elbow is enough to guide her into place with a soft groan as she settles against my chest.

My bedroom is only a few steps away and, bad knees or not, I can still do this just fine, easing her down to the mattress. For a moment and then another, she holds tight, pulling me down toward her and I hold firm, stock still until her arms slide away and fall. Letting out a sigh of . . . well, not relief exactly, but something near it, I stand back. While the Pacific spanning the windows just beyond the cliff face is pretty good, it's easily beaten by Francesca Sullivan in my bed, her long blonde hair spilling across my pillow, her soft curves tempting my hands to explore every peak and valley until she's writhing with the torture of it, her fingers curling into my sheets, her voice echoing up into the ceiling.

She lets out a little groan and I frown down at her before reaching over and, without my hands drifting to anywhere she hasn't said they're welcome, I gently unbutton her suit jacket because there's no way that's comfortable to sleep in, and then I pull the covers over her while she burrows into the pillow immediately.

Good, that's better than the couch. She'll get some rest and I'll order us some food while she sleeps even as I slowly go mad at the idea that, when I go to bed tonight, it'll smell of her.

I might never wash my sheets again.

Gross, but potentially worth it.

Quietly, I dig through my closet and find another t-shirt, old and soft, purple and gold, for the Lakers, and fold it neatly before placing it on the nightstand for her when she wakes up.

There isn't much to do except wait, so I busy myself with a little bit of research. Making sure everything is saved, I settle onto the couch and flick through her files on Nakamura.

There isn't a ton known about his personal life. All of his biographies just talk about how he's close with his family, his parents and four brothers, all of whom play baseball competitively. He's the oldest and, so far, the most successful. He's not married and I don't see any evidence of a significant other, which isn't all that strange for pro athletes in Japan. They tend to really protect their privacy. Half the time no one even knows their biggest stars are dating anyone until they announce their wedding.

The background is what you'd expect for a prodigy. Constant training, domination at a young age, an Olympic silver medal, a World Baseball Classic trophy and two Japan Series championships.

Now he wants to play at the highest level, against the best competition in the world, with the best players in the world.

And we have a shot at him.

If we can talk him into taking less money, somehow.

Because we won't be the highest bid. The depth of our ownership group's pockets isn't the question. Every owner in Major League Baseball has enough money to do whatever they want. It's convincing them to cough it up in service to winning that's the issue. Most of them like the idea of owning a team. Very few care enough to do what it takes to win it all.

The Steinbrenners with the Yankees. Steven Cohen with

the Mets, the Guggenheim group with the Dodgers and John Henry with the Red Sox.

And that's basically it.

But Frankie seems to think that Hannah Vinch might be able to make the offer *close* enough. We just need an X-factor. Her pitch will go a long way. I really believe that, but it might not be enough.

Huffing out a heavy breath, I stand, replacing her laptop on the table and stretch out. Still some time left to kill.

The weather is great, warm with a light breeze coming in off the water, so I make my way through the back patio doors and head straight for the pool, chucking off my t-shirt before diving in and barely coming up for air before I start my laps.

It's one of the last forms of exercise I have that doesn't absolutely murder my joints.

The repetitive motion is soothing and mindless, clearing away everything clattering around in there. A new career. A new city. Stew. Frankie. Nakamura. Those kids in Arizona who looked at me like I was some kind of deity come down from on high to make their major league dreams come true. All of it gone. Just my body slicing through the water to the wall and then back again, long and slow strokes to keep my heart rate even and my out-of-shape ass from pulling something or losing my breath.

Finally, with my chest heaving and my muscles tingling, setting off little bells in my head to call it quits, I push as hard as I can through that last lap before surfacing, gasping for air, but feeling like I used to after scoring from first . . . back in the early days of my career.

Flicking my hair back out of my eyes and wiping the water away, I look up and see Frankie standing at the edge of the pool, framed by the ocean and looking for all the world like she belongs on a California beach. Her hair is down, her skirt suit is gone, replaced by the t-shirt I left her tucked haphazardly into denim shorts that are maybe my new favorite thing I've ever seen her wear. Old and worn, shredded edges hitting at just above mid-thigh, her long legs look like they go on forever.

The view doesn't last long. She eases down to the pavers lining the patio and dunks her bare feet into the water.

"How long was I out?" she asks, not looking at me, but out at the ocean.

"Not long. Maybe an hour. You needed it."

"Did you, uh . . ."

"Carry you? Yeah, sorry, but you looked like you could use some real sleep in a bed and not just a quick nap on the couch."

"Just what every girl wants to hear," she says, finally looking at me, exasperated.

"That's not . . ."

"I know," she says, with a sigh, and then stares out at the ocean again.

"Do you miss it?"

"What?"

"Home."

"A little, sometimes. But there wasn't anything left here for me."

"No, me neither."

"Well, if we lose Nakamura to the Dodgers, you could always sell him this place."

"You like the house."

"What's not to like?"

"The traffic to the stadium."

"I did always wonder why you chose to live all the way out here. I figured you surfed or something. Or you liked long drives to clear your head before and after the game."

"You thought about that?"

"I'm an analyst. I think about everything, Charlie. Haven't you figured that out yet?"

"Sullivan, I think maybe I could know you for the rest of my life and I'll never have you all figured out."

"Probably not," she agrees, and smiles brightly at me, like keeping me confused as hell makes her happy. That's fine by me. "Thanks, though, seriously, for just letting me sleep. When I got the call about Nakamura I booked my flight and didn't sleep at all on the plane. I . . . you're right, I needed that, especially if we're going to do this right. The hotel rooms should be ready by now. Do you want one or . . ." she trails off, gesturing back to the house.

"I'll stay at the hotel," I finish for her, heaving myself up and out of the pool and grabbing a towel from the basket near the edge of the patio. "Who else is flying out?"

"Not Stew, though he wanted to," she says, standing up as well and I toss her one to dry off her legs, trying and failing completely not to watch as runs the terrycloth over her damp skin. "A couple of guys from media relations, Javy's on a flight later today, plus you and me. I don't want to overwhelm him with new faces. I figure we keep it simple, make real connections with him as the people he'll be working with once he gets to Spring Training and then once we break camp. I had a jersey made up with the number 18 on it for him to have, the number they give their aces in Japan."

"Nice touch," I say, taking the towel as she offers it back to me and dumping it into the empty basket for the cleaning crew.

"Gift giving is a massive part of Japanese culture; I'd be remiss if I didn't have something for him. I'm sure the other organizations have done the same. It's going to be about trying to differentiate from everyone else, especially since we'll be able to make a competitive offer, but I doubt it'll be the highest one," she says, following me as we head back into the house.

"Do you think . . ." I trail off, wandering into the kitchen, knowing there'll be a fully stocked fridge and at least a few decent options for lunch.

"What?" she asks, leaning against the countertop and I match her pose, opposite her against the large island that separates the kitchen from the living room. "I'm open to ideas."

"What if I called up Hannah Vinch and asked to extend the budget?"

Frankie furrows her brow. "Why would she agree to that?"

"Well, I've been known to have a certain effect on women of a certain age."

Her laughter is instant, but then she stops when she sees my face. "You're serious?"

"What could it hurt?"

"First, I've had enough of your negotiation skills for one life time," she says, and though there's still humor in her tone, I can see a little bit of real offense in her eyes.

I cringe. "And second?"

"Hannah Vinch is gay, Charlie."

"She is?"

"Very much. Married to her wife for twenty years. They have two kids."

"So that wouldn't work."

"It would not. We have a couple of days. We'll come up with something that won't require you to, what was it . . . have an effect on women of a certain age?"

"Shut up," I say, shaking my head at her with a grin, embarrassed, but mostly just glad I said something to her before trying it and truly humiliating myself in front of our boss.

"Make me," she shoots back, her grin matching mine and

I lift an eyebrow at the challenge, thinking of one particularly effective way I could make that happen.

The silence stretches out between us and, the longer it goes on, the more I want to make good on the images flashing through my head, remembering with crystal clarity what it's like to kiss her thoroughly, to make her body meld into mine, to trace the fullness of her mouth with my tongue and feel every nerve ending in my body respond to her.

"Maybe we should," she finally breaks, "maybe we should skip lunch and just go to the hotel. We can have everything set up when the rest of the team arrives and we can get started right away."

"Yeah, yeah, that's a good idea," I hear myself agreeing out loud, when I don't actually agree at all. I want her and I know she wants me, and I don't know how much longer we're going to get away with pretending that isn't true.

Chapter 15

FRANCESCA

My Japanese is rudimentary, despite that Duolingo streak, but I don't need it to talk to Nakamura's agent.

Daniel Wilson, the same guy who got Ethan Quicke to use our offer as leverage to squeeze some extra money out of the Dodgers, is on the other end of the phone when I call to schedule an appointment for an initial conversation.

Pacing back and forth, the plush carpet of our suite at the Four Seasons is soft under my toes. It's not their most expensive room, but has a decent-sized sitting area and a dining table with an okay view of the city, but not too good. Don't want him to look out the windows and think, yeah, fuck Brooklyn, it's LA for me because we're too close to the beach or the mountains or something. Just some streets below us, hustle and bustle.

That's all.

I sit down on one of the dining room chairs and pick at the frayed edge of my shorts, studying the purple Lakers shirt that I still haven't changed out of.

Working in clothes that don't match the job I'm supposed to

be doing feels wrong. Like the uniforms I used to wear on the field, my skirt suits and silk tops are armor for the job I need to get done. But the clean scent from the t-shirt must be the laundry detergent his housekeeper uses, I realize now.

I want to be annoyed at myself for it, for liking it and being so freaking aware that I like it.

And that he's aware of it too.

Would it be so bad?

He was right, that one time: we're equals. Him on the field. Me off the field.

And yet I made that promise to myself a long time ago. I wouldn't be that girl.

But . . . would I still be that girl?

The girl everyone whispers about, the girl who slept her way to the top. The girl who, ultimately, was just another girl who doesn't belong.

I made it.

I'm where I want to be.

Being with Charlie and, yeah, I can admit that's what I want, would it undo the decade plus of hard work I've put in? We're both adults. Fully consenting adults. Enthusiastic consent. Barely even a conflict of interest.

But it would look like . . . something.

Something that could derail everything.

And like I told him, if things went sideways, I'd be the one who faces the consequences.

Not him.

Just like what will happen if I don't land Nakamura.

"I'm honestly surprised that you guys are in on this," Dan says, as I refocus on the real problem, not whatever romantic fantasy I'm inventing in my head.

"Well, you'd know better than anyone that we're in the

market for a starting pitcher, Dan," I shoot back, and the asshole chuckles, but then he gets down to business.

"We want to thank you for submitting your initial interest bid. I'm happy and, frankly, surprised that the it's within the range we've determined as a good start for negotiations. He's narrowed his focus now to teams that will have the opportunity to pitch him in person here in Los Angeles and make their case and offers. Obviously, we reserve the right at any point to withdraw his interest from any particular organization."

"Obviously," I agree, and roll my eyes while I try to keep my tone as even and professional as possible.

"Excellent. You're up first. We have you scheduled for tomorrow, nine sharp."

First. The sacrificial lamb. Or . . . an opportunity to set the bar so high that no one else can clear it?

It'll have to do, though.

"Sounds good, Dan. See you tomorrow."

"Good luck," he says, just as I'm ending the call.

I turn to the team we have assembled.

"We have approximately eighteen hours to prep for this meeting. Let's do it."

Gregory and a couple of guys from the media relations department are on the presentation, assembling footage of Brooklyn then and now, the neighborhood, the people, the food, the energy, giving Nakamura a sense of exactly where he'd be signing up to play, since we don't have the advantage the Dodgers do of hosting the negotiations in their own city.

Javy and Charlie are going through video of Nakamura's highlight reel, pulling out the baseball information they'll need to talk to him about, what he'd bring to the organization's pitching staff and where we see him as he develops in the majors.

And me? All I can do at this point is wait.

The wait might kill me.

My phone buzzes in my hand and I smile at the screen.

Stew.

"Hey, boss," I say. "Isn't it nearly bedtime?"

The doctor was clear: he needs a lot of rest, time to let his body really recuperate.

"You watch your tone, young lady," Stew scolds, with laughter in his voice.

"Yes, sir. How are you feeling?"

"Fine, fine, progress is good. Doctors are thrilled, but that's not why I called."

All business then. Okay, that must mean he's feeling better.

"What can I do for you?"

"Checking in. I spoke to Hannah Vinch."

"Did you?"

"Yeah, it sounds like she gave you just enough rope to hang yourself."

"That was my read on it too."

"Shit. I'm sorry about this. I meant for you to take my job, but in a couple of years when you had some more experience under your belt, when they wouldn't axe you for one false move. I told Hannah that you aren't going to be doing anything that I haven't expressly sanctioned, but the thing with Ethan Quicke really got the board's shorts in a twist."

"I appreciate that, but we both know it won't matter."

"We'll get you another gig."

"Yeah," I agree, though I'm not sure it'll be as easy as that.

And it definitely won't be easy if I'm hooking up with our manager.

"Okay, well, when's the meeting?"

"Tomorrow morning."

"First?"

"First."

"Fucking Dan Wilson."

"I agree."

Stew laughs again. "And how's our boy?"

"Your boy?" I correct, and Charlie's head perks up from his conversation with Javy. "He's here."

"Let me talk to him."

"Avery," I call out, the last name now a little unfamiliar on my tongue. "You've got someone who'd like to talk to you."

He pushes up from his chair, swatting at whatever Javy said to him as he does, and I hold out the phone.

"Hey, Skip," he says and I grin, remembering those boys in Arizona who already call him that. "What's up? How're you feeling?"

Standing beside me, he's listening to Stew intently and I fold my legs beneath me, turning back toward my laptop where my meeting notes are still sitting, waiting to be reviewed for the billionth time.

"Yeah, she's doing great," Charlie says, and I diligently ignore that they're talking about me, all while my eyes fail to take in any of the words on the screen. "I'll remind her. Tell Rita I'll be over for dinner when we get back and I'll drag Frankie along too. Okay, go get some rest, old man."

A warm hand lands on my shoulder, squeezing lightly.

"He sounds good, right?" I say, when he offers the phone back to me.

"He does, really good. He'll be back before we know it."

"But not soon enough to do this."

"No, definitely not. Would you really even want him to?"

"Is it bad if I say no?"

"No," Charlie replies, shaking his head, his thumb stroking at the nape of my neck, catching on the collar of my shirt . . .

his shirt. "Because you got this. I know you do. What else do you need from me . . . from us?"

"Nothing. We're ready. We've been ready. It's just a matter of waiting now."

"And waiting's the worst."

"It really is."

"Okay, then let's get out of here. Go do something."

"Do what?"

"Anything, you grew up here, I lived here for nearly twenty years. There's gotta be a place you want to go eat or just hang out?"

It hadn't even occurred to me to leave this hotel suite. There's so much riding on this it felt like the only thing to do was sit here and let the seconds tick by, but he's right. We have nearly an entire day to wait. Might as well go out and do something.

"Okay, let's do that. What were you thinking?"

"You've been gone longer than I have. You pick."

And suddenly I know exactly where I want to go.

"A taco stand?"

"The best taco stand in the city. Manuel's tacos are perfection and he always has Mexican Coke too. You know, in the glass bottle? You lived here for how long and you've never been to Manuel's?"

"I couldn't really go to taco stands," he admits.

"Too famous?" I tease him, as I park my rental car down the street from Manuel's, just like I did back in high school after every game. "Couldn't make your way down to Los Feliz with the regular people?"

"This neighborhood is not regular," he insists.

Fair enough. Gentrified isn't a strong enough word, but the neighborhood has kept some of its charm over the years.

"It was when I was growing up. My parents' house is just a few blocks away."

"Do they still live here?"

"Oh, no, they're . . . they passed away. My mom when I was in middle school, my dad a few years ago."

"Shit, sorry."

"No, it's okay."

"My parents are gone too."

"Yeah, I know."

"Of course you know," he says, and then hesitates. "Is that part of your analysis too?"

I cringe, but nod. "Yeah, it's part of it. Not the dead parents thing, but more a . . . support system thing."

"Right, and what does that say about Kai Nakamori's?"

I'm really grateful for the change of subject. "It says that he's likely to struggle a little bit without a support system."

"Is that part of why you want those kids up in the big leagues next system? You figure they could be a part of his support system."

"He's learning."

"He pays attention when you speak, Frankie. Always have."

I blink at him, at a loss for words, just like I always am whenever he drops something like that on me, something that makes me pretty sure that we would work together, that we'd be great together, that all my hang ups about relationships, no matter who the guy is, would crumble to dust as soon as I decided to give him a chance to prove me wrong.

There's no one I recognize working at the counter at Manuel's, which isn't surprising. Manuel retired years ago and I'm pretty sure none of his kids wanted the business, but at least the place looks the same and smells the same too.

Armed with three tacos each and Mexican coke for me and

a Jarritos Mandarin for Charlie, we end up at the Mulholland fountain.

"Shit that's good," Charlie mumbles around his carnitas.

"Right?" I say, washing down a bite of my pulled chicken with ice cold Coke.

"Can't get tacos like this in New York."

"They're close, but no," I agree, "The Italian is way better, though."

"I don't know, I'm gonna have to try that."

"There's a place, by Javy actually, we'll go when we head back. The pesto gnocchi actually melts in your mouth."

"Now that I have to try."

There's something about sitting in silence with this man, less than a foot apart, not even looking at him that has me reconsidering everything. Every time we're close – hell, every time we're in the same room – there's chemistry, a magnetism, something that makes the air spark and my body desperate to be closer.

I glance over to find him already looking at me, Jarritos halfway to his mouth, but he stops when our eyes meet. Then his gaze flicks down to my lips and the air electrifies around us, sharp and hot against my skin, already warm from the after-noon sun.

"Hang on, you've got . . ." he trails off, and I feel like I'm in some kind of extremely earnest nineties romcom as he reaches out, hesitating just before the callused edge of his thumb lands at my bottom lip. "Can I?"

And it's so familiar, his need to know if I want him to touch me, if it's allowed, that I find myself nodding and then, when the rough pad of his finger brushes against me, a shiver flows through my body at the slightest contact.

I could be imagining it, but I think maybe he starts to lean in, the tips of his other fingers ghost against my neck, making the shiver into a surge of pure fire in my blood.

How is it possible that it's getting more intense?

Reaching up, my hand grasps his wrist, simultaneously holding him close, but stopping him.

He lets his hand fall away and I release it as he does. Shaking my head, I let out a heavy sigh. "Every single time."

He laughs and then takes that sip, before saying, "There are worse things in the world."

"True," I agree. "But at some point . . ."

"We're both adults, Frankie. We'll ignore it until it goes away."

"You think it's going to go away?"

"I think . . ." he trails off, "I think we have to hope that it does, unless . . . you've changed your mind."

And there it is. The ball is in my court and I can admit that it has been ever since I hitched a ride with him back from JFK in the wee hours of a rainy New York morning.

"Then here's to it going away," I say, raising my glass bottle for him to clink his against.

"No offense, Sullivan, but I'm not drinking to that."

And now I'm the one laughing. "Fair enough. We should get back."

"Yeah. Do you mind if we go back to my place first? I didn't bring anything with me and, if we're going to be camping out at the Four Seasons for a few days, I'm gonna need a change of clothes."

"Sure, but I pick the music."

"You drive a hard bargain, Sullivan. Dan Wilson doesn't a stand a chance."

The drive is long. It's never easy to get from one side of LA to another, but rush hour has us in the car for nearly an hour.

"Isn't this a little . . . obvious?" he asks, when I tune up *California* by Phantom Planet.

"I will hear no blasphemy about this song."

"I marathoned this show once."

"Really?"

"When Javy and I were in the minors, we had no money, there wasn't anything to do, so one season we just mainlined *The O.C.* from beginning to end."

"Okay, moment of truth then, Marissa . . . better dead or alive?"

"Alive. It was so fucked up when they killed her."

"Right? I remember being enraged. Like, was she annoying, sure, but that was the point. It never worked right again after they killed her off."

"So which one were you?"

"What?"

"Ryan or Seth?"

"Ryan Atwood is one of the greatest male characters ever written. Second maybe only to Pacey Witter. Teenage me was absolutely ruined for real-life teenage boys."

"Wait, who, Paste??"

"Stop, if you watched *The O.C.* then you watched *Dawson's Creek* too. That's more your era than mine."

"You are not that much younger than me."

"I'm enough younger that I didn't watch that show when it was airing."

"It's weird, isn't it?"

"What?"

"You're what? Five years younger than me and you're just on the upswing of your career, meanwhile mine is pretty much over?"

"I'm sorry, did you check into the nearest old-age home?"

"You know what I mean."

"I do. I always imagined it'd be pretty surreal, to not even be forty and to be retired, and you managed to play longer than most guys."

"It was . . . it is. Like, this is technically my retirement job."

"Technically. Don't pretend like you're a greeter at Wal-Mart now."

"Okay, so it's a pretty good retirement job."

"One of thirty guys in the whole world who are able to do it. Less than the amount of catchers in the league. If you think about it, it's even more rare than what you were doing before."

"Doesn't pay as well, though."

"Yeah, you're really hurting for money."

"Just saying, and it's not like you're doing too badly yourself. I know what that neighborhood you live in costs."

"Have you started looking for a place?"

"I have, just you know, scrolling Zillow a bunch to see what's around. Somewhere near the ballpark, for sure. Something that makes me feel like I'm getting the whole Brooklyn experience, you know? If I'm gonna do it, I might as well really do it, become a part of the place."

"It's a great neighborhood. The team being there really kept it the heart of the borough, kept businesses alive, made it a place people want to be, you know, even before Brooklyn was cool."

"Brooklyn was always cool, but that's because of the people. None of this matters if you're not surrounded by good people."

"Yeah, you're right."

Something clicks in my head. It's not a fully formed idea, but when I pull up to Charlie's driveway and park my car, it starts to come together, starts to become more than just an idea. It has me thinking back to that presentation that I have memorized, the thing I've had prepared for weeks now, the way I was going to convince Kai Nakamura to come play for us.

And now I want to scrap it all.

Because I have a way better idea.

Stepping into Charlie's house, I look around: it's warm, comfortable, and, despite its size and the clear amount of money that went into making it look that way, it feels safe.

Staring at the view, I know in my gut this is the way to get the job done.

"What if . . ." I start, and try to find the right way to say this. If I can talk Charlie into it, then I'll know for sure. "What if we started the meeting here?"

"We might just convince him right into signing here instead and buying this house from me."

"It's more personal this way, though. Having him in your home. He's a kid, leaving his family behind, everything he's ever known, and chasing his dream here. Let's show him what signing with the Eagles would mean: it would mean joining a family, *our* family, and that we'll treat him that way when he signs with us."

"You think that will work?"

"It will if he's the kind of guy we want around for the next ten or twelve years. If it doesn't work, then I'm not sure he was the right fit for us in the first place. We just got rid of one cancer with Ethan Quicke. I don't think Nakamura is that kind of guy, but it's better to know sooner rather than later. We're going to build around those kids playing in the fall league -~that's the organizations future, and if Nakamura is anything like them, he'll understand what we're trying to do here and he'll buy in."

"And you think he'll be able to tell all of that just from my house?"

"No, that's . . . that's just the first part of it."

It's completely crazy, the plan that just popped into my head, but if I'm right about the kind of player Nakamura is, the kind of player we need him to be, it just might work.

"So what's the second part?"

"It's a little bit insane."

"I'm all ears."

"It's actually really insane."

"Sullivan . . ."

"The kids."

"The kids?"

"Cole, Archie and Xander. What if we brought him to see the kids?"

"You want to fly him to Arizona?"

"I want to fly him to Arizona and sit his ass behind home plate and let him watch an Arizona Fall League game that his future teammates are playing in. We can show him instead of tell him what we're offering."

"And you don't think sitting in a minor league ballpark watching a game that doesn't matter will have him leaning the other way?"

"I think if he sees those kids, guys his age, playing the way they play, wanting the same thing he wants, to come to the big leagues and show the world what they can do and maybe do it together, I think maybe it'll work."

"You're right. It's batshit, but . . . you're also just . . . right. We're not going to be the highest bid. We kind of knew that going in, but this might be crazy enough to actually work."

"You really think so?"

"Yeah, I really do."

"Then call the guys at the hotel, get them over here. I have a plane to reserve."

Chapter 16

CHARLIE

She's back in my house. Not just in it. She's suddenly every-where. Her luggage is in my bedroom, her makeup and perfume sitting on the dresser, and behind the door in the corner of the room, the shower is running and a warbly version of Katy Per-ry's 'Firework' is echoing out from the ensuite.

Not that I'm complaining.

Not at all.

When she waltzed in this morning, it was such a shock that I didn't really get to process it, but now? Now, I don't even want to consider a time when she doesn't have free rein over my space. And I know if I say that to her, I'll destroy the odd sort of tentative in-between space we've agreed to occupy while we work together.

Rapping two knuckles against the bathroom door, her song cuts off followed quickly by the sounds of the water. "Yeah?"

"I've got the flight ready and," I hold out the towels in my arms, like she can see them through the door, "I grabbed you some clean towels. I'm going to leave them on the bed."

The door creaks open a couple of inches and a manicured hand appears along with some tendrils of steam and I hand them over, determinedly looking away just in case.

But she doesn't seem to care because, a couple of seconds later, she's out of the bathroom, towel wrapped around her securely.

"Christ, Sullivan," I mutter, and she shrugs.

"We don't have time for your midwest sensibilities," she says, blithely. "You said the plane is ready. Does the team know we're coming?"

"They do, and we have a car waiting for us at the airport when we arrive."

She moves over to her suitcase and carefully unzips a small bag, pulls free a scrap of black silky fabric and bends at the waist to pull them up under the towel while I do my best to keep my eyes focused up and over her head.

I'm only semi-successful, catching quick glimpses of silky thigh and the curve of her breast as my hands feel the phantom softness and weight of her in my palms. And a bed just a few feet away is not helping.

It's too easy to imagine this is a normal morning, her getting ready while we run through the day ahead of us, back in Brooklyn, down in Clearwater or wherever the game takes us next, the one constant through our lives.

The one constant through all the years ... has been baseball.

I've been in the game too long to not hear that sentence in James Earl Jones's voice, talking to Kevin Costner about the game I've played since I was a little boy. But why couldn't it also be about this, about the constants that baseball has brought me?

Francesca Sullivan has been a constant in my life for years

and now she's crept slowly but surely into nearly every other part of my life. She's a necessity now, as much as the game is.

She pulls on one of her pencil skirts, slate blue like the lettering on the Eagles' jerseys and drops the towel entirely, exposing the smooth length of her back to me as she fishes a bra out of her luggage, sliding it quickly into place – it's not the one from that night in Arizona – nude colored this time, to remain hidden beneath the cream silk camisole she slips over her head.

"Charlie?" she asks, spinning around and raising an eyebrow at my slack-jawed gaping. "I'm going to need you to focus up, Avery."

I snort and she has the self-awareness to smirk just a little bit, but then move on.

"What was the question?"

"The boys have been fully briefed?"

"Javy's on the way there now. He'll make it a couple of hours ahead of us and prep them."

"Am I crazy, to put the fate of this team . . . my entire career really, in the hands on three twenty-one-year-old kids?"

Her voice is steady, but there's an underlying waver in her voice, a ripple of nervous energy that I don't recognize.

"Yeah, but it's the right call."

"Yeah?"

"It's what my gut is telling me," I reassure her, the best way I know how.

"The same gut that used to be my mortal enemy?" she asks, reaching out and giving my midsection a gentle thwack. I'm too quick, though, and I grab her hand, holding it in mine. She's deflecting, but, right now, she needs to deal with whatever doubts are in her mind because there won't be any room for them in a little while.

I've been there.

And I can help.

"Yeah, that gut."

"They'll be here in a few minutes," she says, her eyes flicking toward the bedroom door. "We should make sure everything's perfect."

"Gregory's handling that. Right now, I just need you to take a deep breath."

"What?"

"Take a deep breath and relax your shoulders," I say, firmly, so much so that she does it without questioning it. Huh. Good to know that works and I file it away for when, one day, I really need her to listen to me. I squeeze the hand that I still have possession of gently and then tug on it. "C'mon."

I bend into a squat and look up at her, expectantly. With a quick, but maybe affectionate roll of her eyes she joins me.

"Better?"

"Yeah, a little, how did you . . ."

"That day when I fucked up with the press, before Stew went down, this is what you were doing before you yelled at me. Figured it's something that helps you calm down."

"Yeah, it feels . . . safe."

My knee creaks a little and I shift my weight. "Maybe for you."

"You really should get that taken care of. The longer you put off surgery on one, the more likely it is you'll need it on the other," she says, rising with what seems like barely any effort while I grip her hands tightly and let her help me up before I fall over.

"At some point I will," I brush it off. "Anyway, feeling better?"

"Yeah, it's just nervous energy. I've . . . I've never really done this before."

"You've never pitched an athlete before?"

"Not as the lead person in the room. Stew was always there and, before that, Brandon."

"Shit, sometimes you just come off so fucking in charge that I forget you're new at this."

"Fake it 'til you make it?" she says, shrugging one shoulder.

"Okay, so you're nervous, that's fair. What will help to make that go away?"

"Well, you being so damn calm is more than a little annoying." She laughs, but there's a sliver of truth there too.

"You need me to be nervous?"

"I don't know. Maybe?"

"Not a lot makes me nervous anymore, Sullivan," I admit.

"Great," she quips, sarcasm dripping from that one syllable.

"You . . . you didn't let me finish. One thing does, though."

"Yeah?"

Okay, here goes nothing.

"Can I be honest with you about something?"

"Of course."

Of course, she says, like what I'm about to do isn't the scariest fucking thing I've done in a long time.

"It's been a while since I've felt any kind of way about a woman. And I know what you said, how you feel about something happening between us, but I just need you to know that if that changes, if you decide that you can . . . I'm here."

"Charlie, I . . ."

"You don't need to say anything. It's . . . well, it's not fine, but it is what it is. I just needed you to know that. Right now, you're it for me. You and this team. And, for the record, if it's just the team, if that's the only thing we have together, then I promise you, that's enough. I think we can be great, you and I, on the field, even if we can't be together off it."

The silence is louder than the roar of any crowd I ever played for and, when I finally have the courage to look at her, there are tears in her eyes.

Shit, I made her cry.

Then she sniffs and shakes her head, somehow pulling them back and, a second later, her eyes are clear and the emotion entirely washed away from her face.

That's impressive as fuck.

"Are we okay?" I ask, afraid I might have ruined everything, or made it worse somehow.

"Yeah, we're okay."

"Good, that's good."

"You were honest with me, so I should be honest with you, at least about this one thing."

She's smiling now, a little sadly, so it doesn't give me much hope, but, despite that, I match it with one of my own.

"Okay, what is it?"

"There was a time and, it was not brief, where your poster was on the back of my bedroom door."

"I knew it."

"Don't let it go to your head. My bedroom was basically wallpapered with baseball players."

"Yeah, but you were a catcher and an LA girl, through and through. I bet I was your favorite."

"You were up there and that's all I'll admit to."

Okay, that's better. Her humor is still there, but it doesn't seem like she's using it to hide anything anymore, at least not anything beyond what's happening in this room right now.

Mission accomplished.

"C'mon. Time to go dazzle Nakamura, and I promise I'll buy you a new poster for your bedroom wall."

"I'm never gonna live that down, am I?" she asks, taking my hand as I pull her to her feet.

"Never."

And I know what she did. I bared my soul, made myself vulnerable, and she couldn't meet me there, so she gave me something else, something to break the tension and to keep us okay despite everything.

When they arrive, it's deceptively unimpressive. Two cars, one carrying Nakamura and Dan Wilson, the other a security guard and a guy I recognize from my playing days. Nelson was an interpreter for the Dodgers, fluent in Spanish, Korean and Japanese, since it was easier to have one guy around that could translate for anyone on the team at any given moment.

"Gentlemen," Frankie says, as we march out of my front door. She stops just ahead of Nakamura and executes a short bow, which he follows, then she shakes his hand and Dan Wilson's, followed by the other two men before gesturing back toward me. "You all know our manager, Charles Avery."

"Charlie," Dan says, like we're old friends, which in the broadest sense of the word friend, I suppose we are. "Good to see you."

"You too."

I don't mean it, but I shake his hand and then Nelson's before turning toward Frankie and Nakamura.

He's young, just twenty-five, and looks it, not a line on his face, his eyes bright and a blinding smile spread across his face. He's a big kid, nearly my height, but slender, with a wiry flexibility that's perfect for a young pitcher, athletic without being wound so tightly he's constantly in danger of pulling something. His suit is new and clearly high quality. I've been in the game long enough to know custom tailoring when I see it. He's done well in the Japanese league and he's about to do even better here.

"Avery-*sama*," he says, his bow deep, nearly from the waist, and he holds it for a second and then another before holding his hand out.

"Kai, it's great to meet you, kid," I say, returning his bow with one of my own, then shaking his hand firmly. I can't help but smile when the kids' face lights up even more.

He opens his mouth and starts, "It's . . ." but then he hesitates and looks toward Nelson, who steps forward. He speaks in rapid Japanese for a few moments, looking at me and not at his interpreter the entire time.

Nelson nods along and then says in monotone, "It's such a pleasure to meet you, Mr Avery. I have been a very big fan of yours since I was a little boy and I'm looking forward to talking to you today."

I grin. I'm not above having my ego stroked by a kid who watched me play growing up and I'll be happy to use that to our advantage during this process.

"I really appreciate that, Kai. You can just call me Charlie. I'm excited to get to know you better and hopefully make you a part of what we're trying to do in Brooklyn for the next decade or so."

Nelson translates rapidly, but abruptly, and I wonder how much is actually being communicated. Though, from the way that Kai's attention is still on me, either he's very good at listening with one ear or he doesn't actually need the interpreter.

My money's on the latter.

"Gentlemen, if you'll follow me," Frankie says, gesturing back toward the house. "We can get started."

Gregory has my living room looking better than it ever has, pillows fluffed, trays of snacks and beverages lined up on a serving table that I don't recognize, fresh flowers cut and placed sporadically around the room and my furniture rearranged, not to face the television, but two chairs and my couch in a conversational formation with my coffee table in between. There are notepads and pens for everyone, monogrammed with the Eagles logos.

"We were thrilled to see your offer was as competitive as it was," Dan says, sitting down in one of the chairs and crossing his legs to start the meeting off.

Nelson is translating quietly as he sits beside Kai on the couch. Frankie sits on another chair and I move off to the side with Javy, ready to be called in when needed.

"So, shall we get started?" Dan says.

"Actually, we've decided to go in a slightly different direction for this pitch, if you'll indulge us."

That gets Kai's attention clearly before Nelson even starts translating.

Good.

I don't trust that translator guy as far as I can throw him, especially if Dan Wilson hired him away from the Dodgers. If he's going to be Kai's personal interpreter, he'll have no interest in leaving LA any time soon and, with only a few voices in the kid's ear, I want to make sure that what we say is actually being understood.

"Go on." Dan prompts Frankie to continue.

"We know what we're up against here. We know that the teams who are vying for your services may have deeper pockets and more storied histories, so our pitch is, perhaps, a little bit different than what you'll be hearing from other organizations. We know what you bring to the table, Kai. I know what you're capable of and I know what you're worth. I saw it for myself in Tokyo less than a month ago. You are exactly what we need to bring a championship back to Brooklyn, along with a few other players we think you'll be excited to have with you over the course of your career."

"I'm sorry, where exactly is this going?" Dan cuts in, even though Kai has leaned forward in his seat, clearly intrigued as Nelson rapidly interprets Frankie's words.

"Arizona. We have a car waiting to take us to the airport, where we'll be flying to see this afternoon's Desert Dogs game."

"The Fall league?" Dan says, but his voice is drowned out by his client.

"Arizona?" Kai asks. "To see a game? The Desert Dogs?"

"Yes, but mostly for you to meet three young men who have the exactly the same dream as you do, who will be making their major league debuts with you and who will be the centerpieces of the dynasty we plan to build in Brooklyn."

"Yes," Kai says, cutting off Nelson as he continues to interpret what Frankie just said. "Yes. We'll go to Arizona."

A private jet doesn't impress the kid. I didn't expect it to, but as we're given our seats, I make sure to slide into one facing him with Frankie at my side while the flight attendant comes around to pour us glasses of champagne.

"No, thank you," he says to the woman, "water, please."

"Same," I say, and then look to Frankie.

"Seltzer and lime," she says.

"What is it like?" Kai asks me, leaning forward in his seat as his agent and interpreter make themselves comfortable in the row across from us.

"What's what like?"

"The Major Leagues. The big leagues. The show."

"You think you're ready for it when you get there. You've played baseball your entire life, so how could it be any different than every game before it? But it is. It's so different. There's no bigger jump than the one you make into the big leagues. The best pitchers. The best hitters. It's grueling and terrifying at first. Everyone's bigger and stronger and knows more, but then it hits you one day, that you belong. And it's like nothing you've ever felt before. The crowd. The stakes. Your teammates. It's everything you ever dreamed of and everything you ever dreaded all wrapped into one glorious season, and one day you'll look back and you'll miss it like hell, so you'll find yourself talking to a rookie who hasn't made it yet like you're an old man reliving his glory days. I can't wait for you to see for yourself, kid. You're gonna love it."

The flight is short. A little under an hour and a half and the drive to Glendale isn't bad either, but my phone is already lighting up with texts, mostly old friends from the game asking if there's any truth to the rumor that we got Kai on a plane to Arizona.

The baseball world is very, very small sometimes and its fans are rabid. There's always someone watching and our secret isn't a secret for very long.

I imagine, by the time the game gets underway, the ballpark will be packed with fans hoping to get a glimpse of the sport's next big thing, but when we pull up, it's still relatively quiet.

The Desert Dogs are taking batting practice and there's a security guard waiting to escort us from the player's entrance through the inner workings of the ballpark, hallways I once knew like the back of my hand, and then onto the field where the bright sunshine, blue skies and the perfect scent of grass, dirt, the wood of the bats and leather of the gloves envelops us.

Cole Davis is already out on the field waiting. I imagine he's usually the first one out on the field, and his reaction is instant, making a beeline for us and, before anyone can perform introductions, he's already talking.

"I've studied the film from the Japan Series," the young catcher says, without preamble and definitely without worrying about the interpreter. I had him do his homework. I wonder if he figured out what I did, that Kai Nakamura understands and speaks perfect English. "You worked your changeup in a lot more than you usually did during the regular season. Was that a deliberate choice to throw off their scouting report or was it just working that day so you went with it?"

To his credit, Kai just goes it with: "I . . . I only use the changeup when all my other pitches are working."

"Yeah? Why's that?"

"Because it is a new pitch and I am building confidence with it."

"A new pitch? When did you start throwing it?"

"Early this season. I knew I would need it for the major leagues and thought it would be important to have it developed fully before I arrived here."

"Well, it's definitely ready to be mixed in more . . . Wait, Xander and Archie are here. Guys, what took you so long? We've been waiting."

The other boys emerge up from the tunnel, jogging toward us in their Brooklyn uniforms, metal cleats clacking against the cement steps of the dugout in unison.

"Sorry, my fault," Archie says. "I almost put diesel in the gas tank and then I thought I *did* put diesel in and we had to call an Uber so the mechanic could make sure I didn't. It's nice to meet you. Your stuff is wicked."

"Wicked?" Kai asks, and turns to Xander and freezes, mouth dropping open, eyes lighting up like he did when he first saw me coming out of the house to greet him.

"Great, he means great," Xander says, holding out his hand. "I'm Xander Greene. This is Archie Esposito."

"Archie," Kai says, nodding toward the other young man, but reaching for Xander's and shaking it slowly, "and Xander. It's . . . it's nice to meet you?"

Neither one of them pulls away. Xander is staring at their joined hands. Kai is simply standing still while their handshake stops and they blink at each other silently.

Huh . . . what . . . oh.

Oh.

My eyes fly to meet Frankie's and it's clear she put the puzzle pieces together as well.

Sparks. I recognize them easily enough and this is . . . well, it's interesting. There's a reason, I guess, that there were no mentions of a girlfriend back in Japan, no mentions of anyone in his life.

And maybe this is why.

I can't blame the kid for keeping it a secret, neither one of them. Baseball isn't exactly the most inclusive of professional sports, but it doesn't make a difference to me who they go to bed with at night, as long as they're bringing it on the field.

And this? This might work to our advantage.

The boys finally let their hands drop and they all fall into a conversation together, Cole and Archie joining in easily as they talk about where they want to live for Spring Training and getting to Florida early in order to maximize their prep time before the rest of the squad arrives.

Frankie moves to my side as we watch it unfold and whispers, "What do you think?"

"I think Xander Greene is going to be one hell of a centerfielder and Kai Nakamura one hell of a starting pitcher in this league, and if they can do those things on the same team while they figure out whatever the hell we just saw was, more power to them."

"You don't think it'll be a distraction?"

"Not in my clubhouse."

"There's never been a publicly out Major Leaguer, let alone one that's going to get the amount of attention Kai is about to get."

"He's not out. Not to us, at least, and unless he is, then our response is no comment. If he decides he wants to make an announcement, we'll support him. What did Ted Lasso say? It matters to us because he matters to us."

"The writing of that episode was super clunky. But, yeah, that was the gist."

"You won't disrespect Ted Lasso to me."

"Oh, don't tell me you're one of those people who were glad that Ted and Rebecca didn't get together."

"I thought it was refreshing to see a platonic relationship on TV."

"We don't have time for this right now, but at some point we are watching that show together and I'm going to make sure you understand just how wrong you are."

"I'll bake shortbread."

"You can bake?"

"I can do a lot of things, Sullivan. Now, c'mon, can't let these boys do all the heaving lifting for us."

She grins and steps away to join the conversation, but before I can follow her, Dan Wilson is next to me.

"This is one hell of a stunt the girl pulled."

"You mean the woman in charge of a billion-dollar company about to offer your player hundreds of millions of dollars? She doesn't pull stunts," I insist, trying to keep my cool, "She does what she thinks will work."

"It won't. Her bid is going to be tens of millions behind the leaders."

"Then why did you even show up today?"

"Price goes up when more teams are involved."

"Really? Or did your client insist?"

I've been around enough fans in my time to know it. Kai Nakamura is a fan. He wanted to meet me. Maybe our initial bid wasn't close. Doesn't mean it won't be the one he takes.

The agent's silence is enough to confirm it.

"He's a hell of a kid, Dan. He's gonna be great. Don't get in his way. Let him make the call."

"It's my job to look out for his best interest."

"Well, let's just see how this plays out," I say, looking over to where the boys and our top free agent target have their heads bent together while Archie shows Kai his knuckleball grip.

"Yeah," he says, "we will."

"And don't underestimate Frankie and what she's trying to do here."

"Don't worry," he says, his mouth lifting into a superior smirk. "I won't."

And as he turns to go, stadium employees dodging around him as he doesn't break his confident stride, I try to ignore the fact that it sounds an awful lot like a threat.

Chapter 17

FRANCESCA

These kids are ready for the big leagues, that much is clear, and if the stats didn't already show it, the way they play when we're there to watch is just another sign.

The Desert Dogs are up seven nothing by the bottom of the third, making the game second fiddle to what's going on in the stands and that's Kai sitting between Charlie and Javy as they go pitch by pitch, talking through the game, his interpreter long forgotten and sitting on the end of the row, while Dan Wilson sits beside me mostly scrolling through his phone looking more than a little annoyed to be in the sweltering Arizona heat instead of in an air-conditioned hotel suite in Los Angeles.

At least it's a dry heat, I think, as I flick my hair over my shoulder and grin out at the field. Cole Davis is up to bat again and the first pitch he sees is launched more than four hundred feet to dead center field over the fence for a home run. His second of the game. He's incredible and he's ours.

"I don't know what you think you're doing here, but I stand by what I told Charlie. This out-of-the-box bullshit isn't going to play once hard and fast numbers make Kai see the light," Dan says, as the fans around us cheer while Cole rounds the bases. Kai joins in with a massive grin on his face when Xander scores ahead of Cole and then points to him in the crowd.

"I don't know, seems like it's working pretty well to me."

"Sounds like code for your offer won't be the highest or you won't be willing to come up over the highest?"

"It's not code for anything other than I'm doing what I can to convince your client that money's great, but the best experience he'll have in the major leagues involves those three kids out there and the two guys up here."

"And you," he adds, with a knowing look.

I snort. He doesn't know shit. Guys like Dan Wilson can't imagine someone *not* being a raging ego maniac. It's what makes them so easy to read.

"I'll be sending over our next offer when you're both safely back on the plane to LA and we'll see where things shake out."

"We will. I'm done. I'm going to find some air conditioning. Notify me when this stunt is over."

"Our plane will be on the tarmac waiting for you."

And with that he slides from his seat, his custom-tailored Italian suit clearly sticking to him as he disappears up the stairs and out of sight.

Kai's phone buzzes in his hand and he glances down at it, his expression unchanging before he flips it face down on his thigh and refocuses on what Javy is saying to him about – if his hand shape is anything to go by – a grip for a knuckle changeup.

As subtly as I can, while I'm sure Kai is focused on Javy, I lean toward Charlie in the seat beside me, nearly resting my chin on his shoulder as I murmur, "How do you think we're doing?"

"Having second thoughts?" he whispers back.

"Wilson's not on board."

"We knew he wouldn't be."

"True," I agree, but I can hear the doubt in my own voice. He must hear it too.

"Hey," he says, his hand finding my hands, clenched tightly in my lap over my crossed legs. He loosens their grip easily enough and then squeezes one warmly. "We got this."

I squeeze back. "Yeah, we do."

"What do you think, Charlie?" Javy says, from around Nakamura, and draws him back into their conversation, his hand sliding from mine quickly, but not fast enough for Javy not to see. I try to avoid his wide eyes, but it's too late and he shoots me a wink before refocusing.

Damn it, he caught me.

I turn my attention to the game and do my best to stay focused there for the remainder of it while keeping one ear on the conversation beside me. Nakamura is a baseball junkie, that much is clear, as obsessive and exacting as Charlie and, as every innings passes, they get deeper into the weeds about the development of higher spin rates to make sure the pitches he throws move as much as possible before they get to the batter and in-game biometrics analysis that can tell a manager when a pitcher is fatiguing before it becomes apparent through a bad result on the field.

"Is that something you use?" Nakamura asks, and I'm happy to chime in when Javy and Charlie look to me.

"All the teams are using it, but I've incorporated that into my predictive algorithm. Plus it's been updated to take that data into account, to help prevent injuries, especially the ones associated with overuse."

He nods thoughtfully. It makes sense he'd be concerned about it. One of the major issues Japanese players sometimes have when they come over the States is getting used to a five-man rotation instead of six, plus an extra eighteen games in the regular season.

By the final out, I'm more sure than ever that this risk was absolutely the right call.

We wait for most of the crowd to empty out and our boys jog over to the stands, at which point Nakamura is allowed onto the field by security to chat with them.

I watch carefully, while Javy and Charlie chat beside me, as a soft flush appears in Kai's cheeks when he types his number into Xander Greene's phone, and the wide, silly grin on the centerfielder's face as he does.

Well, if nothing else comes of this, they're pretty adorable, and I'll be able to say I was there the day they first met.

"Ms Sullivan," Archie says, jogging over to us. "Do you think we could go grab some tacos again? Kai said he'd be down to come with."

He reminds me of a little kid asking his mom if he can have a sleepover with his friends.

"You don't have to get back to LA?" Charlie asks him.

"My next meeting is not until tomorrow," Kai says, with a shrug, like he's wildly unconcerned about whatever is happening at that meeting.

And I'm feeling even better about my choices, grinning as I imagine Wilson cooling his heels back on the plane, waiting even longer for his client.

"Okay, let's go get some tacos."

It's the same Mexican place as the last time we were here, a little hole in the wall buried in a bland strip mall not far from the ballpark, but the drinks are strong – I'm definitely only having one margarita – and the food is as good as I remember.

Kai Nakamura seems to agree as Xander hands him a bottle of Cholula to add to his carne asada tacos, and utters an uncontrolled groan after a bite that has Xander blushing again the way he did back at the field.

"Did I mention this was brilliant?" Javy says, wiping his face and settling back against the booth seat, across the table from me, while we watch the kids at the table next to us and Charlie is at the bar grabbing us more drinks.

"You didn't."

"You gave him a glimpse of what his life will be like, surrounded by these kids, feeling comfortable here before he even throws a pitch."

"We'll see if it matters more than the check the Dodgers or Yankees will write."

"Can't control that and we can't worry about things we can't control," Javy warns. "You know that better than anyone. It's what you used to tell me all the time whenever I whined about run support. I remember you saying, clear as day, *I can't control for every variable, Javy. Suck it up.*"

I ignore his terrible impression of me. "You never whined about run support."

"I was doing it in my head and you always knew. That data of yours, you always knew shit was going on, sometimes even before we did."

I can't help my grin at the compliment, whether he meant it as one or not. "The things we can't control are the most frustrating, though."

He nods and then clicks his tongue, leaning forward. "And speaking of frustrating, I gotta ask you a question."

His eyes light up and I can already tell where this is going.

"You can ask," I say, "doesn't mean I won't tell you to fuck off."

He lets out a sound that's half laugh, half snort. "When are you going to put my boy out of his misery?"

"I don't know what you're talking about."

"I think you do," he says simply, "and you should be glad it's me asking you and not my wife, because she wants to call dibs on designing your dress."

I choke on a sip of my drink at that last part of his sentence. "My dress?"

"We talked about it before I left and we haven't seen Charlie like this in a long time, not since . . ." He trails off, like he said too much.

"No since what?"

"You know he was married before, right?"

"Yeah," I say. He hesitates and I let out a frustrated breath. "If you want to say something to me, Javy, just say it, otherwise, leave it alone."

"Gemma . . . she fucked him up. They were together since high school and then she just reneged. Wanted a different kind of life."

"Okay, so, what does that have to do with me?"

"I haven't seen him this happy since, I don't know, the early days, when we still had our careers ahead of us, when we thought we'd win over and over again and that it would never end, you know?"

"Yeah, I do," I agree, remembering my freshman year at Cal.

"And then we didn't and then Gemma left and things got rough there for a minute. He got over it, moved on, but then the game, it started to catch up to us, me first and then him. So to see him like this again, after all this time, and we haven't even gotten on the field yet. It means something. *You* mean something to him."

"He means something to me too," I admit, watching him

balancing our drinks – two beer bottles and my margarita that I insisted I wasn't going to drink – as he heads back to the table. "But I have a rule about office relationships and it's served me well the last decade. What would that make me if I broke it now?"

"It would make you human," Javy mutters, but that's all he's able to get out before Charlie arrives.

"Another round, on me," Charlie says, about to slide into the space beside Javy, but his friend nudges him back, leaving the booth.

"Gotta hit the head and then call the wife," Javy calls over his shoulder, leaving us very much alone, and I have a feeling he won't be coming back any time soon.

"You alright, Sullivan?" Charlie asks, as I take a very, very long sip from my drink.

"Did you know your best friend is incredibly annoying?"

"Shit, what did he say?"

"Nothing, just . . . he reminded me of something."

"What?"

"My divorce."

"You were talking about your divorce with Javy?"

"No, he was talking about *your* divorce and it reminded me of mine."

"I thought you said the guy cheated on you?" Charlie asks, furrowing his brow. "Gemma didn't . . . at least not that I know of."

"No, it was more about making promises and then not keeping them." I stop, but he tilts his head, silently asking me to continue. "Shane and I, we had our lives, he worked in finance, I was with the Dodgers. We were, you know, doing what we set out to do, we were happy, it was what we talked about, what we said we both wanted. Putting off kids until later, if ever, climbing to the top of our careers and then, one day, he just reneged and, before I knew it, he was quitting his job and playing house."

"So not the same, but definitely not completely different," he says. "Gemma wanted kids and didn't want me to travel so much and, to this day, I really wonder if she thought I was going to quit baseball, even though she knew that it was the only thing I ever wanted. Or maybe she realized that I wanted it more than I wanted her."

"That's what Shane said. That he couldn't compete with my job and he didn't want to."

"And now here we are, however many years later . . ."

"Three."

"Ten for me," he admits, "alone."

"Alone, together," I correct him, and then nod to the other table. "Three kids. Maybe four."

He snorts. "Twenty-six of them once the season gets going, overgrown teenagers with more money than they know what to do with and more energy than I can ever remember having."

"I'll drink to that," I say, raising my glass, and he clinks his beer bottle against it.

When I put my glass back down, after a much shorter sip than before, my phone lights up on the table. It's Dan Wilson.

Done holding my client hostage?

I'm half tempted to snap a picture of the four guys at the table, laughing and having a great time after pounding a few tacos and a couple of beers each, but I manage to restrain myself.

"Someone's getting cranky," I say, showing my phone to Charlie.

He snorts. "Does Kai turn back into a pumpkin soon?"

"That would definitely put a dampener on contract negotiations. C'mon, let's get him back to the plane before Wilson leaks this to a reporter that we'll have to deal with."

We send off our three kids in an Uber and all very deliberately turned our backs or focused on our phones while Xander and Kai's handshake and one-armed hug went on a beat or two longer than the ones he exchanged with Cole and Archie.

Javy and Kai pick up that same conversation about developing a knuckle curve during the ride back to the airport.

"Thank you very much for today," Kai says, slowly, clearly choosing his words carefully despite his obvious fluency. "It has given me much to consider."

I smile at him and extend my hand for him to shake, which he does firmly. "I really appreciate your willingness to come out here today and see what our plans are, long term. And know that, no matter what you decide, you have three fans in us. If you ever need anything, you reach out, okay?"

"You work on that knuckle curve grip before Spring Training. Send me some video if you need feedback," Javy says.

Then Kai turns to Charlie and pulls something from the inside pocket of his jacket. "Before I go, will you sign it?"

It's a baseball card, an old one, encased in thick plastic to protect it from even the slightest wrinkle.

"Of course," Charlie says, and I produce a pen from the recesses of my bag, while Kai unclasps the plastic gently.

With great care, Charlie scribbles his signature at the bottom of his picture, baby faced with thick stripes of eye black at the top of his cheekbones, looking as fierce as an eighteen-year-old rookie possibly can. The card was worth a lot a moment ago and now, as Nakamura takes it back and closes the case, it's worth even more.

"Thank you, Avery-*sama*," Kai says, staring at it, before

looking up sheepishly. "Don't tell Mr Wilson that I asked. He advised me not to."

"Your secret's safe with us, kid. And not just this one," he says.

Kai freezes, looking from Charlie to Javy to me, and then back to Charlie again, before his shoulders relax and he smiles, wider and brighter than he has all day long, and that's saying something. "I appreciate that, very much."

"No problem, kid," Charlie says, clapping him on the shoulder. "Now come on, we have a plane to catch."

Once we board, Wilson shuffles his client to the other end of the plane, probably to grill him on what happened during the hours they were apart, but I won't even let that bring me down.

Today is exactly why I got into this business, a chance to bring together players and coaches, to see them make connections and find that spark between them, the spark that ignites a team through a grueling hundred and sixty-two games and then into the post-season, keeping the flame alive until that last out.

I can see it, clear as day in front of me, the boys spilling out of the dugout at Russell Field, a dogpile on the pitcher's mound with Charlie and Javy embracing each and every one of the players that finally got them to the pinnacle of their careers, and I'm there too, probably pacing the tunnel just beyond the dugout during the last three outs, not watching, just listening, knowing the crowd will tell me what happened and then, when that deafening final cheer goes up, I can sprint out to the field and be with them after we've brought a World Series home to Brooklyn, the first one since 1955.

That moment will be so sweet, beyond everything I can even imagine.

And it feels like I took one step closer to it today, but now it's out of my hands and the only thing I can do is wait.

For a moment, one blissful moment when I hear my cell phone ring on the nightstand in Charlie's guest room, I think that maybe, just maybe, Nakamura's already made his decision, that he's forgoing all the other meetings and will sign with us after we sent over our very generous offer the night before.

But then I realize it's not even two in the morning and I've only been asleep for an hour and the number lighting up my phone screen definitely isn't Dan Wilson's or even Nakamura's himself.

It's Hannah Vinch.

My heart sinks into my stomach.

Stew.

I can't think of any other reason why she'd be calling this late or even calling at all. She never has before.

"Hello? Mrs Vinch? Is . . . it Stew?"

"What?" she asks, her voice clipped and sharp on the other end of the line. "Oh, no, Stew is fine, as far as I know. Chomping at the bit to get back to work, but fine. Did I wake you?"

She knows she did.

"No, of course not," I insist, sliding my feet out from under the covers and turning on the sconce mounted to the wall beside the headboard. "What can I do for you, Mrs Vinch?"

"You can tell me that the information I was given tonight is false."

"Information?"

"That you didn't stick to the presentation the ownership group approved for Kai Nakamura and that instead you flew him and his agent to Glendale on the team's private jet to watch a minor league game?"

"Arizona Fall League," I correct, without thinking. My brain is still sleep fogged.

"That is beside the point," she snaps back. "Clearly we were hasty in appointing you interim general manager during Stew's absence if you can't even conduct yourself as a professional during a negotiation as important as the one with Kai Nakamura."

"Did you, by any chance, speak to Daniel Wilson tonight?"

"It doesn't matter who I spoke to." That confirms it. "You haven't denied it and, frankly, Ms. Sullivan, you're trying my patience every second that ticks by."

"We did. We . . . I," I correct, because it was ultimately my decision, "I decided that our best chance to sign Nakamura was to show him exactly what he'd be choosing if he signs with the Eagles, who he'd be playing with, the kind of coaches that would support him, a team that will have his back during his big-league career."

"And you didn't think to run any of this by anyone, not me, not Stew, you just went off on your own and made a mockery of our organization."

"That's not . . ."

"That's *exactly* what it was. You took the prize free agent of the off season to a Desert Dogs game to eat bad ballpark food and then to a strip-mall taco place for what, two for one margaritas, blowing any chance we had to sign him out of the water?" When she puts it like that, it doesn't sound great. "I won't have it and neither will the rest of the board."

"But . . ."

"You're fired, Ms Sullivan. Effective immediately."

The phone goes dead and, with it, so goes my career.

Chapter 18

CHARLIE

When I'm home, I'm used to near absolutely silence at night. The house is set up high enough that the traffic noise from the Pacific Coast Highway doesn't reach my bedroom, not even when I have the floor-to-ceiling windows open. It's so quiet that it took a few Brooklyn nights to get used to the near constant noise that would echo into the dawn when I was staying with Javy.

Here, though, the reverberation of the diving board followed by the splash of someone slicing into the pool, just steps from my bed, is enough to wake me from a dead sleep.

There's a glow emanating up out of the water, blue tinted as it reflects off the pool's liner and, as I slip out of bed and pad across the room, a blurry shape is still under the water, swimming a strong breaststroke toward the far wall.

Frankie.

Quietly, so I don't wake Gregory or Javy, who are camped out in the living room just beyond my door, I ease open the sliding door and stand at the edge of the pool, breathing in the cool night air that's coming in off the ocean in the distance.

It's a clear night, barely a cloud in the sky, a nearly full moon and stars twinkling down at me, way more so than in New York. The city lights up the night there, instead of the stars. Though, truly, it doesn't matter to me either way.

Frankie surfaces at the edge of the pool, gasping for breath while she holds on to the stone-edged coping, her chest heaving up out of the water.

"Night swimming?" I ask, keeping my voice down. I don't want to startle her.

Her shoulders tense and she doesn't turn to face me, not right away.

"Frankie?"

"Yeah," she says, finally. "Couldn't sleep."

"Worried about Nakamura? Don't be. I think we've got it in the bag."

"No, it's not that," she says, finally twisting around in the water, her hair slicked back, and I try to focus on that and not that she's clearly swimming in her bra and panties. It doesn't cover any less of her than a bathing suit would, but still, my dick doesn't care: it knows the difference.

"Then what's up?" I ask, settling down on the pavers, with only my boxer briefs on, letting my feet dangle into the pool, the water perfect as it laps against my shins.

"I got fired."

The words at first don't actually register for me. *I got fired.* They're absolutely the last thing I ever expected her to say, but then when they hit me, the only thing I can feel is pure unadulterated rage.

"Dan Wilson. I'm going to beat the shit out of that motherfucker."

"No, not Dan Wilson," she says, lifting herself up out of the pool, and I'm so enraged that I don't even fully appreciate the long line of her body glinting in the moonlit. "Me. It was my fault. Nobody's fault but mine." She wraps a towel around herself.

"You're telling me he didn't have anything to do with it?"

"He definitely did. I'm sure, while we were watching the game with Nakamura and handing him watered-down minor-league beer and shopping-center tacos, he was on the phone with every single member of the Eagles board, who then called Hannah Vinch to let her know I blew the deal and that's that. I'm done and it's no one's fault except mine."

That has me on my feet in an instant. "Bullshit. He's just a dick who's afraid his star player is going to take less money to sign with the team he wants, instead of the team Dan tells him he wants. The one that would earn Dan a bigger cut."

"Yeah, but that's the job, isn't it? Dealing with assholes like Dan Wilson, making sure you don't alienate them, making sure you woo them *and* their clients. That's what I was supposed do, that's what Stew entrusted me with, and I didn't do that, so I lose, game over."

"No, no, I don't accept that."

"You don't have to. It's already done."

"Fuck, well then I'm gone too."

"No!" she practically shouts, but then shakes her head and continues, her voice lower, "Don't do that. Don't make it like that. I want you to stay with the team. Those boys, they need you and you need them. I know you're gonna do great things with the Eagles and you deserve your ring."

"You deserve it too. More. You're the one who started this, building the team since last season. It's your team, Francesca."

"It was supposed to be." Her voice hitches and, as I take a

step closer and then another, it's clear the droplets of water now running over her cheeks are tears. "But it's not anymore. It's yours."

"C'mere," I say, reaching out for her, a hand at her shoulder gently guiding her forward into my chest. She takes a small step and then just collapses into me, her body heaving in quiet sobs as she cries, her tears hot against my skin.

"You have to promise me," she mumbles against my shoulder, as her arms come around me, holding tight ,and I press a hand to her back to keep her close, her towel rough against my fingertips. "You have to promise me you'll win the whole damn thing."

"Okay, okay," I say, as I feel her breathing start to even, warm exhales over my chest that make the hair there stand on end while goosebumps rise over my skin. "I promise."

"Good, and wherever I land I'll be doing my best to make sure that doesn't happen," she says, leaning back in my arms and looking up into my eyes, her gaze satisfied, but still not shining with that brightness I love.

Love.

Shit.

I love her.

I don't even know when it happened.

There's no moment I can pinpoint, no bolt of lightning to my heart or tidal wave of feelings.

It's been there for so long, I didn't even notice, until right now when she was crying in my arms, and there's absolutely nothing I can do to fix it.

The last of her tears fall and I reach up to wipe one away with the pad of my thumb

"Francesca, I . . ."

But she cuts me off, pushing up on her toes, a hand already

buried in my hair as she pulls my mouth down to meet hers and I half expect it to match the last time this happened, hard and rough, mostly pleasure, but just the right amount of pain.

But it's not.

As soon as her lips find mine, the kiss turns hesitant, gentle even. And if that's what she wants, that's what I'll give her, but first . . .

I pull away with every ounce of restraint in my body and pull in a gasping breath. "Before we do this, I need to know something."

"Anything," she whispers, her lips ghosting against mine as she says it, close enough to send a firestorm of sensation over my skin.

"Do you really want this or is it because . . . because of what happened tonight."

"I thought . . . I thought you knew . . ." she says, blinking up at me. "It was always there for me, the whole time, hovering in the background. Every time you fought with me over some stupid point in my analysis, every time you did something exactly the opposite of what I'd told you and, especially when you followed my game plan, when you listened."

"You liked when I listened to you *and* when I didn't listen . . ." I say with a laugh, and a quick peck to her nose, ". . . so always?"

"Always," she says, and laughs too, a light, airy sound that makes something in my chest loosen. I hate what happened to her, but she's going to be okay.

"So, this isn't just because you're upset that you got fired and you need a distraction . . ."

"Charlie?"

"Yeah?"

"Shut up," she says, and kisses me again, bracing herself

against my shoulders and then leaping up into my arms, knowing, instinctively somehow, that I'd take her cue and catch her.

My hands wrap around her thighs, my thumbs landing in that clever little crease between them and her hipbones. I could spend a lifetime exploring the soft skin there, running my fingers over it, tracing it with my tongue, sucking a bruising kiss into it, in a place that only she'll see.

And suddenly I don't care why she wants this now. She wants me and that's enough.

I ignore the creaking protest of my knee as I turn back toward the house. We're too exposed out here. I make it through the slider, managing to close it behind me when the internal creak turns into a scream and I have to toss her away from me onto the bed as I collapse beside her onto the mattress with a huffing laugh.

"Are you okay?" she asks, leaning up on her hands to hover over me, the damp strands of her hair tickling my shoulders and chest.

"I'm good," I assure her, cupping the back of her head and drawing her down for a long, lingering kiss, just like I've always wanted to.

I nudge her bottom lip with the tip of my tongue and then she groans into my mouth while letting me deepen the kiss, the sound echoing down into me, setting my body alight and my hips softly thrusting up off the mattress into hers.

The bed shifts around me as she tosses a leg over mine and settles down against me, her legs on either side of my thighs, her ass sitting round and full and soft against where my dick is growing hard and hot encased in the cotton of my boxer briefs.

The towel falls away as she starts to set a rhythm, long and slow figure eights that have my hands gripping her hips, along for the ride with her. She pulls away from the kiss and sits up, her head thrown back as she keeps up the pace, giving me a view that even the long stretch of the Pacific Ocean can't match, the dips and curves and peaks of her body completely intoxicating

The light pink lace of her bra and the matching panties are still wet and dark against her pale skin and I run a hand up from her hip to slide my fingertips along the underside of it, before cupping the weight of her in my palm, while my other hand traces up her spine to the clasp.

Her eyes open as she looks back down at me and nods, pressing her chest deeper into my grip and running her hands up and down my chest before bracing herself there to get a better angle. My hips are rising to meet hers of their own volition when, with a twist of my fingers, the hooks are undone.

She laughs lightly, leaning down to nip gently at my lips. "It should probably annoy me that you can do that one handed."

"But it doesn't, does it?" I ask, already knowing the answer.

"Nope," she says, popping the "p" sound and then pressing a lingering kiss to the underside of my jaw and then to my neck while I gently lower the straps of her bra down to her elbows. She lingers there for a moment, her mouth working hard against my pulse point as I grow even harder against her stomach.

Finally, she sits up and lets me draw the lacy scrap of fabric from her body entirely, before tossing it away and rising up from beneath her to bury my face against the soft mounds tipped with dusky nipples, already rock hard and waiting for my mouth.

A quick circle of my tongue has her gasping and burying her hands into the back of my hair, urging me forward. I match the pressure of my mouth with my fingers at her other breast, taking my time, exploring the salty sweetness of her skin made even more so from the salt water from my pool. Her hips begin to collide against mine with more urgency, and when my teeth gently graze against her, her entire body gives a gentle shudder, a sweet, soft orgasm that has her breathing out a gentle moan against my ear.

She's so responsive to my touch, it's incredible, and seconds later as she recovers, she grins at me before pushing at my shoulders with one hand, another at my sternum before following it with her mouth, her tongue tracing the long line that leads to my bellybutton. It used to be a little bit firmer, a little more defined, but she doesn't seem to care as her fingers slip under the elastic of my boxer briefs and give them a little playful snap.

As if I'm going to say no her, crawling down my body, ass in the air while her soft cheek rests against my hips.

"You want to?" I ask.

With a smile and nod, she bites her lip and carefully pulls down the briefs as I spring free from the fabric confines, she reaches for me as I kick them off, training her manicured fingertips along the underside of it and I almost lose it then and there.

"Fuck," I rasp out, and she laughs. "You keep that up, this'll be over before we really get started," I warn.

"So, I can't touch you?" she challenges, with a small eye roll.

"You can, but first I want to touch you," I counter, and before she can answer back with that smart mouth of hers, I hook a leg around her and flip us over on the bed, pressing her deep into the mattress and holding her there with the weight of my body.

I'm not sure I thought this through, though, because as I land on top of her, into the cradle of her hips, my dick slides against the fabric of her panties, hot and damp and not just from the pool water.

"Remember what I said that night before Stew's call interrupted us?"

"Yes," she gasps, as I shift my weight and then grind against her.

"What did I say, Francesca?" I ask, flicking my thumbs over her nipples as I do.

"You said you," she manages, before letting out a little moan from the back of her throat at the contact, "you said you wanted to suck my clit until my thighs are shaking around your ears and my voice goes hoarse from screaming your name."

"An exact quote," I chuckle. "I'm impressed."

"Charlie, are you trying to give me a good grade in foreplay or are you gonna . . ." she trails off, more than a note of desperation in her voice.

I snort because, despite her protest, I know I've turned her on. I can feel it in the way her body is strung tight, arching against me.

"You can't scream, though, or you'll wake them," I say, flicking my head back toward my bedroom door. "You have to keep quiet. Can you do that?"

"Yes," she whispers, "for fuck's sake, Charlie, yes."

I shoot her one last grin before I bend to my work, hooking my thumbs up under the sides of her panties and, in one motion, yanking them down her legs, tossing them in the vague direction I sent her bra. Up on my knees, I stare down at her, my tongue flicking out against my bottom lip at how utterly gorgeous she is. I want to taste every inch of her, worship every rise and dip, every freckle and I want to do it for the rest of my life.

Shit. No time for that now, not when she's staring up at me, her eyes hot and desperate, her body laid out for me to explore.

Running my fingers down her legs, I raise one up before

leaning down to press a hot, open-mouthed kiss to the inside of her knee, feeling her body tremble just slightly at the contact. I inhale the scent of her, that salt sharper and tangier than before, after she came from just my mouth at her tits.

I burn a trail of kisses over the inside of her thigh, grinning against it at the soft keening noise she's clearly trying to suppress as I get closer and closer.

"Please, Charlie," she whispers on an exhale, and I give in, leading with my tongue to exactly where she wants me, to the sweet little bundle of nerve endings that I know will drive her mad, but in reality will be my own undoing.

My fingers join my mouth, my thumb exploring, finding her as hot and wet as the last time, as I hold her open gently while above, my lips and tongue work her over.

Her hips rise off the mattress and my free hand spreads across her lower belly, holding her in place, a fine sheen of sweat breaking out on her heated skin. Soft, muffled noises of mounting pleasure echo in my ears as her smooth thighs tighten around them, her body tensing and bowing until finally she's shaking again, a hand gripping my hair, her heels pressing into my shoulders, keeping me there while I ride out the waves with her.

I've had tens of thousands of people chanting my name, but it has never sounded sweeter than *feeling* her say it from between her thighs.

Her hold on me loosens as she finally sinks into a languorous stillness and I rise up to my knees, licking the evidence of her away as she watches me from beneath her lashes.

Fuck, she's gorgeous, her skin flushed, laid out this way over my sheets. I didn't think it was possible to be any more fucking turned on, until she smiles gently up at me and says: "I love you."

Chapter 19

FRANCESCA

How is it possible to feel this content when my life has gone to hell in the last few hours? Finally giving in to the tension that had been building for weeks, for years, if I'm really being honest with myself: it's even better than I imagined.

It doesn't fix what happened, not even close, but it's one hell of a consolation prize.

No. That's not right. He's not a consolation prize. He's everything I've ever wanted.

Which is how, in maybe one of the most intense post-orgasmic hazes of my life, three little words that I've only ever uttered to a handful of people slip out of my mouth.

"I love you."

The panic rises almost instantly, not just because I said it, but because I meant it, wholly and fully, without reservation.

I love him.

I *have* loved him, maybe for years, and now he knows.

And he's not saying anything.

He's just staring down at me, hair a riot from the absolute

vice of a grip I had on it just seconds ago when his mouth had sent me over the edge, just like everything else about him does, in all the best ways. Most of all, it's how much *belief* he seems to have in me. It's startling, every single time. And it doesn't feel possible.

"Frankie . . ." he begins, and then stops, his eyes meeting mine with a question in them, like he's not sure if I meant it or if I want to take it back or if maybe, just maybe, I'm terrified that he doesn't feel the same way. So, he lets us both off the hook. "My mother always told me never believe what a woman says after you make her come twice."

The tension eases and I can feel it as I leaves my body, though the sparks of pleasure from his efforts are still brushing up against my skin from within.

"Your mom was a wise woman."

"It wasn't actually my mom."

"Shocking. Was it Javy?"

He shrugs one shoulder in admission of the truth.

"Same thing, then," I tease, and love him even more because this is how it should be, an intoxicating mix of lust and friendship and knowing each other, maybe better than we know ourselves. That's love. That's what I want with him.

Charlie snorts and then falls down to the bed beside me and I roll over to rest my chin on his chest, looking up at him as his eyes fall shut, not in sleep, but in satisfaction, and when I press my lips to his skin and then trail a path down the center of his body to where his dick is still resting, hot and hard and leaking against his stomach, I watch him swallow roughly, clearly holding himself back, letting me take control.

When my hand finally circles around him, he lets out a wavering exhale and a soft, muffled groan.

Crawling down his body, I settle over one of his powerful

thighs, the muscle well built from years behind the plate and perfect against me as I lean over to run my tongue along the sharp cut of his abdomen down to the underside of his dick. He's thicker here than I imagined and my body clenches at the thought of him inside me, stretching me, filling me. My hips find a rhythm against his thigh as I lower my head to him with purpose now, a solid grip at his base as I finally take him into my mouth. I raise my eyes to his and watch him, watching me.

I've never felt more powerful than in this moment, with him at my mercy, the weight of him in my mouth, the salty tang of him on my tongue and the fire in his eyes as I slowly drive him to the same heights he brought me to.

"Fuck," he grinds out. "You're so fucking pretty like that."

And I punish him for it just a little bit with just the slightest nip of my teeth before I take him as fully as I can once more, losing eye contact as my hair falls over my face and my hips lose the rhythm I set before, wanting him to lose it, to come down my throat.

But before I can make that happen, his hand tangles into my hair, pulling me off him and meeting my mouth with his in a frenzy of lips and tongue and teeth. And when he releases me from the kiss, he dives straight for my neck, mumbling into the skin as his arms circle around me, pulling me closer, his dick trapped between us.

"I wanted—" I manage to gasp out.

"Later," he insists, his mouth now at my breasts again, giving both equal attention. "I need to fuck you. Do you want me, Francesca?"

"Yes," I whisper, pressing closer, my mouth at his ear. "Fuck me."

His hands span my ass, holding me to him as my hand

falls to his dick again, fingers trailing along it as he lets out a long hiss.

"Like this," I say, bracing myself on his shoulder with my free hand and he lifts me up with ease just so I can lower myself down onto him.

My mouth falls open as my body stretches to accommodate him, a sweet tinge of fullness as he slides in completely. And it's so, so good: my breasts against his chest, his thighs holding me up, my arms around him, his wide shoulders bracing me as his hands grasp at my hips while I grip him tightly inside.

"Jesus Fucking Christ," he growls out, and with a thrust of his hips, he pushes just a little bit deeper and at just the right angle so that I see stars.

We find a rhythm, slow and grinding, sweat-soaked skin sliding against each other and gasping moans filling the air, no longer concerned with being overheard, just lost to sheer sensation and the overwhelming rightness of finally being together this way.

"What do you need?" he asks, as I keep circling my peak, but then losing it.

"I . . . I don't . . ." I manage to stutter, for once in my life unable to find the right words.

"I've got you." And in one smooth motion that I'm too far gone to really understand, I'm beneath him, pressed into the mattress again, with him still inside me. He slides free and then reaches above my head for a pillow. "Lift up," he says, with a hand at my hip and I raise them just enough for him to slide the soft cushion under my ass.

"Like that?" he asks, a hand across my stomach pushing down just as he presses forward again.

"Yes. Oh God, Charlie, yes," I ramble, as he sets a punishing pace, his body hammering into mine and hitting just the right spot inside of me over and over again. It's so good my back arches up off the bed, my head thrown back, completely unconcerned with the scream that tears from my throat as my entire body convulses around his when his thumb finds my clit. I'm still so sensitive from his mouth and it's more than enough to launch me onto another plane of existence, my soul crashing up and out of my body as I take him with me to a place where it's just the two of us and this rapture, forever.

When I finally come back to myself, it's to the sound of gasping breaths, his and mine. He's collapsed, half on top of me, like his strength gave out when he came, but he had just enough judgment left to shift aside so he didn't crush me completely.

"Holy shit," he slurs, almost drunkenly, the words like kisses against the place where my neck and shoulder meet. "You're fucking incredible."

And my mind is still barely functional enough to manage, "My best friend always told me to never believe anything a man says after he comes inside you."

His body hitches with silent laughter. "You should, though."

"What?" I ask, half losing track of what we're talking about as a sweet aftershock slides through me.

"You should believe me," he murmurs, "because I love you."

Struggling to blink my eyes open, I shake my head. "You don't have to . . ."

"I do, though." His voice is suddenly firm and clear. "Look at me." And just like it has for the last hour, my body obeys his every command. My gaze meets his, warm and serious. "I love you. I think I've loved you for years, but I know I've loved you every damn day since I saw you climb into that car on a rainy morning at the airport."

His hand slips over my ass and down my thighs before tracing his fingertips back up over the curve of my waist and the underside of my breast before pressing into the center of my chest, right above my heart.

"I love you, Frankie Sullivan, and I'm sorry I had to tell you on the worst day of your life."

"It is, isn't it?" I ask, covering his hand with mine and holding it tight, warm and calloused and mine. "But things are looking up."

"Yeah?" he asks, somehow still unsure, and I hate that so much I can't let it stand.

"I love you. I said it and I meant it, and it might be the worst day of my life, but you're the one I want with me for the worst days and the best days and the exciting days and the boring days."

He makes a disbelieving sound in the back of his throat. "I know one thing – boring isn't something we have to worry about."

A laugh bubbles out of my throat and then another, which is joined by a chuckle from deep in his chest, and I love this too, laughing together: our bodies still stick with sweat, his come still staining my thighs and mine all over his mouth and jaw.

I nudge his hip and he takes his cue, just like he has every other one tonight, and lifts up so I can slide out from beneath him to go use the bathroom. We didn't use a condom and, even though I have an IUD, that's pretty irresponsible of me and, without the warm weight of his body and his breath against my skin, it's easier to remember that.

I stop at the doorway to his bathroom and turn, bracing my hip against it, catching him watching me, propped on his side, his hand holding up his head.

"Protection next time," I say, simply, "and we're both getting tested when we get back to New York."

"My last one was clean," he assures me.

"Mine too, and I have an IUD, but it's still a good idea, for the both of us."

"No problem," he says, smiling, and it's all I can do to turn back around and close the bathroom door behind me, because if I run back into that bed, I won't be getting out of it again for hours.

He knocks on the door just after I flush the toilet and start washing my hands.

"Come in," I say, and then add, "also I'm not into the *pee in front of each other* kind of relationship."

"Me neither," he agrees quickly, "but I was thinking."

"Always dangerous," I say, as he comes up behind me and wraps his arms around my waist and I dry my hands on the towel next to the sink before looking up at us in the mirror.

Holy shit. My thoughts echo his words from a few minutes ago as I watch his reflection bury his face into my hair and breathe in while his hands slide around to cup my breasts.

"Shower?" he murmurs, as one hand skips over my belly to between my legs.

I don't respond, just stop his hand and lace my fingers between his and squeeze, wishing I could freeze this moment and just live in it until I'm ready to face the world again. Maybe a few months will do the trick.

"Shower," I agree, and slip from his grasp to turn to the massive glass-encased shower behind us.

There are so many knobs and handles that I don't even know where to start. All of my toiletries are back in my bedroom, and I'm *not* leaving this little world we've managed to escape to just so I can smell like lavender. Though for a half a minute, when

I eye the three-in-one shampoo, conditioner and body wash in the corner, I *almost* change my mind.

He convinces me to stay, though, holding me back against his chest as his fingers slide between my legs.

I let out a soft hiss at the contact on the sensitive skin.

"Too much?" he asks, lifting his hand away gently.

Humming a yes, I spin in his arms and trace the patterns of his chest hair, flat and dark, pasted against his skin by the steams of water, as his large hands span my back and then slide down to squeeze my ass gently.

"There's something I want instead," I say, one hand slipping lower to wrap around him, already semi-hard again and his groan rumbles out of his chest, nearly drowned out by the water still spraying behind me.

Leaning in, I press an open-mouthed kiss to his sternum and then trail down a line of matching kisses to his navel, dropping lower and lower as I do, falling into a squat not unlike what we both used to do behind the plate. Then I lift my eyes to him, my cheek against his thigh. His jaw is clenched, the tendons of his neck straining as one hand lifts to brush the backs of his fingers against my cheek. That gentleness in him that always seems to reveal itself at the most unexpected moments is one of the things I love most about him.

"Yours knees," he protests.

"As we've discussed, *I* didn't spend twenty years in the majors," I tease lightly, running my fingers along the underside of him, his arousal growing by the second.

That's the only protest he's able to manage and he gives himself over to me. He's large in my mouth, a satisfying weight there, salty and slick as his hand settles onto the back of my head, wrapping my hair around his fist. Looking up at him, eyes wide, I wait and his expression flickers in surprise understanding.

Slowly, he uses those powerful forearms I've always admired to guide me ever so gently, my mouth taking him deep while I relax my throat against the intrusion, feeling myself clench tightly between my legs, my body wanting more of him, despite how tender it is. He only stops when I give a gentle tap to his calf, taking his cue perfectly as he pulls back. There's a hypnotic rhythm to it, one that lets me study him carefully as he drives himself mad using my mouth, the strain in his body to keep himself under control, the way his muscles ripple with the motion and the way his skin glows against the steamy air, rivulets of water finding paths I intend to memorize.

He finishes, calling my name, and it echoes over the steady beat of the water against the tile and I taste him on my tongue, salty and bitter, but worth it to watch his head throw back in complete surrender to it.

And when I finally let him fall free, his arms immediately wind around me, pulling me into his chest in an embrace that somehow feels more intimate than anything else that's passed between us in the last little while, even the words "I love you". Holding each other under the water for I don't even know how long before we both clean up and rinse off without a word exchanged between us.

His towels are soft and massive, thankfully, because it hits me then that I don't have any clothes, just my bra and underwear, which are probably still soaking wet from the pool.

"You need something to sleep in?" he asks, though he knows the answer.

"Just a t-shirt will do."

"Ah, so you can add to your collection? You never gave back the last two."

"And I never will."

"Good," he says, and obviously we're talking about a t-shirt and *not* talking about a t-shirt at all.

I have no idea what I'm going to do next, but at least I know that.

I barely remember collapsing back into his bed, curled up into him with his thighs lining mine, one of his arms carelessly tossed over my hip and another cupping my breast beneath his Los Angeles Dodgers National League Champions t-shirt from three years ago (that I will definitely be keeping, as I never actually got one that night).

That's how I wake up, though, sun already pouring through the skylights, with Javy pounding on the bedroom door. "If you two are done fucking each other's brains out, Stew has been trying to call both of you for hours!"

Charlie groans into my hair and then blindly reaches out toward his bedside table to grab his phone.

He holds it out so I can see it too, a dozen missed calls from our . . . no, his, boss.

"Are we calling him back?"

"It's Stew," I say, already way more awake, sitting up fully and leaning against the headboard while he makes the call, putting it on speaker.

Stew picks up in two rings.

"Nice of you to answer your fucking phone, meat," Stew says, using an old nickname for rookies in baseball.

"Sorry, Skip," Charlie says, immediately and sincerely apologetic. "I've got Frankie here with me on speaker. What's up?"

"It's a fucking shitstorm is what's up. Frankie, we're going to fix this."

"I appreciate that, Stew, but Hannah Vinch seemed pretty clear about . . ."

"Things have changed or are about to. I've got some feelers out there and there's nothing official yet, but I just need you to hold tight, okay? Get yourselves back here and we'll figure this thing out."

He sounds good, way better than the last time I spoke to him, invigorated and lively and tough, just like he's always been.

"Okay," I agree. If trying to get me my job back is gonna make Stew feel better, who the hell am I to argue with the old man?

Charlie ends the call and then looks at me, seriously. "You think he can pull this off?"

"No," I say, with a half shrug and a smile to match. "But if he wants to be a pain in Hannah Vinch's ass, I'm all for it."

"Alright then, back to Brooklyn it is."

I don't even try to look ashamed of myself as I step out of Charlie's bedroom, his t-shirt hanging down to my knees, my hair in long damp locks down my back and a challenging glare aimed at Javy and Gregory, neither of whom look up from packing up their stuff, thus ruining the effect entirely.

Back in my room, there are also a dozen or more missed called from Stew, but also one that I absolutely cannot believe is there.

Elliott Forbes.

Vice President and General Manager of the New York Yankees.

And not just a missed call, but a follow up text.

Call me back when you get this. – EF

I don't know him that well personally, but well enough to have his number in my phone. Not really to use, just to have. He's been a stalwart of Yankees baseball for as long as I can remember, worked for the organization since college, an early adopter of analytics-based scouting and team building, but old school, hence signing his text messages. The curiosity is too much for me and I call him back.

"Ms Sullivan!" he says, in that booming voice he's famous for. "I hear you might be looking for a job?"

"News travels fast," I say. "I haven't even had an exit interview yet."

He snorts heavily, a man who, by reputation, probably doesn't quite believe in extremely standard Human Resources practices. To be fair, when it's the New York Yankees, they probably don't much care.

"What can I do for you, Mr Forbes?"

"Elliott," he insists, but then pushes forward. "I have an opening here that I think you'd be perfect for."

Ah. Right. One of his Assistant GMs, also their analytics department head, just got hired by the Mariners for their top job and he probably wants me to step in.

It's flattering.

"You want me to come in an interview for Caleb Rivera's job?"

"No, Frankie. I want you to come in and interview for *my* job, and then after we interview a couple of more guys for appearance's sake, I want you to take it."

Chapter 20

CHARLIE

It feels too good to be true.

I love her. She loves me.

And we live happily ever after, right?

Isn't that how it works?

Is the charmed life I've lived up until now about to somehow get even better?

That's what it feels like as we fly back across the country, sitting side by side in the massive seats on the Eagles' private jet (which she nearly refused to get on and I had to call Stew, interrupting him in the middle of his quest to get her un-fired, from the tarmac to insist she hitch a ride back with us).

She's got her laptop open, scrolling through some documentation she has on the current Yankees roster with one hand and the other is firmly in mine.

We're probably over Kansas or Missouri when her fingers squeeze, tightly and not that affectionately.

"What's up?" I ask, leaning into her a bit.

She points to a message on her screen from an unknown number with a +81 at the beginning.

A Japanese number.

—*Daniel Wilson is no longer my agent. I will be in touch soon.*

Kai Nakamura. It has to be.

I knew that kid was special. He saw through Wilson and fired his ass before they even inked a deal. It takes guts. It takes balls. And that's the kind of player I want playing for me for the next dozen years.

"It worked," she whispers. "The plan, taking him to the game, introducing him to the boys. It . . . fucking worked. I knew it."

Lifting our joined hands to my mouth, I press hard there in place of what I really want to do, pull her out of her seat and into my lap and kiss her until she's breathless from it and – if it were just the two of us in this cabin – join the mile high club right here in my seat.

But we've traumatized poor Javy and Gregory enough for one day.

She's still staring at the screen, expressionless, until she laughs.

"What?" I ask, confused, and she turns to me, laughing so hard that tears start to form at the corners of her eye.

"I managed," she says, inhaling and trying to fit her words in around her laughter, "I managed to nail the top free agent in the last five years and get fired in the process, only to get a job with the cross-town rivals. We'll probably have to face him in the World Series in October. God, baseball is always so incredible, even off the field."

I think back to Stew, waiting for us in Brooklyn, probably jumping through a shit ton of hoops to get in front of Hannah

Vinch today after she axed Frankie, to try and make it right. I know my old manager. I know what he's capable of. And I know it won't be long until the news that Nakamura fired the top agent in the game is everywhere.

And the thought pops into my head and then out of my mouth before I can stop it.

"What if you didn't leave?"

"What?" she asks, brow furrowed. It hadn't occurred to her, at least not yet. And I'd be thrilled to be ahead of that incredible mind of hers just once, if it didn't mean what I think it means. It didn't occur to her because, as far as she's concerned, she's already gone.

And why not? After the way Vinch treated her. Of course she wouldn't really consider coming back, not when she has another option and that option is actually a major step up from where she is right now.

But it's too late. I can't take the words back, so I double down.

"Stew's going to talk ownership around, especially now that Nakamura is probably headed to Brooklyn. What if you stayed with . . . us."

Not us, me. Stay with me.

She knows that's what I'm saying.

Stay with me. Win a championship with me. Marry me.

All of those things. Together.

"I . . ."

"Did you guys see this?" Gregory cuts in, from the other side of the cabin. "Nakamura fired Dan Wilson this morning. It's everywhere, beat writers had it first, but now it's confirmed out of Nakamura's camp, from his old team, the Yomiuri Giants. They say that he still firmly wishes to sign with a major league team and that there will be an update on his decision in the coming days as the prospective teams send in their final offers."

Frankie doesn't say anything about the text she got. And neither do I.

Which leaves Javy and Gregory to speculate on where they think Nakamura might end up.

But she knows.

And it might change everything.

There's nothing to do but wait. We land in Teterboro, get in the cars and head back home. Javy and I in one car back to his house to drop off our stuff, Frankie and Gregory in another.

Javy's texting Maria that we're on our way when I blurt it out.

"I told her I love her."

He drops the phone and, by the time he's managed to fish it up, I take control back over my own freaking mouth.

"Well, that's good, right? Especially after all the shit I had to listen to last night. Fucking like a couple of kids who can't keep their hands off each other or their voices down." He mutters something else in Spanish that I *almost* understand, but choose not to think too hard about. "Did she say it back?"

"She said it first."

"Knew she had bigger balls than you."

"No argument here."

"So, what's the problem? This is good, right?"

"It is. It's good."

Javy lets out a low whistle. "Even better. Same city, though you might want to split the difference, live in maybe Upper West Side or some shit."

"Man, real estate? Really?"

"Yeah, sorry. So what's the problem? Is it just that you're

a fucking greedy bastard and you want her near you all the damn time and fuck the Yankees?"

"Yeah, exactly. Fuck the Yankees."

"You gotta let it go, brother."

"It's more than that, though."

"What?"

"She's got a thing about being with a guy in baseball and, when she got fired, that's when . . ."

"So you think she won't want . . ."

"I don't know, I'm actually kind of afraid to ask, and she hasn't said anything."

"Shit," Javy mutters. "What are you gonna do?"

"I can't stand in her way. This is the only thing she's ever wanted. I'm gonna . . . I'm gonna head over there and tell her that. That she should take the job and it'll . . . it'll be fine."

Javy clicks his tongue. "I'm sorry, man."

"Yeah, me too."

The driver takes Javy home first and then drops me off at Frankie's place.

I buzz her a few times. She should have beaten us here, until it hits me. She wouldn't have gone home. She'd have gone to the Stadium, to clear out her office, because . . . because she's done and it was fucking unfair as all hell for me to ask her to not be.

I jog back down the steps of the brownstone and nearly run into a guy turning into them.

"Sorry," I say, shifting around him.

"Hey, aren't you . . . Charles . . . Charles Avery?"

"Yeah, that's me."

"Shane Sullivan," he says, with meaning, and holding out his hand like I'm supposed to know who the hell he is.

"Have we met?"

"No, no, but you used to work with my wife. Francesca Sullivan."

"Ex-wife," I correct, instantly. This is the dickhead that followed her across the fucking country and moved in downstairs like that wasn't fucking insane.

"Yeah, obviously," he says. "What are you doing here?"

"Frankie and I are working together again."

"That's right." I'll give him this, he plays dumb very, very well. Too well. "You took the Eagles manager job. Good for you. I was always a big fan when you were in LA, but maybe I should root for the Eagles now."

"What?" I snap, trying to keep the voice in my head that's bellowing for me to just knock this guy into next week under control.

"I said maybe I should root for the Eagles now. You know, living in Brooklyn it just makes sense."

"You're a Dodgers fan, though."

"Well, yeah, but . . . "

"You don't just do that."

"Do what?"

"Switch alliances. You're a Dodgers fan. That's who you cheer for. You don't just fucking decide one day to root for another team because it's convenient."

"*You* switched teams."

"It's my job, that's what I do. You're just a fucking scumbag who can't be trusted to honor a promise he made."

"Listen, I don't know what Frankie told you . . ."

"Save it, shithead. Don't root for the Eagles. Or the Dodgers. Baseball doesn't fucking want you and neither does Frankie."

And with that I know exactly what I need to do, and it might not make everything right, but it'll be a decent start.

*

A few phone calls and a couple of hours later, with my plan set into action, I head for the only place I think she could be: Russell Field.

Gregory's camped out at his desk, as usual, and he sends me back with a flick of his head and pleading eyes. I'm not sure if he wants me to talk her into staying or if he just desperately hopes I don't intend on defiling her office while he has to listen.

She's not at her desk but standing up staring out the windows onto the field, but once I move to stand beside her, I'm not sure she's even seeing it.

"They don't have views like this from their offices in the Bronx."

A soft huff of a laugh answers me, but not much else. Glancing around, her office doesn't look any different. Nothing is packed, the desk is organized with her laptop there, open and waiting for her, the phone beside it. No boxes or storage containers. She's even dressed for work, in one of her pencil skirts with a long-sleeved blouse tucked into it, not the jeans and t-shirt that someone would probably wear to clear out their office.

"Is this what you've been doing all day?" I ask, tentatively.

"No, I . . ." she trails off and finally turns to me.

"Did you go to the stadium?"

And the way I say it, she knows the difference. Lots of teams have stadiums, including this one, but when you're in New York and you say, *the stadium*, you mean the big ballpark in the Bronx.

"I did. I didn't want to give Forbes a chance to change his mind. I went there and we had a good long talk and he offered me the job."

"And did you take it?" I ask, trying desperately to keep my

voice neutral. Her little smirk is enough for me to know that I didn't succeed.

"Not yet."

"Not yet?"

"I wanted to talk you about it first."

"Frankie, I . . . I don't expect you to . . ."

"I know, I know you don't, but this is how I operate. I'm in your life now and you're in mine, right?"

I hesitate and open my mouth, but no words come out.

"Is that . . . not what you want?" she asks, her voice small, and that jolts me into action.

"Absolutely not. I just thought . . ." I trail off, not able to form the words.

"What?"

"I thought you might not want this anymore."

"Charlie?" she says, "No, no way. We're together. I'd call you my boyfriend, but it feels like the wrong word for a guy pushing forty."

I roll my eyes at the jab at my age, but reach out to take her hands as I say, "You can call me whatever the hell you want, but, yeah, we are together."

"So, if that's the case," she says, looking up into my eyes, "then when big life things happen, big decisions and choices, then I want to talk to you about it beforehand."

"You should take the job."

"Charlie . . ."

I release her hands, but only to raise mine to her face, cupping her cheeks softly, my thumbs brushing against the soft skin. "It's everything you've worked for. You earned this and more than that. You had to work twice as hard and do it in heels. Take the job *and* be with me."

She leans into the touch with a little sigh of relief.

"But on the plane you said . . ."

"I was being an idiot, a sentimental, selfish idiot."

"Hey, that sentimental, selfish idiot happens to be my boyfriend."

"I thought I was too old to be called boyfriend?"

"Man-friend?" she says, and then immediately screws up her face in disgust. "God, no, that sounds like someone your divorced grandma brings around. Significant other? Partner?"

Husband.

I don't say it aloud. It's way too soon. Way too fast.

Though . . . if the time in LA counts . . . it doesn't, though. It can't, but that's where I'm headed, if I can make sure not to screw this up. I never thought I'd get married again. Never thought I'd want to, but the only thing I want more than a World Series ring is one she'll slide onto my finger one day.

"*Amor.* Lover."

She's still going with the labels, but finally I cut her off by leaning in and smothering whatever ridiculous suggestion that was coming next with a kiss.

One thing I love about her is that she gives as good as she gets. When we used to go at it over a scouting report, she used to use her mouth to twist me into knots and she still does that now, only it's a lot more fun when she dips her tongue into my mouth and yanks me to her by my shirt, backing up as she goes until her thighs hit the edge of her desk.

Another thing I love about her is the cues she gives me and, with just a quick nudge of her hips against mine, I know she wants me to lift her onto the desk. So I do, palming her ass, the memory of that soft skin grinding against my thighs back in my bed firing through me as she raises one leg to hook around my knee to draw me between her legs.

"Can you be quick?" she asks, trailing her mouth from against my ear to the underside of my jaw.

"Here?" I choke out, trying to think clearly even when her tongue traces the line of my neck and her hands slip under the hem of my t-shirt. Glancing to the door, I just know Gregory has his earbuds in place with the music cranked up as loud as it can go. "Really?"

She pulls back and bites her lip, so I reach up to caress her cheek with my thumb and then gently brush it against her mouth to make her release it. It's so rare to see her unsure, that I step in.

"C'mon, I have a better idea."

"Better than fucking me on my desk? I *know* you thought about it back in the day."

"You did?"

"Well not then, but thinking back, I know it now. You used to get that look in your eye."

"What look?" I ask, curious. No one's ever said that to me before.

"The one you're wearing right now. Brow furrowed just a little, mouth set and your jaw twitching." She trails her fingers softly against it again, sending a shiver through my entire body at just the barest touch and my dick jumps against the fly of my jeans. It would be so easy to just hike up her skirt and take her right here, staring out at the baseball field where I thought our dreams were going to come true.

But that dream feels like it's dying.

Still, a new one can take its place.

"I mean it, I know a place we can go that's way better than this. C'mon."

I reach out a hand to her and she takes it, no hesitation at all.

We leave the office hand in hand and Gregory seems

incredibly relieved as he pops out his earbuds and sends us off with a wave before refocusing determinedly on his computer screen.

"So, where are we going?" she asks. "Oh, wait, did the realtor find you a place?"

"Something like that," I admit. "I want your opinion. Your honest opinion, and if you hate it, I need you to tell me, okay?"

"I mean, I can't imagine that I'm going to hate it, but sure, I promise, my honest opinion."

The neighborhood is even more bustling than usual, given that it's the weekend and the weather is still clear, though the chill in the air is crisper than it was a couple of weeks ago.

Shit, my life has changed so much since then, I can barely remember what it was like.

Single. Living in LA. Retired.

Lonely. Isolated. Adrift.

"Wait, we're walking. Is it right around here?" she asks, when I lead her down Ocean Avenue, the park on our left, the rest of Brooklyn stretching out to our right.

"It's just up ahead," I say, nodding down a side street that's extremely familiar to her and she goes completely quiet the further along we go, until finally I stop at our destination.

"Charlie?" she asks, unsure. Maybe she doesn't quite know what question to ask is and I get it, it's confusing.

The brownstone we're standing outside of on this tree-lined block, a calm retreat in the middle of a bustling city, is hers. At least the second and third floor are.

And now the bottom two floors are mine.

"Let me explain?" I say, worried that maybe it was too much.

"Yeah, that's . . . that's a good idea."

I take a deep breath and then let it all out in a flurry of words. "I know you're the kind of woman that solves her own problems and doesn't need a man to handle things, but this was the one thing I knew I could do. I could get that dipshit out of your life. I bought the bottom unit. Offered him double what he paid if he would get out today. I put them up at a hotel in Manhattan, a whole borough away."

"You're learning the lingo," is all she says, at my casual use of the word *borough*, but nothing else. And I can't read her expression. It's entirely neutral.

"Yeah, well, I plan on sticking around for a while," I say, rubbing at the back of my head. "I don't have to live here. I can sell it again or even sell it to you, if you want. I think you're probably about to get a pretty decent raise."

So, I've explained and now the only thing I can do is wait.

I'm getting really good at that.

Chapter 21

FRANCESCA

No one has ever done anything like this for me before.

I've never wanted them to. My whole life *I've* been the one to solve my own problems and, to be honest, everyone else's. It's what I'm good at.

I should maybe be feeling a little annoyed. Maybe more than a little. Especially after that speech I gave him about us being together and making big life choices together, but I don't have it in me to be anything other than relived and grateful and, yeah, maybe a little bit turned on by it.

There's something extremely hot about a man who sees a problem and fixes it, without any waffling or handholding or without expecting to be crowned master of the universe for it.

In fact, Charlie seems to realize that, generally, doing stuff like this all the time would be a bad idea.

That's even hotter: a guy who knows exactly when it's time to get things done.

This is definitely one of those times.

I've been silent for too long.

He's rubbing at the back of his head and rocking on his heels and with his bottom lip caught between his teeth, he looks genuinely nervous. It's kind of extra hot, honestly.

Finally, I manage to come up with something to say.

"We don't have to decide right now, but I need you to know that this is the nicest thing anyone has ever done for me."

His shoulders sag with absolute sheer relief.

"Really?"

I push up to my tiptoes and brush a kiss against his cheek. "Really," I whisper, barely getting the word out before he turns his head and catches my mouth with his.

"You're completely insane, you know that, right?" I say, when I pull away gasping for air.

"Yeah, I know," he admits, and then I grab his hand and lead him toward the front steps and through the front door.

It's awkward, trying to run up the stairs to the second floor holding his hand and, halfway up, he gives up, braces himself against the wall and swings me up into his arms. I let out a little shriek at the sudden weightlessness and the momentary spark of fear that we're about to go tumbling back down the steps, but then he shifts my weight against his chest and we're moving again, up to my door, where he reluctantly lets me down so I can unlock it.

"It would have been cooler to carry you in," he mutters from behind me, his arms twining around me as I try to maintain enough focus to actually get the key into the lock. It's hard with his mouth pressing hot, wet kisses down the line of my neck while his fingers untuck my blouse from the waist of my skirt, darting beneath it and rising to cup my breasts, gently weighing them in his hands.

With a shuddering breath, I manage to slide the key into the stupid lock, twist it and the doorknob in one motion and then stumble into my apartment with him at my back. The door slams shut behind us and I drop my bag and my keys to the floor as he spins us around and pins me against it, his mouth immediately finding mine while his hands grip my thighs and lift me, my legs tightening around his waist as one shoe falls off and the other dangles on my toes until I kick it away. He slides my skirt up over my thighs, but the bottom isn't wide enough to push up over my hips and he growls at the delay.

Using his body to brace me against the hard surface and while his mouth sucks gently at my neck, his fingers find the zipper to my skirt before he deftly slides it down and sets me on my feet to allow it to fall the rest of the way.

"Fuck," he bites out, tossing the skirt away while I slide out of the suit jacket and then go to work on the buttons at the front of my shirt.

Why the hell did I pick a blouse with so many buttons this morning?

After I undo the first few, he grows impatient and lifts it over my head, sending it to join my skirt.

"Bed?" I suggest, but he shakes his head.

"No way," he mutters, and drops to his knees. My panties go the way of my other clothes and then he's running a hand along the back of my thigh and then along the inside of my knee, and I let out a light giggle. Charlie lifts my leg over his shoulder and repeats the action, drawing more laughter, clearly intrigued at finding a ticklish place, but not wanting to be diverted from his goal just now.

"It's my only spot," I insist, and he snorts his disbelief, but allows it, pressing a kiss there.

"Hold on," he instructs, and I do, a hand in his hair, the other at his shoulder as his mouth trails a hot path up the inside of one thigh and then, skipping where I want him the most, licks a slow stripe up my lower abdomen to my belly button.

"Don't tease," I ask, just this side of begging.

And then he doesn't. His mouth and his hands are everywhere, fingers filling me – though not nearly enough now that I know what it's like to have him inside of me – his mouth at my clit, my thighs closing around his ears, just the way he likes it. My fingers twist in his hair at the incredible sensations firing through my body so fast it feels like being a teenager again, when every touch is new and heightened and so intense you think you might explode into little bits of nothing before it's all over.

My heel finds the space between his shoulder blades as he works me through the arching release of my body, holding him there until they finally begin to subside.

And when my brain starts working again after luxuriating in pure sensation, I manage to say, "If that baseball thing didn't work out, you could have done this professionally."

He tilts his head in adorable confusion. "That's a compliment, right?"

"Yeah, I think so," I answer, still not entirely sure that, if he lets me go, my legs will be able to hold me up.

"Good," he says, wiping at his face with his thumb before sucking the mess he made away.

"I don't think I can stand," I admit, when he starts to shift back.

"I'm not sure I can either," he says, sitting back on his haunches as my leg slips off his shoulder to the floor.

"We're a complete mess."

"We are."

"Okay, let me just," I test the strength of my legs and they seem okay, if a little more unsteady than normal. I brace myself on his shoulders and he lets out a hiss. The wood floor must be doing a number on his knee. I manage standing on my own and then lean back a bit against the wall, offering him my hand to help him up.

He manages it without falling over, but he's clearly in pain.

"You need surgery."

"Yeah," he agrees.

"We'll go to the doctor after Thanksgiving. Get it scheduled."

"Yeah," he says, without protest, which must mean he's in way more pain than I assumed.

"Good." I reach up to brush the hair out of his face and my smug smile fades at the heat still in his eyes.

"Please tell me my fucking knee didn't ruin the mood,"

"It didn't."

"Thank God, because I'm still as hard as a rock and I fucking need to be inside of you."

"Come on," I say, taking his hand and leading him just a few more steps into my bedroom. I give him a gentle shove down to sit at the edge of the bed and then stand in front of him as I undo my bra while he looks up at me from beneath his lashes. "God, you're gorgeous."

His mouth lifts at the corner into a mischievous smile. "Is that why you had my poster on your wall?"

I give him that one. "That's exactly why." Lifting his t-shirt up over his head, I send it to the corner of my bedroom while he presses kisses into my stomach and the underside of my breasts and then it's my turn to fall to my knees, undoing the fly of his jeans and taking them and his boxer briefs off in one long motion after he kicks off his shoes and socks.

He clearly doesn't want to test his knee, so after I retrieve a condom that I'm pretty sure hasn't expired from my nightstand drawer and slide it onto him while he watches slack jawed, I simply climb into his lap and allow him to press up into me, my body more than ready for him, but still reveling in the sweet stretch of having him inside of me.

"So good," he grits out when my ass hits his thighs and his palms span across me, guiding my body into a grinding rhythm, and it doesn't take long until my eyes fall shut and my mouth falls open while every twist of his hips creates the perfect friction against my clit and he presses up inside me, hitting just the right spot.

"Yes, right there," I manage, between the gasps emanating from the back of my throat, getting close again so quickly after his complete undoing of me against the door.

Then, his hips start to thrust up off the bed and I hold on for dear life as he finds the strength to push up off the mattress and deposit me back on it, leaving me on my hands and knees, ass in the air and when I look back over my shoulder at him he lets out a noise from deep inside that makes my entire body clench in anticipation.

"Your knee," I protest, but weakly.

"Fuck my knee," he dismisses, and then he's filling me from behind, while he presses down at the center of my back, the other around to find my clit again and as he pounds into me, hard and fast, a punishing rhythm, and that's when white hot energy crackles through every part of me, exploding behind my eyes and at my core, my hips mindlessly thrusting back into his while I collapse down into the mattress, only for him to flow, his thrusts suddenly uneven and short until he gives over to it entirely and we land together, a sticky, gasping heap of exhausted pleasure.

When I finally come back to myself, I'm still catching my breath with the soft cotton of my sheets sticking to my sweat slicked skin. I don't remember rolling to my back, but I must have, and Charlie's arm is thrown carelessly over my waist, his face half buried in the pillow and half into my shoulder. I glide my fingertips up and down the sinew of his forearm as our breathing syncs and then slows, both of us drifting into a doze.

But then my phone vibrates from my bag, across the room, where, somewhere in our mad dash to my bed, I dropped it on the floor.

"Don't answer it," he murmurs, his words like a kiss against my skin. "Rest."

"If it's going off it's because it's someone important."

The vibration stops for a moment and then another before picking up again.

Charlie groans as I slide out from under his arm and he buries his head more completely into the pillow. Though, when I stand to walk away, he lets out a chuckle. "Never mind, stay just like that. I like this view very much."

I'm already too far away from the bed to throw a pillow at him, so instead I just wiggle my hips, shaking my ass back at him and grinning at his bark of laughter.

This is how it's going to be and I love it.

I'll take the job with the Yankees. He'll manage the Eagles. We'll live here in this house and we'll build a life. It'll be different than what we originally planned, but at least we'll be together. And no one will bat an eyelash at our relationship.

Because that's what it is now, a relationship.

I love that man. More than I even thought I'd let myself love anyone ever again. I had my career and for a long time and I thought that was enough. And it would have been, if he hadn't come back into my life. And now I can't imagine a day without him in it.

My phone has stopped vibrating by the time I find it, bending over just right while I dig through my bag to give him a view that elicits a tortured groan.

There are two missed calls, but from different numbers.

The first was Stew.

The second was that Japanese number that I saved into my contacts as KN.

And while my phone is in my head, a text pops up from KN.

I am told you are not with the Eagles. Please update?

Here we go.

I call Stew back first as Charlie slides from my bed into the bathroom to dispose of the condom and, before I can really appreciate that view, Stew picks up and skips the pleasantries. "You are a royal pain in my ass, you know that? Did you take the job with the pinstripes?"

"Not yet."

"Yet. So you're going to take it."

"It's not like I have another option."

"You do," he insists. "Or you will in about an hour. Someone leaked to Nakamura that Vinch let you go. His new agent called today to start negotiations on some of the finer points of our offer and, when you weren't around to take his call, they freaked out. Ownership is in an emergency meeting. If you get down here now, I think we can spin this into something special."

Charlie's pulling his clothes back on, but he looks entirely like he just rolled out of bed after fucking someone within an inch of her life. Accurate, but not the best look for work, and when I catch a glance at my reflection in the mirror in the corner of my bedroom, I'm not much better.

"I'll hear them out," I say, finally. "I'll be there in a half hour. Charlie's on his way too."

"And how *exactly* do you know that, young lady?"

"I'm hanging up now," I say, and end the call, cutting off his laughter.

"What's up?" Charlie says, handing me a robe he found hanging on the back of my bedroom door. I slip it on as he turns to find his shirt, now a crumpled lump of cotton lying across the other side of the room.

"Nakamura found out they let me go. It's a mess. Stew wants me to come back to the office. I think they're going to offer me my job back."

"Oh," he says simply, and I can practically see the wheels turning in his head, like he used to look when his pitcher was struggling and he needed to figure out a solution to get him through the rest of his start.

"I'll hear them out," I say, with a shrug that sends one side of the robe slipping down my arm.

Charlie reaches out to right it, his fingers lingering against my neck for a moment and then another. "What do you need from me?"

"Go there and stall? I can't show up looking like this."

"You look great."

"I look . . . ravished."

He snorts and then nods in agreement. "Exactly."

"I need to shower, at least."

"Okay," he says, and then leans down to press a soft kiss to my cheek and then to my lips. "I got you."

"I know you do."

One more kiss, this one a little more lingering and bit more handsy, and he's out the door.

I forgot how good it feels to be wanted like this. To be needed.

But now I've got to focus.

Clothes.

My closet is full of options. Most of my clothes are for work, but when I catch a glimpse of a navy-blue pinstriped skirt, the choice is made for me. If I'm going in there, they're going to be reminded of exactly what they're up against the entire time.

A shower, cold to really make sure I'm fully awake, and a quick blow-dry to my hair, twisting it up into a bun and then, after staring at myself in the mirror for longer than I normally do, letting it down again.

A different look because they need to know they're dealing with a different woman today than they were yesterday.

My heels that were left carelessly by the door when we crashed through it slide into place, nude patent leather, with the white and navy pinstriped skirt, a stark white camisole and the matching suit jacket and I'm good to go.

Walking down the stairs of my building, I glance at the door to the apartment beneath mine, the apartment that no longer houses my ex and his family, and I wonder if the co-op board will let us make the house into one single unit. If not, maybe we move until we find something big enough for two.

But that's a problem for another day.

There's a car waiting for me when I step outside and I grin at Vladimir, who smiles back, wide and toothy. I haven't seen him since that day at the airport.

"It's only a couple of blocks," I protest, while he holds the door open.

"Mr Avery insisted," he says, after I slide into the backseat, before closing the car door behind me and jogging around to the driver's side so we can get going.

Of course he did.

Is this what it's like to be loved by a man like him? Not coddled or managed, but taken care of, just because he can.

I can't even try to pretend like it doesn't feel amazing.

I love him. He loves me.

And now, whatever lies ahead, we'll face it together.

Chapter 22

FRANCESCA

When we pull up in front of Russell Field, he's waiting at the staff entrance, t-shirt still a wrinkled mess, his jeans slung low on his hips, the autumn wind tousling his hair when he steps out of the stadium's shadow to meet me.

I thank Vlad and watch him toss Charlie a little salute before he drives away.

"They're all there," Charlie says, shoving his hands into his pockets as he falls in beside me, matching my stride with his as security lets us through the entrance. "The entire owner-ship board and Hannah Vinch. Stew's up there with them now, trying to find a solution."

"The solution was not firing me in the first place just because Dan Wilson is a little bitch."

"That's the gist of Stew's pitch."

"They can't undo it."

"No, they can't," he agrees, simply.

"So, I listen to what they have to say and we go from there."

His eyes twinkle at me as we wait for the elevator and, when the doors open, Gregory is there.

Stew's assistant – turned my assistant – looks me up and down carefully and then nods, like he was afraid I was going to show up as raggedy-looking as Charlie.

Charlie's hand falls from the small of my back; the comforting weight had been there since I arrived and I hadn't noticed, but the loss of it, the sudden emptiness, that makes me stop.

"You're not coming?" I ask, as Gregory holds the elevator. He's taken a step back from me.

"Nah, they know where I stand and this is your show. Go do your thing. You got this."

With a final nod, I step into the elevator and Gregory straightens his shoulders before pressing the button for the top floor. We ride in silence for a few seconds before he spins in place. He blinks at me and clocks the pinstripes in my outfit, maybe for the first time, and then he grins. I'm not sure I've ever actually seen him smile before. It's a nice one, a little hesitant and a little shy, but nice.

"I want you to know," he says suddenly, "that if you're going elsewhere, I'd like to come too, if . . . if that's okay with you."

"More than okay. You're my first hire."

His shoulders relax and the elevator arrives at the intended floor.

"Good luck."

"Thanks," I say, stepping out, seeing Stew waiting for me about halfway down the hallway.

"I mean for them," he mutters, and I just manage to control my sputtering laughter as the elevator doors hide his.

Who knew Gregory had a dry wit?

At least there'll be one familiar face in the Bronx with me when I get started.

"Stew," I say, thrilled to see him, and I suddenly have a pang of regret for not making more time to go and visit him in the last couple of weeks. "How're you feeling?"

"Fit as a fiddle. Got the doc's clearance to get back to work soon, so there's that. Rita is thrilled to get me the hell out of the house."

"That's great news."

"Yeah, well, the no red meat, no caffeine and no salt diet she has me on isn't fun, but it was the only way she'd let me out of her sight."

"It's because she loves you."

"Yeah, she does," he says, "God knows why."

"She's a true saint among women."

Stew snorts, but doesn't contradict me. "Where's the kid? I sent him down to get you."

"He thought I should do this on my own."

His forehead crumples in surprise, but then, inclining his head, he considers it. "Yeah, you two will do just fine."

"Do what?"

"I was born at night, but not last night, young lady. I don't know who either of you thought you were fooling now or even back then."

"What?"

"Weren't you two an item when you were with the Dodgers?"

"Absolutely not. There was nothing going on."

"I mean I just assumed you broke up at some point there, maybe when you left to come here, but I thought . . . we all thought it was . . ."

"It was what?"

His cheeks stain red and I never thought I'd see Stew blush, not if both of us lived a hundred years. "Foreplay," he mutters, "all those fights, you know? It does it for some people."

And now it's my turn to flush in embarrassment, because *that's* not a word I ever thought I'd hear him utter.

"We weren't," I clarify.

"But now."

"Yes, now we are."

"Good. I don't know who would put up with either of you for the rest of your lives, stubborn mules, the both of you."

My brain finally fully catches up to the completely insane conversation we're having just outside the door of the Brooklyn Eagles board room.

"Wait, so . . . who exactly thought that? About Charlie and me?"

"Everyone," he says, with casual shrug and a sniff. "Anyone who was around you together, most of the league, probably"

"And this whole time I thought . . ." I trail off.

I'd been worried about ever being perceived as *that girl*, as someone who shit where she ate and took advantage of being an attractive woman in an industry full of men, sleeping my way to the top and not earning it.

But, apparently, no one cared.

I got promoted with the Dodgers, twice.

I got this job.

The Yankees want me to be their next General Manger and, all this time, I was worried, for nothing.

Second-Place Sullivan to the core, I didn't even realize that I'd already won.

"I'm such an idiot."

"You're not," Stew admits. "You're just so damn good at your job no one cares who the hell you're sleeping with, kiddo."

"Every girl's dream," I say, wryly, and then with a deep

breath and a sharp exhale, I look to him. "Okay, let's get this over with."

Stew chuckles. "That's the spirit."

Nancy, the woman who I met a couple of weeks ago, is there to open the door and she gives me a firm nod of acknowledgment and waits for me to respond. I do, smiling to let her know I appreciate it and straighten my suit jacket before another nod signals to her to open the door.

Hannah Vinch is there at the head of the table, already standing and moving around it to shake my hand, two rows of men, mostly white and aging, line both sides of the long mahogany boardroom table, shined to a glossy finish. None of them look happy to be here.

I can relate.

"Francesca, I'm so glad you were able to join us today," Hannah says, reaching out a hand for me to shake and I do.

"It's the least I could do for the organization that gave me such an incredible opportunity to build my career for the past two years," I say, neutrally.

A tight smile is her only response and she gestures toward the chair at the foot of the table, directly across from hers.

"Can I get you anything?" Nancy asks from behind me.

When I turn to face her, I whisper "Vodka" under my breath, and she winks before I say "Just water, thank you."

I take my seat, water glass placed in front of me, and Nancy closes the door after Stew moves into the room and sits in the empty chair beside Mrs Vinch.

"I'm sure you know why we've called this meeting," she begins, and I have to immediately interrupt her.

"I'm sorry, but no, I don't."

There's a ripple of disgruntled murmuring from the men.

"Didn't Stew tell you?" Hannah says, looking to her left with a questioning brow.

"It wasn't my place," Stew says, simply, sitting back in his chair and crossing his hands over his protruding belly. "I'm technically still on leave."

"Ah," Hannah pivots smoothly, though I know her voice well enough now to know she's ruffled. "Then, I suppose the honor falls to me."

"Honor?" I ask.

"We held a board meeting last night and this body has determined it's within the organization's best interest, both in the short and long term, to offer you your job back."

Exactly what I expected. "Like I said earlier, Mrs Vinch, while I'm truly grateful for the opportunity Stew gave me when he brought me on," – I'm not about to give her any credit in this moment – "at this time, I have to respectfully decline."

"I told you she wouldn't take it," Stew says, leaning fully back into his chair. I half expect him to prop his feet up on the boardroom table.

"Can I ask why not?" Hannah says.

"I've been offered another job," I say, simply, but make sure to pluck at the wrists of my suit jacket. Pinstripes.

Another wave of discontent flows through the men between us.

"Another job?" she prompts me.

"Yes."

She's no fool. She didn't get to where she is now through anything other than sheer grit and determination. Just like I did. She knows *exactly* who has offered me a job. "We'd very much like a chance to counter that offer, if you'd be so inclined."

"You can certainly try."

"Stew?" She says, with an elegant gesture of her hand, giving him the floor.

He straightens in his seat and grins at me, wide and proud. "What do you say to Vice President and General Manager of the Brooklyn Eagles?"

I didn't see that one coming. Not in a million years.

"I'm sorry, isn't that . . . that's your job," I sputter, and I'm half annoyed at him, because throwing me off my game has made Hannah Vinch smile.

"The doctor cleared me for work today, but I had a long talk with Rita and we decided it was time for me to take it easier, slow down a little, but, you know me, I couldn't retire completely. I'll be around as a senior advisor, for whatever you need, but let's be honest with each other, Frankie, this has been your team since you got here. We'll just be making it official. Whatever those bastards uptown offered you, we'll beat by a year and at least ten percent."

I'm not sure I've ever been more stunned in my life and, given the last few weeks, that's saying something.

"I have a question, if you don't mind?" I ask, directing my words to Hannah. She nods. "When, *exactly*, did you rethink firing me?"

It's a test and I wonder if she knows it. Will she be honest?

"When Kai Nakamura called and was effusive in his praise of your pitch. And then when he expressed his desire to sign here was no longer guaranteed if you weren't at the helm."

Honesty. Excellent.

"So, all of this was at the whim of a twenty-five-year-old kid with a lightning bolt for an arm."

"That's baseball," she says, and smiles, shark-like, but it's a familiar one. I've seen the same exact expression on my own face countless times before. Good. We understand each other.

"It is," I agree, and stand from my seat. Something in the last handful of minutes must have shifted because, when I do, all of the others follow suit, except Stew, still lounging in his chair. "You've given me a lot to think about. When do you need my answer?"

"When you have one," Stew says, interrupting whatever Hannah was going to say, probably to try to save some face before the meeting is over.

"You'll hear from me soon," I promise, as I turn on my heel and stride out of the boardroom. When the door clicks shut behind me, it literally vibrates with the level of grumbling that kicks up once they're sure I'm gone.

"Well?" Nancy says, expectantly from her desk, like she wasn't probably listening in anyway.

"We'll see," I say, "but you'll hear it from me first."

"I better," she warns. "Gregory thinks he runs things around here, but I'm not dead yet."

And I leave, thinking about how Gregory's work nemesis is a woman old enough to be his grandmother and, honestly, watching that play out for the next few years adds a little pro to the Brooklyn Eagles column in the rapidly building pro/con list in my head.

Because now I have a choice.

A choice with no right or wrong answer, just a decision to make, one that will change my life entirely going forward, and there's only one person in the world I want to help me make it.

He's there waiting for me, chatting with the security guard at the main desk, who he says goodbye to quickly with a casual dap and I wave goodbye as well.

"How'd it go?" he asks, as we step out onto the sidewalk, the stadium looming high in the air at our backs.

"Did you know what Stew had planned?"

We walk slowly and I wave off Vlad, who tips his cap and drives away.

"He didn't explicitly tell me, but I had a feeling he had something up his sleeve. Did he offer you his job?"

"He did," I say, shaking my head, still in disbelief.

"What did you say?" he asks, his hand falling to the small of my back and I notice it this time as we wait at the corner for the light to change.

"I asked for some time to think about it."

"Okay," he says, simply, as he follows me across Washington Avenue and down Park Side to Ocean, the same path we'd take to get home, but instead of hanging a right, I lead him into Prospect Park.

"You're not really dressed for this," he says, but I keep walking and he follows, and when I step closer, his hand comes up from my back and his arm slides around my shoulder, holding me to his side as we slowly make our way down the pathway.

The trees are almost entirely bare now and the leaves are mostly gone, blown away by the wind or crushed under the feet of walkers and joggers and bird watchers and kids cutting school.

He might think we're just wandering, but I know exactly where I'm going and, thanks to my heels, I take the fastest route there.

"Really?" he asks, when the ballfields come into view as we round a corner.

They're deserted, obviously. Even the diehard fall leagues like the guys we saw a few weeks ago are done as November creeps closer to December and baseball feels like a distant memory for most people, even when it's still an everyday reality for us.

"I do my best thinking on the field," I say.

"Is that a fact?"

I keep a decent hold of him as we leave the concrete trail for the uneven grass and then eventually the dirt near the home plate of the first field. There are a handful of others in the distance, but this one will have to do. And despite the Louboutins on my feet and the Veronica Beard label inside my skirt, I squat behind home plate and let the tension seep out of me.

It's basically the view I had for my entire playing career, the only defensive player to see the entire field in front of them. They call the catcher "the field general" for a reason. We direct the defense. We call the pitches. And when things go wrong, it's on us. At least I always felt that way.

"Been a while since I had a view like this," Charlie says, settling beside me with only a slight groan from taking the weight off his knee.

"What do you think I should do?" I ask.

"It's not up to me."

"No, it isn't," I agree, "but I'm asking. What would you do?"

"The Eagles offered you more money, right?"

"Yeah, but it's the Yankees, I'm sure they'll match it and, besides, it's not about the money, not at this point."

"I know that feeling," he says. "So, what is it about?"

"It's about . . . I don't know. Respect. A chance to win. Building a team I can be proud of. Winning a championship. Winning more than one. Being happy."

"Those are the most important things."

"They are."

"And what makes you happy, Francesca?"

"You."

"You have me, either way," he says, and I know that. He

said it before, but it's nice to hear it again. I rest my head on his shoulder and take one of his big, calloused hands in mine, holding it in my lap, for comfort and for warmth, because as poetic as this felt before I sat down, the ground is freaking freezing.

"Cold?" he asks, but doesn't wait for my answer, he just wraps his arm around me and holds me closer. "Better?"

"Yeah, but still no idea what I should do."

"I can't decide for you."

"No, but it's nice that you're here," I say, and he hums his agreement, and then it hits me, my conversation with Stew earlier, and I ask, "Did you know people thought we were together back in LA?"

"What?"

"That's what Stew said. Said it was pretty universal."

"Huh, maybe we should have been? Feels like we wasted a lot of time."

"I mean, we were both married and, after Shane, I'll be honest, I wasn't ready."

"Not because of the working together thing?"

"That too, at the time. I was in a different place in my career. I still had so many things to learn, so many mountains to climb to prove myself. It would have been career suicide."

"But everyone thought it."

"Yeah, but nobody *knew*. It was just a thing to say, a thing to think. If we'd been like this . . ." I trail off.

". . . they wouldn't have taken you seriously."

"No, they wouldn't have."

"So, you're not worried about being with me and working for the Eagles?"

"No, not anymore."

"Then it's just that it's the Yankees."

I let out a groan, my knees finally unable to support me on these heels anymore and I sink down to the dirt with him.

"It is and it's funny, because I hated them growing up. Hated their stupid pinstripes and their dumb no facial hair rule for the players and how, no matter what you say to their fans, they're just entirely smug that they always have a chance to win and all the money to make it happen."

"You grew up a Dodgers fan."

"Yeah."

"You had the same things."

"Twenty-seven championships," I mutter, in a mocking tone. "As if they were alive for all of them and they personally watched Babe Ruth hit his 60th homer at the old stadium."

"And yet . . ." he trails off, knowing I'm not done.

"It's the *Yankees*. The greatest franchise in the history of modern sport, and I'd be their general manager, their *first* female general manager."

He lets out a low whistle. "That is something."

"It is. It really is."

"So, Frankie Sullivan, what's it going to be?"

Epilogue

Three months later . . .

I've never been the kind of man to just lay around in bed. My entire life there was always been something I could be doing. A practice, a workout, a game. Even after I retired, I'd be up with the sun, for a swim or a walk on the beach before my I got my day started.

Now, though? Now I don't mind it, not when every morning I wake up with Frankie beside me, blonde hair everywhere, spread over my chest, sometimes in my mouth, but always close, her warm curves pressed into the harder angles of my body. It's been months now and I'm still not used to it. I'm not sure I ever will be.

As the sky starts to brighten outside, the sun rises up over the building and promises another epic sunset over the Gulf of Mexico tonight. Just like we have every day since we made our way from Brooklyn down to Florida to prepare for the upcoming season.

This morning is a little different. Instead of giving in to the urge to start the day just like we ended the last, I slide out of bed, careful not to jostle her too much and get ready as quietly as possible, letting her sleep in while I head to the field.

My favorite day of the season was always the first day of Spring Training. There's nothing like it, everything is possible, no wins, no losses, a chance to start fresh. And that's true for both of us. Despite spending our entire adult lives in baseball, we're taking on new challenges as the calendar marches on toward Opening Day.

I always like to get to the ballpark early, when there's still a slight chill in the air, even in balmy Clearwater, Florida, when the dew hasn't burned off the grass and the dirt still smells fresh, ready to be scraped under the cleats of the ballplayers who've been gone all winter.

Little Russell, the nickname for the Eagle's training facility, is nearly deserted when I arrive and I'm so early that the clubhouse guy hasn't even turned the lights on yet.

My office isn't huge, not like the one I have back in Brooklyn, but it'll do for the next six or seven weeks while we get ready for the long season ahead. There's a uniform hung neatly in the locker at the back of the room, fresh gear laid out the night before for everyone's arrival today. But I don't need it right now.

All I need now is to get out onto the field.

Because today is one of the most important days on the baseball calendar.

It's unofficial start of spring, giving the people freezing their asses off in the north some hope that the end is near and that the national pastime is on its way to thaw them out after a long winter.

Pitchers and catchers report today, a week or so before the rest of the team, but a handful of them have been down here working out for a few weeks. There was no keeping some of the boys away. I spent most of the off season in New York, with a couple of trips back to LA, first to spend Thanksgiving with Frankie and her best friends and then again when my house finally sold.

Construction just got underway to convert the brownstone that I impulsively bought part of, given that both of us are in Florida. The contractor swears the remodel will be done by the time we get back to New York. I'm hopeful. Frankie's skeptical.

But that's nothing new.

We balance each other.

And it becomes more and more obvious every day.

Like right now, when I step out onto the field, and some-how she's already waiting for me and I allow my eyes to slowly take her in, up from her toes, encased in wedged sandals to the hems of the white linen shorts, paired with a matching blazer and a muted blue cami underneath, her one nod to the Florida heat, though going entirely business casual just isn't in her.

I have no idea how she beat me here, but I've long since stopped questioning when Frankie does something that amazes me.

"Happy Pitchers and Catchers," she says, a broad smile spreading across her face as her eyes fall shut and she inhales deeply, taking it all in, just like I came here to do.

I clear my throat and keep my face serious as I hold out a phantom microphone. "Francesca, how does it feel, your first Spring Training as General Manager of the Brooklyn Eagles? Some in the sport are already counting your team out. A rookie manager, a rookie ace just imported from Japan, a rookie catcher and centerfielder, plus another rookie starter – no team has ever had as little major league experience as the one you're about to field. What do you say to the doubters?"

She smirks at me and steps closer, near enough for me to

catch the lavender scent of her on the soft morning breeze. "People have a lot to say before there's even been a pitch thrown. I think I'll let our play speak for itself."

"And a follow-up question, if you don't mind?"

"I suppose I have time for one more."

"What's the goal for this season?" I ask, dropping the fake mic and reaching out for her left hand, entwining it with my own.

"A ring," she says, as the solitaire diamond I slid onto her finger just a few weeks ago catches the sunlight, blinking starbursts onto the dirt below our feet. A promise of a future, no matter where the game takes us.

"Another?" I ask, raising that hand to my lips and pressing a kiss to the inside of her wrist.

"This one's fine for now," she allows, "but when October rolls around, I expect another, one for you too."

I pull back and quirk a brow at her. "We are still talking about a World Series ring, right?"

"What other kind of ring would I be talking about?" she asks, eyes wide with pretend innocence, and then she pulls away from me, laughing, striding toward the dugout and calling over her shoulder. "C'mon, Charlie, the season starts right now and I intend to win it all."

So do I, but, deep down, I think, I may have already won.

And as for the rest?

That's baseball.

HEADLINE ETERNAL

FIND YOUR HEART'S DESIRE...

VISIT OUR WEBSITE: www.headlineeternal.com

FIND US ON FACEBOOK: facebook.com/eternalromance

CONNECT WITH US ON X: @eternal_books

FOLLOW US ON INSTAGRAM: @headlineeternal

EMAIL US: eternalromance@headline.co.uk